*"Have you ever trust_____
She tilted her head_____
face. "Have you eve_____
with all your heart . . . unreservedly?"*

"So serious, suddenly." Bold honesty never led to anything good. "By the by, the ribbon on that, ahem, *hat* matches your eyes to perfection. But, why in the name of God of all bonnets are you wearing grapes and kumquats on one side and a trio of crows on the other side?"

"They are lovebirds, you idiot. And everyone knows fruits on hats are all the rage right now."

"But not an entire fruit stall. Are those violets tucked in back?"

She studied him silently for a moment. "I've never known anyone so capable of managing conversations via diversion, wit, or flattery. The last it has not been my privilege to ever hear from your lips, I might add. But, I would advise you to save your breath, for I think I've proven I'm quite immune to your ways. Now then, are you going to answer my question or not?"

"The love question?"

"Precisely."

Romances by **Sophia Nash**

THE DUKE DIARIES
THE ART OF DUKE HUNTING
BETWEEN THE DUKE AND THE DEEP BLUE SEA
SECRETS OF A SCANDALOUS BRIDE
LOVE WITH THE PERFECT SCOUNDREL
THE KISS
A DANGEROUS BEAUTY

Sophia Nash

THE
Duke
Diaries

AVON
An Imprint of HarperCollinsPublishers

AVON BOOKS
An Imprint of HarperCollins*Publishers*
10 East 53rd Street
New York, New York 10022-5299

Copyright © 2013 by Sophia Nash
ISBN 978-0-06-202234-9
www.avonromance.com

First Avon Books mass market printing: March 2013

Avon Trademark Reg. U.S. Pat. Off. and in Other Countries, Marca Registrada, Hecho en U.S.A.
HarperCollins® is a registered trademark of HarperCollins Publishers.

Printed in the U.S.A.

10 9 8 7 6 5 4 3 2 1

To
my cousins and their families

Acknowledgments

Great thanks to my readers and to all who inspire me: Peter and Alexandra Nash, Georgiana Warner Kaempher, Arthur and Kim Nash, Philip and Renata Nash, Emily Morse, Lisa Nash, Philip Mallory Nash, Jean Gordon, Len Lossaco Fogge, Philippe and Christina Gerard, Laurie and Eddie Garrick, Kim and J.P. Powell, Marie Odon Jacobe, Le Comte et Comtesse d'Aurelle de Paladines, Barbara Kehr, and to a very special circle of girlfriends: Amy Conlan, Mary Lee Reed, Eloisa James, Sarah MacLean, Jeanne Adams, Christina Dodd, Anne Kane, Fairleigh Killen, Kathryn Caskie Parker, Annie Abaziou, Lanette Scherr, Pam Scatteragia, Lisa Schleifer, Cathy Maxwell, Nora Roberts, Irene Schindler, Christine Hill, Kathy Ashy, Barbara Casales, Tessa Dare, Vicki

Witter, Donna Mortel Evans, Anne Waldron, and Heather Maier.

Very special thanks to Lyssa Keusch, Harper Collins Executive Editor, for her unflagging support and extraordinary professional guidance. Thanks also to Carrie Feron, Liate Stehlik, Pam Spengler-Jaffee, Susan Grimshaw, John Charles, Michelle Bounfiglio, and Emily Cotler, for continued encouragement.

And to my mother and children, thank you for continually showing me the meaning of joy and life!

THE
Duke
Diaries

Prologue

Befitting her first name, Lady Verity Fitzroy began chronicling life's truths at the tender age of three and ten. Her initial efforts, she knew, were rambling at best, and puerile at worst. The problem was that her life was beyond dull. Nothing of importance ever happened at Boxwood, the ducal seat of her brother, the Duke of Candover. Or, rather, since she was not out yet, things happened in this bucolic corner of Derbyshire, but she wasn't privy to them. It was astounding how swiftly her elders could button their lips when she entered a chamber.

And so Verity was reduced to writing volumes about topics such as her dislike of peas, her mare's dislike of hoof picks, her governess's dislike of spirited horses and young ladies who did not eat certain vegetables (even if peas were a legume and so not truly a vegetable). Indeed, Verity sought refuge in her writing for there was no one who truly appreciated her outlandish opinions.

Oh, she had female relations, to be sure. She was positively drowning in sisters—two younger still in the nursery, and two older, officially out and not officially floundering in society. That left Verity alone, in the middle, forgotten.

It was very convenient, in fact. There were days like today, here in the shaded perch of her favorite ancient pine tree next to the lake, that she could spend hours lost in her writings and relish being utterly and completely by herself.

She had her down-filled, pine-tar-stained cushion on which to sit, two fig tarts on which to nibble, and, most importantly, her diary in which to scribble news and the secret longings she harbored in her young heart. Verity glanced down at her latest entry.

Cousin Esme paid a call with her mother yesterday. It was, of course, the highlight of the day. No, the highlight of the week. It would have been the highlight of the month if not for the return of Rory. Unfortunately, R has not actually been seen, as my brother grasps every chance to escape our petticoats by visiting R at Rutledge Hall, where I am sure the only petticoats to be seen are the ones gentlemen refuse to discuss in my presence.

Oh, for a glimpse of dear R's eyes! Yes, I am ridiculous. But that is to be expected at my age according to my governess.

But, at seventeen I am to become mature whether I like it or not, she insists. And after three Seasons, if I'm still unmarried, Miss Linhurst warns I will become an ape leader in hell. So, as I understand it, a lady is ripe for the plucking for three years, after which, if she does not accomplish her only mission in life, she will be pickled, preserved, and stored on a shelf, where she will molder with other devilish gorillas—although Faith informs that an ape is not necessarily a gorilla since a gorilla is just one type of ape.

I don't understand why my sisters always laugh at my observations. They do not seem to mind being wallflowers. Then again I have always been different from them. I don't mind being the shortest, but I shall never understand why they are so obsessed by complicated algorithms and science which always leaves me with an aching head. Why am I not like my brilliant naturalist mother or my father who everyone described as a genius of the first order when he was alive? I am but a bat or a cuckoo in a nest of brilliant blackbirds. Mother hates when I tell her this, but what can I expect? She is a mother blackbird stuck with a fig-loving fledgling whose nest mates gobble peas without gagging.

What utter drivel. She crossed out the last, refusing to sound like a mewling infant. Verity made an exasperated sigh. What she needed was adventure. Smoke-filled battlefields. High seas. She smiled. *A pirate with pea-green eyes.* Better still, a gaggle of pirates. Did pirates come in gaggles? No, a *crew* of pirates. Or an African tribe in an ape-free dense jungle filled with exotic animals such as lions, pythons, elephants, and—

Just then a sound broke her concentration. Two people atop horses raced through the gap of trees circling the large lake on her family's famed estate.

Verity inched forward to get a better view, only to see her old chipped straw hat fly from her head in the effort. It tumbled past the outermost branches to land half hidden in a bit of tall grass. *Botheration.* The riders galloped toward her well-leafed secret bower. Past the large old oak a dozen yards away from her, they broke into a trot, then stumbled to a stop.

She inhaled sharply. Rory in the flesh, and surprisingly, Miss Catharine Talmadge in tow.

The young lady screeched with laughter. Yes, when Catharine laughed, she sounded like a cheetah. Of course, animals did not laugh, but it was only fair to mock her, as everything else about Catharine was Venus-like. She was an exquisitely formed model of femininity. A graceful, amusing, kindhearted young lady (at least when any gentle-man was afoot), but an aloof, cool miss who never made any effort to cultivate friendships with other females (when the gentlemen were not). Yet her grace and beauty trumped all. The proof could be spied on the faces of every man, gentle or not, who stood in Catharine's presence—especially in the visage of Verity's brother, James Fitzroy, the premier duke of England.

But right now? Well, the proof was in the face of *that person*. Yes, one Rory Lennox, Earl of Rut-ledge, the most darkly handsome, charming, and disarming lord in all of Christendom.

Verity sat straighter on her lumpy cushion. What on earth was going on? Why was Catharine with the earl? She was all but formally engaged to James. Not that Verity questioned Rory's in-tentions. He and her brother had been more like brothers rather than best friends since childhood.

Verity forced back a wave of something very akin to jealousy masquerading as filial outrage. The ill feeling flooded her stomach, which forever ached since she took pains to hold it in. Peas she might not eat, but tarts were altogether another story.

"I'm not going swimming," Catharine shrieked. "You cannot force me, Rory."

A wicked smile flashed as the earl kicked away

his stirrups, threw his lovely muscled right leg over the front of his saddle, and jumped to the ground. He discarded his hat without a care and advanced on his objective. His cropped dark hair dovetailed in a perfect fashion as he ran his hand through it. Verity, mesmerized, made not a sound.

All Catharine Talmadge had to do was turn her mount's head to the east and flee. But did she? Of course not. Artifice was Catharine's middle name. Instead, she batted her ridiculously long eyelashes and tittered, a determined flirt through and through. Why did gentlemen fall for such obvious ploys?

As he reached her, Rory left a trail of masculine articles in his wake. He discarded his blue superfine coat made by Weston, his neckcloth again by Weston, and his white-tasseled Hessian boots made by a private cobbler whose workmanship equaled Weston.

Verity sighed in disgust. It was amazing he did not look like a fool hopping on one foot and the other while removing them. It was a testament to her devotion that no matter what he did or said, she could not shake her sensibility toward him.

"Come along then, Cat. A true lady accepts her losses with grace," he coaxed in that gravely voice of his that in Verity's view made most ladies behave stupidly, herself included. "Look, we can accomplish this the easy way or . . ."

"Yes?" Catharine whispered, her eyes dancing with the promise of mischief.

". . . the hard way, which is the way you really want to do it."

He lifted one of his razor sharp brows and the sunlight chose that moment to emerge from behind a cloud to strike his face. His green eyes shone like a panther's. The ridiculous simile was the best Verity could do. The one about the cheetah had been far better.

"Impossible," Catharine cackled. "It will ruin my habit, Rory. And I know how much you like it," she purred.

"Perhaps you should have considered earlier that the wager involved water," he rumbled. "It's obvious the opportunity of winning blinded you to failure. I've always said this is the sort of foolish thinking that leads to hardened gamblers with pockets to let—or wet, in your case." He shook his head.

Verity's chest ached as she watched him advance on his objective.

"James would never insist," Catharine breathed, tilting her head in that provocative way of hers. "He is a gentleman."

"Yes, but he is not here, and I am not him. And you've had a lifetime to understand the difference.

You've made the right choice and I am happy for you. My friend is a lucky fellow." He sighed heavily. "As long as you keep that desire to wager in check."

She sniffed, but ruined the effect by breaking into a wide grin.

Verity felt like casting up her fig tarts.

"Cat," he growled, "enough. We both know how this will end"—his hands went about her tiny waist, and the cheetah did nothing to stop the panther—"so come along now. I say, Cat, you've never said if you liked the idea of my engagement present to you and James."

"You know I do," she whispered, with excitement peaking from her lovely face as she looked down at him. "Since you obviously won't let me try to win your horse again, the next best thing is the present of a filly or colt by him next summer."

"Good," he murmured. "I'm glad."

A gust of wind flirted with the edges of Catharine's pretty lace veil and her form-fitted sapphire blue riding habit, which revealed that this feather-light lady had never had to hold in her stomach since she never ate too much of anything. Catharine draped her arms about his shoulders as he disengaged her from the side-saddle and lowered her to the ground, her body brushing against his.

The beautiful couple stared at each other in the golden light of the afternoon. She reached up to stroke the dark locks of his hair, but he pushed her hand away.

"I won't be able to go through with it, Rory," she whispered. "I only wish . . ."

And in the time it would have taken Verity to spell *fickle fiancée*, three things happened. First, Catharine Talmadge leaned toward him, her lips pouted. Second, Rory muttered a dark curse and scooped the lady into his arms. And three, he carried her squawking and kicking form into the lake and unceremoniously dunked her.

After, he dove under the surface away from her and did not appear again for a long time.

It was obvious Catharine had never imagined Rory would go through with his threat. She marched out of the water, her skirting heavy with muck and a bit of algae trailing down one side of her head, all the while caterwauling like, ahem, a *cheetah* very unused to braving the elements.

She spewed a highly unladylike oath that Verity had only heard the new stable hand from London's West End shout when he had been relieved without references for putting a horse away wet.

It took all of Verity's fortitude not to make a sound as she watched the drenched female bluster about "a certain abominable person who does not know how to behave like a gentleman, unlike the far superior character and station of the gentleman she would most definitely wed considering this latest action." Catharine awkwardly remounted just as Rory emerged from the lake shaking the water from his head.

He saluted her as she trotted away, without taking proper leave of him.

Verity sat transfixed as the one-and-twenty-year-old earl, a man with his prime years ahead of him, stood motionless at the sight of Catharine, her back rigid with anger, riding away from him. His breeches and fine white lawn shirt, wet and translucent, clung to his form in a fashion that left Verity with a far better understanding of the male form than ever before. She darted her head about to get a better view from her perch. She was, indeed, shameless.

Rory watched Catharine's retreating figure far longer than she was in sight. It was very odd behavior.

He finally moved to retrieve the clothing and boots he had tossed helter-skelter on the ground. He suddenly paused, his gaze settling in the direction of Verity's misshapened straw hat in the sprigs of tallish grass.

She froze.

His head swiveled to the left. And to the right.

He crossed to retrieve her hat and studied it. He did not look up into the tree. Just when she thought she might be lucky and breathe again, he spoke.

"One could hope," he promised, "you know how to hold your tongue and preserve your anonymity. However, if you are considering dishing out scandal-broth at the next opportunity, show your face now for I shall do worse than a mere dunking if I hear a peep out of you." He paused. "Are we agreed?" Another pause. "Good. I shall keep this ahem, *lovely* thing as guarantee. I'm certain you understand."

And as the most impossibly handsome man Verity could possibly ever know threw his leg over his horse and galloped into the distance, she took a good, hard look at the pathetic diary she held in her hands. Ever so methodically, Verity started ripping out the pages. She then reached into her book bag and retrieved the lovely new red diary she had meant to start today.

She opened to the first page, fingered a newly trimmed quill, feathered her face with the other end of it, and dipped into her tiny ink pot to scratch in the following words:

The Duke Diaries
or
How the Far More Interesting Half Lives . . .

Little did she know how her life would change after that monumental moment.

1. Verity Fitzroy would refine the art of eavesdropping, especially after her brother's circle of friends became known as the royal entourage. Yes, all of James's acquaintances, now dukes, bore their ducal strawberry-leaved emblems with pride and celebrated their unrivaled superiority in the ton by extraordinarily entertaining, ofttimes wildly excessive actions.

2. Her brother would not marry Catharine. (However, his next choice for a bride fourteen years later would be no better. This current fiancée suggested all of his sisters should be packed off to a nunnery. It made Verity reconsider the merits of cheetahs and pray for divine intervention. Her wishes and those of her sisters, Faith, Hope, Chastity, and Charity, would soon be answered.)

And 3. Verity's own secrets, in the end, would rival the combined actions of all the dukes of the royal entourage.

Yes, the very public fall from grace of more than a handful of Graces, and her part in it would

prove to Verity that her stories of small green veri-
fiable legumes, hoof picks, and governesses with
irrational dislikes, would have been far superior
diary topics after all.

Then again, the best of heroines are usually
known for dabbling in disaster.

Chapter 1

There was a reason Rory Lennox, the former Earl of Rutledge, and now first Duke of Abshire, didn't drink. It wasn't because it left his palate tasting like the bottom of a parrot's cage. It wasn't because his cottony tongue felt three times larger and his brain sloshed in his now thirty-five-year-old nob. No. It was because disaster never, ever, *ever* failed to lurk on spirit's coattails.

And last night?

The royal entourage's celebration during the final hours of the Duke of Candover's bachelorhood prior to committing marital doom had obviously been a cock-up of the first water. Rory knew it within seconds of waking to the sound of a fist pounding on his door as if Napoleon's own army was paying a call. Yes, he thought, as he tried to pry open an eyelid and then thought the better of it, he really didn't give a damn who was making such a nuisance of themselves.

He was now a goddamned duke, for Christsakes, and if he couldn't at least get a good night's sleep in return for prior service to the Crown, well then, what was the point of risking one's life? Not that he had ever risked a hair on his head for the reward of a good night's sleep. He'd had his own bloody reasons.

Thank God the pounding stopped. His eyes closed, yet fully awake, he knew better than to move. For the life of him he couldn't remember any of the events leading to this splendidly awful state of postinebriation, but he knew the only recourse was to remain like a petrified oak until his former military batman, now valet, made an appearance, carrying a crystal snifter filled with the hair of the mongrel that had bitten his arse to the bone last eve. He almost retched as he remembered the absinthe the Duke of Kress had provided in amounts capable of pickling half of Wellington's regiments.

In fact, the only part of Rory that did not feel like it had been turned inside out and burned in a cauldron was his hand.

What was that lovely, soft, warm sensation coursing through his fingers? He smiled. Well, at least part of last evening had gone as planned.

The lovely Countess of Velram had hinted she would find his bedchambers in the Prince Regent's pile, Carleton House, and quite obviously the young widow had succeeded. It was only too bad Rory couldn't remember a single moment of the interlude. He gently gripped the lady's hand, and received a sensuous squeeze in reply.

It was odd, actually. He never touched people's ungloved hands. It hurt his brain box too much to remember why.

And then the pounding recommenced with the force of a log battering a well-garrisoned and fortified Portuguese fortress. The door to the regal bedchambers gave way to the man who would surely regret it.

Rory pried open his eyelids to find three things:

1. His former friend and current archenemy, the premier duke, Candover, breathing fire and brimstone in his direction.

2. Three royal servants peering around the broken doorjamb.

3, And lastly? Not the Countess of Velram in flagrante delicto beside him in the bed. Of course not. It was one of bloody Candover's *sisters*.

And he was holding her hand.

He released her fingers as if they were hotter than the hinges of hell, and wrenched his body upright, his head screaming in revolt. His nemesis barked something to the servants behind him and closed the door, a considerable feat given the ruined state of the frame.

"Get up," Candover said, ice threading the syllables. "And get the hell away from my sister, you sodding bastard."

Rory lurched to his feet on the side opposite his former friend, only to notice his clothes were wet, including the water-logged boots hugging his clammy legs. In the next instant Candover's sibling sighed in her sleep, smiled, and turned to burrow deeper into a pillow.

Rory blinked, trying desperately to make out which one of the five sisters had entered his chambers last night. They all looked so damned alike with that voluminous dark hair and aristocratic mien that matched their brother's. Pretty was an adjective rarely used in their direction—although, to be fair, Rory had always found them tolerable, far more intelligent than most, and no giggles to plague the ears.

But right now the lady in question looked more like a mummy trussed in lace from head to toe. Honestly, there were nuns in France who showed more flesh. This he knew firsthand.

He squinted at her during the three seconds

Candover's visage turned from sea green to purple. Lord, he hoped she was not the algorithmist whose only conversation concerned totient functions that would have boggled Euclid. He exhaled. Ah, it was the middle one, Verity Fitzroy. The one who had always dogged Candover, the Duke of Sussex, and his own heels whenever she could manage it as a girl. Well. He vaguely remembered she had wit, but obviously not a great sense of direction in terms of bedchambers. Well, if it had to be one of Candover's sisters, he was at least glad it was not one of the mathematically inclined ones.

"I should have put you out of your misery years ago," Candover seethed, his words seared with contempt. "You refuse to suffer as you should. I shall ensure it now. Dawn tomorrow. You know where."

"Yes, I'm certain your bride would prefer an uninterrupted wedding night," Rory retorted calmly. "Primrose Hill it is."

"I'll not grant you your choice of weapon, for you don't deserve a show of tradition. It will be daggers so I can gut you like the eel that you are."

Rory cleared his throat and stared at his nemesis. "All right," he replied. "Although, I should like to know why your sister is in my apartments and sleeping like the dead."

Candover's eyes narrowed, flashing mercury. "My sister's sleeping habits are not your affair and these are *her* rooms, you lunatic."

Rory coolly glanced toward the corner, only to find that the burled walnut armoire that should have been there was now in the center of the opposite wall and it was made of rosewood and considerably larger. There was also one more telltale clue as to the bona fide resident of the chamber. The apartments were decorated in very fine pink and yellow *toile de joie.* Every last inch. Very unlike the burgundy and gold wall pattern of his apartments.

Despite Candover's green about the gills demeanor, the premier duke appeared ready to dispatch him on the spot. Instead, the head of the royal entourage took five very long strides to his sister's side and shook her. "Verity . . . Verity, awake." When she did not stir, he tried again and failed. He finally grasped a glass of water on the nearby rosewood table and dashed the contents on her innocent face.

She gasped, sat straight up in bed, a sole long dark brown braid snaked around her neck and shoulders like the marital noose she would soon feel. The heels of her palms rubbed her eyes as she yawned so widely her jaw cracked inelegantly. Eyes never opening, she paused and dropped back onto the pillow. Her brother gritted his teeth, grabbed her reticule nearby and extracted a small container of smelling salts.

He wove it around her nose and finally, blessedly, she pushed away his hand and balefully opened one eye.

"James," she said with a sleepy voice. "Whatever are you doing here? Where is Amelia?"

"I haven't the faintest idea where your abigail is but I shall sack her when I see her—of that you can be sure."

Verity, beginning to fully awaken, gave her brother a long-suffering look. "How ridiculous. You adore Amelia." She rubbed her forehead. "We shall chalk this up to wedding day nerves. Oh, my head is splitting, James." She suddenly appeared agitated. "I must find Amelia. What time is it?"

"Half past ten. But that is the least of your problems," he replied, stiffly. "You are in far deeper—"

Her eyes widened in shock. "But the wedding was to start ages ago. Oh, James, why did no one wake us?"

"An excellent question," Rory drawled from the far side of the bed. The suspense was almost killing him and so he had to put it out of its misery.

She jerked her head to face him, and scrambled from the frame, taking almost all of the bed coverings with her. "What are you doing here?" she breathed, her brown eyes huge in her face.

"Missing the Wedding of the Century and the after breakfast, along with you, too, apparently," he replied casually. "And providing your brother the chance to finally live out his fondest desire. All in all, a fairly mundane beginning to the week, no, my sweet?"

"Don't you dare address my sister so cavalierly, Rutledge—"

"Abshire," Rory corrected.

"I keep forgetting you blackmailed Prinny for a duchy."

Rory tilted his head and said not a word. There were times silence was the best answer of all.

"Enough," Verity said while wrapping the heavy bed covering about her. "You haven't answered my question. And why are you both wetter than ducks?"

Rory scratched the back of his aching head and peered at Candover, who while maintaining an air of superiority, appeared just as much at a loss for words as he. "I haven't the foggiest."

"You haven't a notion why you're wet or what you're doing in my chambers?"

"Both," Rory replied, "although I'm certain it had something to do with Kress's French drink of the devil."

She turned to her brother. "Where is everyone else? We haven't really missed your wedding, have we?"

Candover's face was as pale as the underbelly of a royal swan. Just the thought jarred loose in Rory the wisp of a memory last night of a web-footed, white monster aquatic bird chasing the premier duke on the banks of the Serpentine. He half smiled in remembrance until the motion made his face hurt. He swayed. God, he would have swooned if his manhood would not have been called into question.

A cold sweat broke out on Candover's prominent forehead. "Lady Margaret, her family, and half of London apparently waited at St. George's for ninety minutes before the Spencers whisked her away. There's no hope for making amends."

"James," his sister whispered, "oh, I'm so very sorry—"

Candover cut her off with a look.

"But why weren't we woken?"

Rory cleared his throat. "One could guess from past history that Prinny commanded that none of us be disturbed. The last servant who disobeyed him . . . well, the poor fellow regretted it."

Candover narrowed his eyes. "The Prince Regent is waiting for us to join him in his chambers. The *Morning Post* just printed a second edition for the first time in its history, which is full of damning evidence of larking about last night."

Larking about, indeed. Sudden flashes of hideous scenes flooded Rory's mind. Lord, he might have even broken down a door in the wee hours to enter White's Club, where all of London's aristocracy won and lost their fortunes many times over. "Prinny will be bent on exacting a pound of flesh from all of us even if he was likely with us each step of the way."

Candover's ashen face turned dark as he glared at Rory. "That's nothing to this . . . this . . . You'll marry her today, and then you and I shall have a meeting of the minds, you sodding blackguard—"

"Don't be ridiculous, James," Verity interrupted. "We'll do nothing of the sort. This is just a stupid misunderstanding. Nothing—"

Her brother continued, one index finger stabbing the air at the start of the never-ending series of righteous demands. "Verity, you shall immediately have your affairs packed, mouth vows you will not have to keep, and then you will depart for Derbyshire this very afternoon."

"I most certainly will not."

He had to admire her spirit.

"Don't worry," Candover continued darkly. "You won't have to live with him."

"Really?" Rory inserted. "That's not how I've heard this marriage business limps along."

"Enough," Verity insisted. "James, did you not say Prinny is waiting? This can be sorted out later. Besides, no one will ever know."

Candover shook his head. "I had not thought a sister of mine could be so naïve. There are a bevy of servants just outside your damn door."

"And they will not breathe a word," she said as she rearranged the bed covering, then grabbed her discarded gown and slippers from the scrolled footstool at the end of the bed. "This place is riddled with secret passageways. I'll just use the one I discovered over there"—she nodded toward the east wall—"to go to Isabelle's chambers, where we'll all agree I passed the evening." She rubbed her forehead yet again.

Rory examined her shrewdly. He would bet his last farthing that she had sampled Kress's bloody absinthe.

Candover appeared at the end of his rope. The small tic near his right eye was the sign. "It won't do. You will marry him today."

"I will not." Verity turned away from her brother and eyed him. "What say you? Are you willing to be trapped so easily? Where is the rakehell we all know and revere when we need him?"

"Standing before you." Rory bowed with a

flourish and nearly lost his footing. "You know very well once a rake, always a rake."

Candover rounded the edge of the bed, and Rory did nothing to stop him. It didn't hurt. For three seconds the blinding pain meted out to his eye was held in suspension. He nearly cast up his accounts when his brain caught wind of the blow.

"Pardon me," Verity said so quietly that both men turned to her. She picked up a nasty-looking pistol from her nightstand and pointed it at them. "Can you not both wait until tomorrow? You did say Prinny is waiting, James."

"Why on earth do you have . . ." James said, stunned.

She paused for just the slightest second. So briefly, another man would have missed the precursor of a lie in the making.

"Perhaps Prinny keeps these in ladies' chambers to ward off intruders," she said in an overly lofty tone. "Exquisite, but lethal, no?"

The hue of Candover's face became paler, the effects of the evening evident. "For the love of God, put that down."

"No."

Candover sighed, crossed the room and came to a stop near the door, which was as far away as the other man could get from Rory. "Verity, like it or not, you will marry the bastard. You will obey me."

She lowered the pistol and jutted her chin forward. "Why ever would I start a bad habit like that? And you are a fine one to talk. Did you not just stand up your bride in front of half of London? You have far more important things to worry about than a spinster sister who has never had any intention of marrying—as you well know."

A glimmer of sadness invaded Candover's face, before he wiped it clean of any emotion. "Promise me you will depart for Boxwood today," he replied quietly. "Promise me, Verity. And you will not leave Derbyshire until this is sorted out to my satisfaction."

"I will go, brother," she capitulated. "If only to avoid the storm and not add to your epic disaster."

Candover eyed the two of them. "Verity, take the passage. Dress as fast as you possibly can and I shall arrange for a carriage. Amelia will stay to pack your affairs." Then Candover looked at Rory as if he was nothing more than the eel he had suggested. "I suggest you follow me after I divert the servants. Over there"—he nodded to the newspaper he had tossed on the table when he'd entered in a rage—"you'll find recommended reading before you join Prinny and the rest of us."

Verity had gathered a few articles and disappeared through the concealed door.

Rory's eye hurt like a thousand devils. He did

not turn a hair. "Your power of control over a female is inspiring, Candover. I salute you."

The premier duke narrowed his eyes. "I should have almost enjoyed witnessing how you fared with my sister. But I shall enjoy finishing you off even more . . . after you say your vows."

The premier duke Rory had once considered a brother turned on his heel and departed with far less violence than he had arrived. His head throbbing like a thousand devils, Rory glanced at the newspaper on the table and retrieved it. He turned to "The Fashionable World," the section read by the aristocracy who participated in social folly, but more importantly by the legion of lower classes who wished they could partake. His head swimming in devil's brew, he fought the pain to scan the column, his chest tightening.

> In a continuation of the regular obscene excesses of the Prince Regent and his royal entourage, not one of the party made an appearance at St. George's much earlier this morning, with the exception of our Princess Caroline, darling little Princess Charlotte, and Her Grace, the young Duchess of March. His Majesty's absence and that of the groom and groomsmen caused all four hundred guests to assume the worst. And indeed, this columnist has it on the very best authority, partially one's own eye-

witness account, that not only the august bridegroom, His Grace, the Duke of Candover, but also seven other dukes, one archbishop, and the Prince Regent himself were seen cavorting about all of London last eve on an outrageous regal rampage. Midnight duels, swimming amok with the swans in the Serpentine, a stream of scantily clad females in tow, lawn bowling in unmentionables, horse races in utter darkness, wild, uproarious boasting, and jesting and wagering abounded. Indeed, this author took it upon himself to retrieve and return to White's Club their infamous betting book, which one of the royal entourage had the audacity to remove without even a by your leave. In this fashion we have learned that the Duke of Kress lost the entire fortune he so recently acquired with the title, although the winner's name was illegible.

Even the queen's jewels were spotted on one duke as he paraded down Rotten Row. Yes, my fellow countrymen, it appears the English monarchy has learned nothing from our French neighbor's lessons concerning aristocratic overindulgence. As the loyal scribe of the Fashionable column for two decades, you have it on my honor that all this occurred and worse. I can no longer remain silent on these reoccurring grievous, licentious activities, and so shall be the first plain-speaking, brave soul to utter

these treasonous words: I no longer support or condone a monarchy such as this.

Lord above . . . Rory crumpled the paper in his
hand. The same hand that had been holding Lady
Verity Fitzroy's quite possibly through the dawn
hours. And all the sordid, bloody, dangerous,
soul-shattering events in his past came roaring
back into his head with a vengeance.

Chapter 2

So this was banishment.

For the first time in her life Verity had not even one hint of family or friends in sight here in Derbyshire. And not one thing to do. The official mistress of the family by default, she had not one dinner menu to approve, not one social occasion to plan or accept, and she had completed the annual inventory for Boxwood in record time.

It was ridiculous.

Her brother had never been an ogre in the past. How could he blame her for sleeping her way to disaster and then send her away? Everyone in the family knew she slumbered like a hibernating bear. And had not James slept like a *drunken ox* through his own wedding?

Well, she refused to feel sorry for herself. It never brought happiness nor changed the past.

She should know.

Verity glanced nearby toward her brother's favorite horse, which she had ridden to this corner, who was deliriously munching on the forbidden grass of the garden. James would be furious.

Using the tattered end of one of her ancient bonnet's faded scarlet ribbons, she swatted at a tiny insect navigating her forearm. She sighed with frustration. Even her very best friend and cousin in Derbyshire, the widowed Esme, Countess of March, was gone. Gone to the Continent to pursue her one passion and great talent: art.

Which meant that for the first time in her life, aside from the thirty-seven silent, or mostly silent, servants, Verity was finally granted the one thing she had always sought: peace.

The only problem was that like most other long-cherished wishes, once tasted (and she had tasted far too much quiet for five long days), the appeal flagged. About the only good thing to say about tranquility and privacy was that she could write to her heart's content anywhere she pleased, unlike her prior crowded life.

But for the first time ever she had nothing to write.

Verity glanced down at her newest diary open on

the garden table under the three-hundred-year-old oak tree, bordering the woods beyond the estate's most distant lower gardens. She wondered how many scandals the tree had shaded with its massive branches. Certainly not as many as Boxwood's infamous maze or the pine tree of so long ago.

The woods and surrounding moors beckoned with the fast tattoo of woodpeckers competing with the lovely song of the pied flycatchers and redstarts. The shadow of a sparrow hawk in flight, his cream-colored legs hidden in formal gray and white striped down tail feathers, preceded a crescendo of alarm calls from robins and thrushes hidden in the dense woodland.

Verity closed her eyes as silence descended, and a few long moments later the skittering of a bank mole or wood mouse intruded.

Lord, she was sure to go mad in the beauty of this solitary confinement.

Beneath her fingers, two dozen pages written through and through fluttered in the slight summer breeze. She had written them during the journey northward and had made a point to read them every day, as the scene in her guest bedchambers at the Prince Regent's Carleton House the eve before her brother's wedding still seemed surreal in her mind. Had she really spent hours in the same bed as Rory? Of course, only she would achieve what she had longed for in her youth and then sleep through the entire event.

Rory . . . Lord, he had been as magnificent as always that morning—undaunted by the cruel trick fate had played, willing to accept the consequences with a cool head and unflappable wit, and always magnetizing in a fashion that only increased her long-simmering yearning for the impossible with him.

Love . . .

Only once—during a hot summer long ago when she had been seventeen—had her sensibilities been displaced. She pushed the thought to the corner of her mind she rarely visited.

And now, Rory was even more exquisitely handsome than in her days of youth. It had been painfully difficult to meet his gaze and remain unflustered in that chamber. Only her unwavering certainty that she could never wed someone who would never love her as she did him sustained her.

Verity stared down at the ink-spattered pages in her lap. She wished for her other diaries, the ones she kept by her side always. But she had been rendered a complete nodcock in the aftermath of that morning from hell. And Amelia, for the first time in memory, had neglected to pack Verity's most prized possessions in the hasty departure from London. Ill ease filled her as she continued staring at the words on the page. But Amelia was certain to carry them on her person when she traveled north in one of the Fitzroy barouches with the rest of their affairs shortly.

She was sure.

Then again, considering all that had happened that awful night, Amelia was very likely not her cool, calm, collected self at the moment. A frisson of dread snaked up her spine just thinking of Amelia. Verity had not one but two disasters in the making and yet was too far away from everyone involved to try and set things to rights.

Out of the corner of her eye she spied her horse's head shoot up and swing about. She followed its gaze to find a rider in the distance—headed in their direction. Her heart leapt.

She knew it was he by the tilt of his head, glancing toward the wood.

She had prepared herself for the onslaught he might spew forth. He would act the role of his life to charm and pretend he truly wanted her for a wife. And if there was anyone who could play a role to perfection, it was Rory Lennox.

She should know. Had she not secretly witnessed or heard his rakehelly powers of persuasion toward the fairer and more easily duped sex? And they fell in hordes for him time and time again.

Nine times out of ten, all it took was a mere handful of words toward a suitably jaded and very willing female, although never a lady who had anything to lose by a liaison. Rory had refined the technique to its purest, most captivating essence: "Darling, I've tried and tried to fight my desire—but I can no longer stay silent. For weeks I've dreamed of you. I've only dallied with the notion of love once in my life, but I fear . . . fear greatly for my soul . . . that that is about to change."

Following a searing kiss, usually behind a tree during someone's ball, his prey stood not a chance, given his outrageous pursuit coupled with his famously handsome face and unparalleled good fortune.

According to Verity's last calculation, Rory Lennox, former Earl of Rutledge, and current Duke of Abshire, had fallen in lust twenty-six times the last three years since he returned from Wellington's war machine, still churning ever onward without him.

In Verity's well-worn dictionary there were six lines describing a rake, beginning with *libertine* and ending with *seducer*. She would have advised the editors to save space by offering up her own definition: Rake, noun. Rory Lennox.

Most dukes are born into the title. Few earn it. Rory Lennox was of the latter group. But he was not proud of it—for good reason. But after last week's debacle at Carleton House, he was through with any further attempts at escaping the hell of his own mind. And since he was giving free rein to horror, facing the ghosts lurking in that crook of Derbyshire from whence he spent his boyhood seemed like the next step on his trail to purgatory.

Now he would be saddled with a wife, Lord help *her*—the one thing he'd sworn never to have—to whom he would have to feign concern for the rest of his life. He had no bloody use for a wife and absolutely no interest in overseeing her welfare until the end of his days and beyond.

And his sodding titles? The earldom would go to a fine third cousin with a preponderance of male progeny at last review. The duchy would die with him. One Abshire was enough.

Rory dismounted a considerable distance from the lady in question—a female he had occasionally seen at the numerous fashionable events in Town the last three seasons, but as he had steered clear of all Fitzroys, he had never spoken more than three sentences to Lady Verity Fitzroy since his return from war. He vaguely remembered he had nicknamed her Lady V during those days she followed without trepidation her brother, Sussex and him when she had been on the cusp of womanhood.

There were only two reasons he was here: he always corrected his mistakes, and she was an innocent and the sister of the man he had once betrayed. If there was one trait Rory had learned too late, it was loyalty. His years on the march with Wellington had drummed it into his once untrustworthy soul.

The mossy green carpet on the edge of the wood sank under his footsteps. The soft murmur of a stream nearby provided the backdrop for birdsong lilting from the dark canopy of trees as he approached. She was seated, and hastily closed a book in her lap.

"Lady Fitzroy." He bowed perfunctorily. "Delighted to find you here."

"Do be serious," she replied, not meeting his eye.

"Lady V"—he pasted his most serene expression on his face—"how fare you?"

"The same as you, I presume, Your Grace. Mildly embarrassed, and wondering how long my brother will insist I endure my own company." She indicated the wood-slatted bench in front of her and he seated himself.

He had to laugh. Thank God she had not forsaken her youthful tendencies to make free with her sentiments. Her chin rose a notch and she finally allowed her brown eyes to wander to his. He noticed that flecks of amber sparked from the centers. The hint of a blush crested her cheeks, as her dark eyes challenged him. The Fitzroy strong features were in full evidence.

"It won't be for long," he murmured. "Indeed, since I'm here, I'd say the incarceration is over. Look, I shall see to the vicar and—"

"No."

"No?" He paused. "No to what?"

"I will not give you the great honor of my hand. That is why you're here, is it not?"

He examined his fingernails. "Look, we can do this the hard way—"

"Or the easy way?" she interrupted. "You could be a tad more original. Clichés disappoint me. And this is the very first time you've had to offer yourself on the altar of eternal wedded bliss, is it not? Not that it will be the last if you continue to be such a nodcock in your bumbling selection of sleeping quarters."

Nodcock? Bumbling? He felt a rare smile tease the corners of his mouth. "Spare the niceties, Lady V. Do tell me what you really think."

She stared at him for a long moment. Thank

God she was no coward. But had she always been quite so outspoken? As far as he could remember, the last time they had exchanged more than five words strung together before finding himself in her bedchamber was when he had lived here fourteen years ago—before he had taken what he had thought would be permanent leave of this hellish corner.

She finally shook her head with a mock look of disappointment. "If you are going to offer, one could hope you would give it a bit more thought and effort. I am James's favorite sister, after all."

"I thought that was Patience or Perseverance."

She tilted her sharp chin up. "There is no Patience or Perseverance in the Fitzroy family."

"Don't I know it," he retorted with a grin.

"*Hope* used to be his favorite," she said.

He gave her a questioning glance.

"Until she made the unpardonable mistake of making James's fiancée look like a fool."

"But she is a fool."

"There, you see? Why is my brother the only one who could not glimpse beyond her infuriating beauty?"

"Because he's a man," Rory said with an owlish expression pasted onto his face.

"Exactly!"

He bit back a laugh. He liked her. She had a lovely, open countenance when she smiled.

She narrowed her eyes. "You do that very well."

"Pardon me?" He made sure to keep a look of cool indifference on his face.

"That way of yours when you speak to ladies."

He was taken aback. "What way?"

She paused to reflect, her eyes staring at the uppermost branches of the trees. "Of agreeing with us. Gentlemen are not expected to ever agree with us. Especially concerning your own sex. I probably shouldn't have pointed any of this out for the sole reason that you will now employ it consciously to dupe a whole new legion of females."

"You look lovely, by the by, Lady V," he murmured. "What is that *fetching* thing on your head?"

"Oh, and your knack for changing the topic is top notch too. That 'thing' is a straw bonnet. Entirely uninteresting to you I am sure."

"There you are wrong, my dear V. It's simply fascinating. Is it from the Georgian or Pleistocene era?"

She refused to be swayed from the topic. "Shall we not have a go at the matter at hand? You know, the one where you are supposed to woo me and wed me in short order to save my soul or more importantly so I will not become the pariah of Derbyshire?"

"You said it, not I."

"Well, you should know the only reason I'm willing to discuss this is to keep my dear brother out of the graveyard. Your war years are too much of an advantage and James would be the worse for the wear should he meet you." She shook her head. "And I hate to arrange flowers. I would feel compelled to lay wilting bouquets on his head-stone every week for the next seventy years, given the longevity of most Fitzroys."

"But you just turned me down. So now I'm able to wash my hands of you." He tilted his head ever so slightly and took a long look at her. He hadn't ever heard so many words from a female Fitzroy. Then again, most of the five nearly identical sisters didn't have very much to say unless it concerned mathematical concepts that put him to sleep.

She pursed her lips. "You could at least try a little harder to convince me," she retorted. "This is your fault, after all."

Women. Would he ever understand them? Then again, he feared he understood them all too well. And it appeared that a large brain box did not take up any of the space for all things contrary. "Look, V, I'll not fawn over you. We've known each other's families our entire lives, and even if ours hasn't been a deep friendship—"

"And whose fault is that?" she muttered.

He stared at her clear brown eyes, which appeared sharp as a whip and yet just like liquid velvet. *What in hell?*

"Cat got your tongue?" She looked at him with a slyness he'd never seen in a Fitzroy female.

"Absolutely not," he replied. "I see you only take offense at others' use of clichés."

"I always allow myself one each quarter. I take care that it is one of the more offensive."

"You know, V, I'm not surprised you and your sisters are still unwed if this is how your brother taught you how to listen to a man's offer."

"Oh, I can do that. When it is politely given."

"I beg your pardon. I meant no offense." He stopped. "Verity, do be serious. Give me the chance to correct the great harm I've done you. We must marry. You know it."

"I most certainly do not. It's as I said in Town," she continued after a beat, "there is absolutely no reason to marry. Nothing will ever come of your stupid mistake in Carleton House—especially since any gossip generated will be far overshadowed by the tales of the royal entourage's night of debauchery. Your only duty to me is to figure out a way to avoid dueling with my brother. You owe me that much, I agree."

This was not at all going the way he had planned. And he knew how to plan. Obviously, he had gotten it wrong. He had thought that almost a week's worth of silent contemplation would convince her of the necessity of wedding him. He had been so certain he had not thought it through. But, of course, she would want to be wooed, even if the end result was not in question. All ladies liked nothing better than wooing.

Even when they knew it would lead to what all gentlemen wanted. And that wasn't wooing.

She looked at him with the oddest expression. One he hadn't ever noticed on a young lady before. Why could he not make it out? He cleared his throat.

"If you will not have me, Verity, the least you could do is allow me the pleasure of your company for a bit each day, since I've taken the trouble to return."

She said not a word. Her eyes still searched his face.

"Your siblings are in London or on their way to Cornwall as we speak. The neighborhood is much changed since I was last here. And I am rattling around the Hall, all alone, while you're becoming a tad starkers wearing one-hundred-and-five-year-old but nonetheless charming hats. Shall we not—"

"You're going to attempt to woo me, aren't you?"

He had to force his jaw to close. "You know, most ladies like me."

"I know." Her eyes had that damn innocent look back in them.

He ground his molars.

"Fear not," she continued. "We understand each other perfectly. Of course I shall see you. We're neighbors. And we must stay until James's ire cools and everyone in Town has forgotten this stupid business." A tendril of her dark brown hair fell to her shoulder from the confines of her hat, which looked rather like a neglected haystack. "You do realize that once the surrounding families know you've come, why, there will be an endless round of routs, dinners, country balls, and the like in your honor to contend with." Her eyes danced merrily. "It will be delightful!"

Rory sighed deeply. Routs, dinners, country balls, church on Sunday, and gossip on Monday through Saturday. "Delightful, indeed," he murmured. He had to retreat before he lost the inch he had gained. He opened his mouth, but she beat him to it.

"Must be off. Lovely to see you." She rose from her chair with her book in hand, and not waiting for him, Verity Fitzroy headed toward her horse without the tittering, coy hesitation of most ladies he knew. With a quickness that surprised, she placed her book in the saddlebag and ascended into the saddle with agility and grace. At the last moment she turned her mount's head about and glanced toward him. "I'm glad you've finally come home. You were missed, Rory."

His hand clenched involuntarily at his side.

Chapter 3

Verity had always liked Robert Armitage, the very tall vicar of the parish. A mere five years her senior, she knew he had a certain admiration for her, even if it could never be expressed, given their respective stations. She respected him all the better for it, as it proved he esteemed her for herself and not her dowry. And while he was a bit shy when he was near her, from the pulpit he delivered his messages with vigor, passion, and sometimes even humor. Yes. She enjoyed spending time with him very well.

And she was sure Mr. Armitage's sermon this morning had been inspiring. It was too bad she had not heard a word of it. Her mind was still whirling with thoughts of yesterday when Rory had appeared in full form. By the end of the service as she rose to leave, she had prayed that she would be able to hold firm to her convictions regarding matrimony. She had long ago accepted that she would probably never marry for many reasons.

1. Marriage without equal love on both sides would be hell on earth. And the chance of finding equal love was nearly nil.

2. Marriage with merely respect on both sides was perhaps tolerable but not worth it if it could be avoided. And she had tried very hard to avoid it.

And 3. Her one near-brush with matrimony had ended disastrously a decade ago. She was distinctly unmarriageable.

Verity came to a stop outside the stone church, which edged the picturesque green in this small village in Derbyshire she loved with all her heart. She watched the various villagers, tenants, and great families of the neighborhood pour through the yawn of the two open doors. Miss Woods, the schoolteacher, spied her and hurried forward.

"Miss Woods," Verity said, smiling.

"Lady Fitzroy," said the gray-haired schoolmistress whose stern manner masked a pudding heart. "Allow me to say how pleased I am to see you. Such a lovely surprise that you are returned from Town. Are your sisters returned as well?"

"No, I have come alone. Is it not a beautiful morning?" Verity could dissemble with the best of them, and managed to turn the conversation. "And how fares the school? Are the children still plaguing you to pieces? You may warn them that I shall send my two elder sisters to spend an entire day teaching algebraic equations, and science again if they play any further pranks."

The smile on Miss Woods's face was so brief, Verity would have missed it if she had blinked. "You are too kind, Lady Fitzroy. Actually, they have been behaving very well. Then again, they have reason."

"Reason?"

"Yes. The promise of an early end of term. I'm needed in Dorset. My sister is in a serious decline and I must go to her. I take my leave of here in three days' time."

"My sincerest condolences," Verity said with concern.

Mr. Armitage strode up holding his hat, while his black vestments fluttered in the strong breeze. He bowed deeply. "What a lovely surprise to see you up from Town, Lady Fitzroy. Are you come alone?"

It was well known that the Fitzroy ladies always

traveled in twos, threes, fours, and most often fives, Verity thought with good humor as she acknowledged him. Again she deflected. "Yes. Miss Woods was just informing me that the school is to close earlier than expected. What shall become of the three boys preparing for Eton's college program next term?"

Mr. Armitage and Miss Woods exchanged glances. "They shall have to wait a year. Their families are relieved, actually," the vicar replied. "They're needed for the harvest."

"But they shall always be needed for the harvest," Verity retorted. "That is entirely beside the point. My brother arranged to sponsor them, as they are the brightest of the parish, and our family promised them an excellent education."

The handsome vicar scratched his jaw. "There is nothing that can be done."

Miss Woods would not meet her eye. "I'm so very sorry to disappoint. But, I fear my sister is very ill, and there is no one to care for her. I took the liberty of writing a letter to His Grace and promised that I shall return as soon as I possibly can."

"Of course you must go to your sister, Miss Woods. You misunderstand. We must simply find someone to continue teaching until your return. Of course, no one is as dedicated or as superior a teacher as you," Verity added.

"The lesson plans for the three boys are prepared," Miss Woods said cautiously. "But finding someone will take time."

"Perhaps I could write to an employment agency in London to see if there are any potential candidates," Mr. Armitage suggested.

"Could we be so bold as to prevail on you, Lady Fitzroy, to forward a letter to your eldest sister to ask her to interview possible candidates?" Miss Woods's old blue eyes studied her like the hawk.

Verity knew what she should offer but held back a moment or two before plunging into the unknown. "Or . . . I could take on the task myself. If the lessons are planned and if it is only a temporary—"

"Oh, would you?" Miss Woods interrupted. The immense relief on the uncompromising schoolteacher's face shone like a beacon of salvation.

What had she been thinking? She might be a capable hostess for her brother, but she was far from qualified to teach even a church mouse. Verity had been famous for shirking her studies as a child. Her sisters' successes had usually eclipsed that fact. "Well, I'm not sure I would be—"

"We accept," the vicar said, his blue eyes sparkling. "With the greatest honor and gratitude. You have always been a paragon of benevolence and selflessness, Lady Fitzroy!"

Well, she could blame no one but herself for wading into this quagmire. She had no more idea of how to teach a roomful of students than how to milk a dairy cow. And at this particular moment the latter held far more appeal. But glancing at the expectant faces of the two people she most admired in the village, she knew she had no other choice but to proceed."

"I think we both know, Mr. Armitage, that I am anything but a paragon. However, I'm willing to very likely make a fool of myself as long as Miss Woods spends a day or two to prepare me to face the—ahem—angels."

"Why do I have the distinct impression you were about to say 'enemy'?" Mr. Armitage's face was lit with amusement.

"I fear you have the right of it, sir. You see, I have the uneasy suspicion that I'm about to be repaid in-kind."

"In-kind?" Miss Woods examined her above her spectacles. "In what fashion?"

"The ghosts of governesses past come back to haunt their least favorite charge, Miss Woods."

"Why, you shall be perfect for the post in that case, Lady Fitzroy," the teacher insisted.

"How so?"

"Foreknowledge and preparation are the main tools of every good teacher. Those that have dished out trouble in the past know what to expect."

Verity was suddenly overcome with a sinking feeling. "That is precisely why I am worried."

Mr. Armitage laughed out loud. "Have no fear. I shall have a word before you start, and you forget the power of your family's name. They shall each of them be quaking in their boots."

"Speaking of which, Lady Fitzroy, the smithy mentioned to the butcher, who informed the draper . . ." Miss Woods took a breath. ". . . that we have the extraordinary good luck that Lord Rutledge—or rather, the Duke of Abshire—is returned to us. Can you imagine, after all these years? Have you seen him yet?"

Both pairs of blue eyes looked at her, wishing her to tell more. This was the life of a small village. Gossip was its life blood, and great pleasure. Even the vicar did not fear its ill-effects.

"Yes."

They willed her to continue.

"He condescended to call at Boxwood."

She could hear the birds chirping on the green.

"And?" The vicar and schoolteacher spoke simultaneously.

"And, he is well."

Mr. Armitage looked at his hands, which held a Bible, in front of him. "Does he intend to reside here for any length of time? No one seems to know."

"I have not the faintest idea of His Grace's schedule. But I should not count on him to stay long."

At their crestfallen exchanged looks, Verity could not help to reverse course. "But, then again, perhaps he will change his mind. You know how these great men are. Fickle. And no one likes to stay in Town the summer months after all." And it was true. Brighton and Bath were the places to be. She certainly wished she could be there right this very moment.

How on earth had she managed to return to the schoolroom? Well, she had no one but herself to blame. Had she not complained about having nothing to do?

But it was hard to feel grateful for the answer to her prayers.

If he could be anywhere this moment, Rory would choose Brighton or Bath. Yes, that or a large house party in a quaint corner where the fast set gathered to privately wager staggering amounts at cards, get blindingly drunk, and do foolish things like fox hunting in a bog, sailing at midnight, and escorting ladies who knew how to flirt and be flirted with.

Instead, he was stuck right back were he began

his journey on this godforsaken mortal coil: in Derbyshire. And it was very likely he would have to remain here for the duration of this campaign to convince a dark-haired, dark-eyed, extraordinarily perceptive Fitzroy female that she must marry him, if only to set to rights a chain of wrongs.

He had no desire to do so, and yet, the whole nonsense was not as terrifyingly distasteful as he had thought it would be. If their first private conversation was anything to go by (and if her brother didn't ultimately kill him), the future occasions they would be forced to share together would not be entirely unamusing. Lady Verity Fitzroy was a refreshing surprise. There was not an inch of coquetry about her. And there was significant charm, and wit. Yes, he had not one doubt that she would never bore him. Her millinery creations were another story.

Balancing precariously on the back legs of an ancient, cracked-leather chair, he stared out the rear window of his father's old study. The play of the late afternoon sun's rays filtering through the verdant branches of the trees dotting the gardens was so familiar to him. And yet, he could not remember ever sitting here with his father. He had seen his mother only a modicum more. But it was the way of it with parents of the Upper Ten Thousand.

He had dutifully answered his parents' few letters over the years, when they had reached him at some far-flung post. He had not returned for their burials. He felt little remorse.

A large shadow moved in the hazy distance, and Rory let the front legs of his chair drop awkwardly to the floor as a shiver snaked up his back. Good Lord. It looked like Nero, his long dead horse. Suddenly the rider slowed the powerful stallion from a gallop to a spirited trot and negotiated the turn to the stables.

Rory shook his head. This was why he had vowed never to return. Too many memories or ghosts and none of them good.

He forced himself to turn and face the small mound of ledgers and two London papers, just ironed, on the desk. But not before he spied the tiny initials he had carved on one of the legs facing the window: RL. He hadn't even received a single lash for that great transgression. That was the problem, he had figured out during all those years following the drum. He had never been punished. For anything in his life.

And he had tried.

Yet no one had bothered to notice.

He skimmed the *Morning Post*'s vast array of advertisements, taking up most of the front page, before he opened the pages to review more important matters such as Wellington's progress, and, of course, given the situation, he finally turned to "The Fashionable World," that outrageous corner of the paper, where the have-nots alternately praised and ridiculed the haves of which he was at the top. He stilled.

"The Fashionable World" is delighted to offer our esteemed readers another rare glimpse at the innermost goings-on of the crème de la crème of the aristocracy—the royal entourage. Just when we all thought there could be no greater evils than those witnessed the botched evening before the Duke of Candover's wedding, we find these events were but a mere candied cherry atop a sinful confection as large as Carleton House. Yes, ladies and gentlemen. It is our pleasure to publish an excerpt from a mysterious diary every Tuesday and Thursday this summer, when things can be a bit dreary and thin of company in Town. Alas, we have unearthed a treasure trove of further proof of the royal entourage's outrageousness. Truly they must each and every one of them be punished—starting with the Prince Regent. The French have shown us the way of it.

Excerpt #1:

There are times when boys will be boys. However, in this case, I must suggest that these gentlemen of my fond acquaintance are actually more like boys being infants.

For what is an infant but a mewling, ill-tempered person unable to speak, walk, and with a tendency to cast up its accounts at very poorly timed intervals in between long stretches of slumber at odd hours.

Yes, I am sad to say, Dearest Diary, that Sussex, Middlesex, Wright, and even Barry were acting thusly not last evening, no. At that time they were all spit, polish, and smiles for their partners. And all shrewd, outrageous bluffing, drinking, and boasting (well, perhaps Barry did not do the last, but we both know he is the stiffest of the crowd) with the gentlemen at Lord and Lady Creighton's ball that kicked off the season.

But why was any of the former remarkable? Really, when one looks at the events quite closely, one must admit that it was but a repeat of a thousand nights before it.

No. The pièce de résistance was when Middlesex insisted on waltzing with one of the scullery maids in full view of Lord and Lady Creighton, with whose daughter he had refused to dance, saying she had far too many names dangling from her wrist and "she should give other fair maids a chance."

Of course, Middlesex cannot be blamed. How could he possibly remember that Miss Gwendolyn Creighton was the reason for the ball? It was, quite simply, her come-out, and on that one day in her lifetime, she should be able to drown in public adoration. Then again, the royal entourage is more often noted for its self-adoration, so they can not be held accountable to us mere mortals.

Rory's fingers were numb, and the newspaper fell from his hand. Rory snatched it up again to look at the paper's date—a mere six days after the infamous evening. At this rate, with the promise of twice weekly additional timber to the revolutionary fire engulfing Town these days, it would be a miracle if the underclasses did not rise up in arms before the end of the summer. Prinny would be a cooked goose if this continued.

Who in bloody hell was the author of this muck?

A tap at the door intruded, and Rory looked up from his musings to encounter towering Towareq, the nephew of a former king of Timbuktu. Stolen by traders and taken to Cairo, Rory had found Towareq as a boy cowering behind a pile of rubble and freed him during the Egyptian campaign against Napoleon.

"Yes, Towareq?"

The young man who had nearly given his life to Rory twice in the intervening years bowed deeply and crossed the polished oak floor. "For you, Your Grace."

Rory pushed aside the newspaper and grasped the edge of a calling card in the highly polished silver salver. "So it has begun."

There was a reason Rory would not travel anywhere without Towareq. He never asked questions. He did not disappoint this time.

"Now that the knocker is up, the hordes will ignore a man's privacy and preference for quiet, all in an effort to ensure that he not grow bored by the country life and so return to London in all haste. Lord, if they only knew how lovely it is to be bored. Show them in, then."

He had hoped to avoid these particular inhabitants of this corner of Derbyshire. He rose as the pair stepped through the open door.

"Miss Talmadge and Mr. Talmadge." His gaze bypassed the blond young man who had most likely just attained his majority, and he nearly started at the sight of Miss Phoebe Talmadge. *God. She was a living, breathing incarnation of Catharine.*

Talmadge bowed as his sister curtsied. "So good of you to see us, Your Grace," the brother began.

Rory steadied his hand and then gestured to the other two chestnut-colored leather armchairs in front of the swept out hearth, and joined them there. "It is my pleasure, of course. Towareq, I'm certain Miss Talmadge should like tea."

The towering dark presence of the Egyptian faded away.

"Thank you, Your Grace," Miss Phoebe Talmadge began, a bit breathlessly. "My brother and I hope you will do us the great honor of accepting this invitation to a ball we are planning Wednesday eve." She extended an elegant envelope, and he grasped it. When he met her glance, he had a difficult moment. Her pale blue eyes were so familiar he felt a drench of sweat under all the cloth layers on his back.

"Wednesday next?" Rory repeated, to gain time to consider.

"Yes, Your Grace," Talmadge began, with awkwardness written all over his young face. "My sister and I hope you will do us the great honor. We wish to formally celebrate your return to the neighborhood. You were once close to our family, especially our dear departed sister before you left . . ." He abruptly stopped after glancing at Rory.

"I should be delighted to attend," Rory lied, wishing he could scream the opposite to the docile gentleman ten years his junior. He continued, "May I ask if the inhabitants of Boxwood will be present?"

The two exchanged glances. "They are in London," Talmadge finally stated.

"Actually, that is not altogether correct," Rory murmured. "Lady Verity Fitzroy is in residence."

"How very odd," Phoebe Talmadge exclaimed, uncertainty coloring her face. "I suppose I heard a vague rumor to that effect."

Rory paused, considering. He knew why she had been excluded. It was due to his own well-known dislike of Candover. "Lady Fitzroy is a treasure of the neighborhood."

Mr. Talmadge glanced at his sister. "She must be included."

"Of course, if it is His Grace's wish." Phoebe looked at him with great expectation.

The brother scratched his chin, uncertain of how to address the obvious. "But we cannot guarantee that she will accept, Your Grace. I am certain you understand that she or her brother might be, ahem, rather put out at the idea."

"Miss Talmadge?" Rory continued.

"Yes?" she said, her eyes huge in her pretty face.

"I would ask the honor of the first set with you, as I'm certain *your brother* will ask Lady Fitzroy for the same." *Would this infernal conversation never end? The silent guard at the palace offered more amusing give and take.*

A shy smile full of lingering coquetry infused

Phoebe Talmadge's face. "Of course we will accommodate your wishes, Your Grace."

The way the young lady's eyes lit up with delight unnerved Rory. She was so much like Catherine physically, but her demure demeanor was jarringly different. And he had the distinct impression that she was hiding her true nature. Did she actually possess her sister's wild, high-flying sensibilities?

Talmadge pursed his lips, his brow furrowed slightly. "But it's very odd that Lady Verity Fitzroy returned just before you, and unaccompanied by her sisters."

Allowing an awkward pause to enter, Rory stared at the young gentleman. "I would take great care in voicing your observations, Talmadge. Nothing can wreak havoc, particularly in a small village, as effectively as gossip. I do hope you are not succumbing to the favorite pastime of the idle."

"Don't be ridiculous, Your Grace!" Phoebe laughed in the identical fashion as her sister, and it was all Rory could do not to climb out of his skin. It was like hearing haunting echoes of days gone by.

Rory's sudden silence cut short any further meddling nonsense.

Talmadge was properly chastised.

The lukewarm tea Towareq served, prepared to Rory's exact specifications to discourage visitors from lingering, had the desired effect, and the brother and sister left in short order. Thank God.

Alone at last, he slumped forward and rested his head in his clenched hands.

He should never have left Wellington in Portugal after all. It was too bad he had not had a say in the matter. But when Prinny made up his mind, there was little to be done to sway him. There were depths to the prince that very few knew.

Behind the royal's dissolute, extravagant mask, the future king's conniving intelligence thrived.

Chapter 4

Verity should have taken the other way to the village, via the lane, but instead she cut through the neighboring property, her mare easily popping over the stile. It had taken longer than expected to ready herself for the first day in front of the class. It was silly how anxious she was.

She attempted to concentrate on the thing about riding that she loved most . . . getting lost in the pure joy and excitement of the moment, forcing all her mountain of worries to fly away with the wind. She urged her mare into a gallop as they mounted the western side of the prominent slope of the Duke of Abshire's property.

A rider and big-boned dark gray horse crested the eastern edge not ten feet in front of her. With extreme luck on their shoulders, each jerked in different directions and avoided collision. Verity's mount kicked out in fright and only a steady stream of soothing words slowed the panicked creature. She finally heaved to a stop.

There were times in Verity's life in which she would have liked to disappear into thin air. Usually those periods had been while her ear had been pressed against an abominably thick door, behind which her brother and his friends communed on the altar of bachelorhood. This was one of those times that thin air appeared very breathable.

Rory's horse reared, and he almost tumbled backward as he wrenched his mount's head to avoid her mare's kick. It had taken considerably more effort to bring his horse under control.

Verity prepared for the barrage. She knew she was at fault. She did not have permission to cross his land, and she should not have been galloping up the slope, as she could not see the other side. But, most days the most exciting thing that would have been revealed over the ridge was a rabbit or two nibbling on rolling hills and hollows of green clover. And it was one mile less to the village than if she had taken the lane.

Reluctantly, she opened one rein to urge the mare toward him. "I'm so very sorry. I'm completely at fault," she stated plainly. "I know I should be horsewhipped for trespassing and for going at such speed without view of the other side."

She could not stop the torrent of words tumbling from her mouth when he would not reply. His face was drained of all color; the pallor reminded her of death. It was embarrassment that drove her speech into the absurd. "In fact, my brother always keeps a coiled whip just for such occasions, I am sure he would let you borrow it. Although, perhaps this incident renders our scores even in terms of disastrous events. And upon further reflection, spooking your horse does not compromise you in any way. Perhaps if you had fallen—in which case it could be argued that it might have bruised your notion of masculinity. But that would not be nearly as bad as the possible blemish on my—" She finally paused to take a breath. "Rory? Are you all right?"

Color had returned to his face. The slow curl at the corners of his lips hinted at his amusement as his beautiful horse pawed the ground. "Do you always talk so much? I mean, before all this sleeping together business."

Shock and surprise paid a call, and Verity suddenly wanted to disappear. "I beg your pardon?"

"As you should. And I accept, even if you have not the faintest idea that a proper apology should not be littered with excuses. But there is one condition if I am to accept your apology right and proper." His words were measured as he dismounted and finally turned his full gaze in her direction.

She sucked in her breath. "Of course," she whispered as she followed his suit by dismounting as well.

"Yes, you will agree to it, or yes, you want to hear it?"

"The latter, unless the former doesn't include marriage," she continued, fiddling with the reins of the bridle. "If it does, I choose the horsewhip. Although, I've never heard that proper acceptances of apologies include conditions."

He glanced at her, and shook his head as he closed the distance between them.

At least he wasn't furious with her. It was always a shock to see him in the flesh. Her cousin Esme might have captured his essence on a canvas once or twice. But it was the grace and surety of his movements that enthralled her. That, and those pea green eyes and the lazy way they gazed down at her, all the while razor-sharp intelligence lurked in his black pupils.

"I do not remember you being quite so vexing when you were an infant."

"Thirteen is not an infant!"

He hooded his eyes further. "And when were you three and ten?"

She sighed in exasperation. "When you were

one and twenty, and thought any lady younger than six and ten was an infant."

"Actually, any woman younger than seven and ten was considered an infant when I reached the advanced age you suggest." He paused for a beat. "By the by, V, you are no novice at changing the course of a conversation yourself."

She would not allow smugness to hollow her cheeks. "I've no idea what you're talking about. And now I am very nearly late. I must be on my—"

"You will paint something as penance," he spoke softly.

"Paint?" Why she was the absolute worst artist not only in her family, but in the whole of Derbyshire, she was convinced. "But, I am very ill-trained, I—" She stopped and reversed course. "Of course. I will paint whatever you like. But really, I must be on my way, I—"

"Actually, there are three things to be painted. Two signs, on either side of this hill, warning riders to slow down."

She laughed in relief. That was nothing. "Of course, if you like."

"And I'm certain you've accepted the invitation to the Talmadges' infernal entertainment? You will dance the second set with me, of course."

"Well, I wasn't actually certain I would attend—" She stopped mid-sentence when his face darkened.

"Of course I shall, if only to make amends." She took care not to agree to dance with him—only to attend the event.

He nodded. "Very good. And lastly, the wood fence surrounding the south field. It needs a good whitewashing."

She widened her eyes. "But it's . . . it's millions of miles long."

"No need to delve into details here and now. I believe you mentioned you're late."

She glanced at his boots to regain her composure. Was it her imagination or were his feet becoming a bit cloven-like?

"Do see to the fence in the next sennight, Lady V."

"I cannot," she replied with more force than she wanted. "I have far more important things to attend to."

"Really?" He raised his brows. "Such as menus for one, horse collisions for two, and embroidery for many?"

"I will have you know that that is entirely not the case."

"I see."

"By that look on your face it's obvious you do not see at all." She knew she sounded like a pretentious ninny, unsalted by the smallest trace of wit. Why was she arguing with him? She just could not stop herself. "I'll have you know that I, alone, am cultivating the next generation of great minds in England."

Not even the smallest muscle of his handsome mouth moved, but she just knew he was laughing at her.

"I see," he finally replied. "Well, then perhaps you will not have time for the next generation of paint on the fences of the south field."

"Precisely," she said, quite proud that not a hint of smugness discolored the word.

"Perhaps, then, you should choose the alternative, less time-consuming penance."

"Obviously. I shall do the signs for your amusement, and I shall write a very formal note of apology to you to promise not to trespass in future, and I shall even condescend to dance with you at the *infernal* Talmadges' as you demand. This is, by the by, far more than you have done for a far greater offense." Her nose rose in the air without conscious effort.

"Perhaps. But I have proper manners, and do not suggest my own penance when transgressions occur. Now then, Lady V, you are in the unenviable position of having to decide if you should prefer to paint, dance, and whitewash—according to you—*millions* of miles of fence, or . . ."

She closed her eyes, and knew what he would utter.

". . . marriage. To me. So I can clean one small corner of my nearly inexistent conscience."

"You're being ridiculous. I've already told you that I will not—"

"I thought you said you were late," he corrected with exasperating good humor. "I cannot bear the thought of taking any time away from the cultivation of the next generation of great minds in England."

She did not know when she had been more exasperated.

"So we're agreed," he continued. "Do let me know your choice at the Talmadge affair tomorrow evening. I should offer to help you remount, but I find myself rather put out in the face of your intractability."

Speechless, she watched him remount his own magnificent animal. She finally found words just as he wheeled about and nodded to her with great condescension.

"I'm so glad you noticed, Your Grace. You are forewarned it's a troublesome trait our children would very likely inherit."

He blinked.

She turned her back to him as she crossed to her horse in an effort to hide the prick of anger that was most certainly mottling her face. "Oh, you needn't look so worried, Rory. You know very well we will never have children together, as

I will never accept you." She quickly remounted her mare. "Not even if you ever truly wanted me, begged me even. You're not the marrying kind, Rory Lennox . . ." She paused and concluded with emphasis, "And neither am I."

She had thought that would render him speechless, but it did not. Just as she turned into the wind, quite brisk now, she heard his words float back to her.

"I do hope you honor your debts, V. Visible pasture fencing or connubial fencing in. It matters not to me. Although, one might be hazardous to your well-being if the past is any indication."

Surreptitiously, he turned his horse about when he was certain she was well on her way to the village. He had hated to say the last, but it was the fair thing to do. She would marry him in the end. Neither had any choice in the matter. There was that sliver of honor that he could not extinguish no matter how hard he tried to smother it. And he had tried. But while they must marry, he would brook no false hope of some fairy tale ending. Love was nothing more than a wisp of a notion soon lost to truth, familiarity, or worse.

Verity felt as rumpled, and her nerves as frayed, as all the governesses had complained whilst attempting to govern her in her youth, which she, of course, had never believed. The truth was always painful, she mused as she gazed at the twenty odd heads bent over the books her forward-thinking, generous brother had provided. There were not many who subscribed to the notion of educating the underclasses.

Oh, it had been a joy to take aside the three young men destined for Eton next winter. Their superior intellect was inspiring as she listened to their lessons. But the second half of the day had involved teaching a large group of the tenant children to read. She had thought she would go mad after three hours of childish primers.

But at least it had distracted her from thinking about Rory . . . and his absurd campaign to do the wrong thing for the wrong reasons when she would only ever do the right thing for the right reasons. And honor had no place in this. It was love or it was nothing.

As long as she could withstand the siege by the very man to whom she would most like to surrender.

Verity glanced up just in time to catch a young boy in the back of the room passing something to another boy, his brother, if she remembered correctly. She gave him a speaking glance, and pointed a finger toward his primer. He immediately complied.

She turned her attention to the next day's lesson plans in front of her at the desk. The vicar would not approve of her sensibilities right now if he knew how she was praying for Miss Woods's sister's quick recovery, all for very uncharitable reasons. She stared out the one window of the simple schoolhouse with the peaked roof. She had one final half hour of this impossible, never-ending day.

The livery stable was suddenly all hustle and bustle when an elegant burgundy and gold barouche conveyed by a matched quartet of gleaming bays came to a halt in front. Who could it be? No one of the neighborhood would travel locally in so fine a vehicle. She craned her neck only to see a ravishingly beautiful lady emerge and accept the aid of a servant while descending.

Verity abruptly pushed back from the desk, causing the chair's legs to make a squealing noise, which drew the attention of the entire class. She quickly crossed to the window without explanation. She knew the lady. She was certain. And yet . . . what on earth was Lady Mary Haverty, best friend of her two older sisters, doing in Derbyshire? She was supposed to be in Scotland, where she was to meet her soon-to-be-husband, Laird MacGregor, for the very first time. Mary's remove from London, the first meeting, the wedding, and the procreating were all to be accomplished in very short order. Then again, Mary had taken a mere fortnight to come to the decision to accept the terms of an arranged marriage to an unknown maternal cousin and powerful Scottish laird. It had been a source of intense debate between the elder Fitzroy ladies and their friend.

Verity glanced at the small gold watch broach pinned to her bodice. Then she studied the silent, expectant faces of the children. What was ten minutes in the grand scheme of things? Was this not precisely the sort of rigid thinking of her former governesses who had made her itch to put amphibians in their beds?

"Go on, then. You have almost uniformly been perfectly wonderful. I shall see you tomorrow, then. Oh, and"—she smiled—"whoever left this lovely welcoming gift for my first day"—she sent a pointed glance toward a carrot-topped boy in the third row before she withdrew an enormous lizard-like creature from a desk drawer using a handkerchief—"my mother once suggested to me that Great Crested Newts prefer ponds to governess's beds. And I do believe they like desk drawers even less. So please return him to his watering hole if you will." She placed the newt in a box on the desk as the boys laughed and made ready to leave. The guilty party sheepishly removed the animal on his way out with the rest of them.

Verity quickly gathered her affairs and the lesson plan that required a bit of revision, and was ready to leave when a sound alerted her to the entrance of a young boy of eight or nine. Tom, was it? He was a little too thin, and she already had a plan for tackling that problem.

"Your ladyship?" he asked shyly, sidling up to her desk.

"Yes?"

"Me brover John and—"

"*My* brother John," she corrected.

"Pardon, ma'am, but John be *me* brover."

She wanted to laugh, but could not muster the energy. "Yes?"

"Well, we be needed for hayin' on the morrow. But John and me, we—"

"John and *I*." She could not let it go.

He scratched his head. "Uh, well, I dunno what your ladyship and me brover did, but John and me wrote this for ye since ye seem so fond of them poems, ye do. Pardon me, yer ladyship."

He placed a rumpled piece of paper on the old desk and dashed out the door, without taking his leave properly.

She picked up the paper.

> *Yer ladyship be so kind.*
> *Yer ladyship be so smart.*
> *Yer ladyship be so pretty.*
> *Yer ladyship like funnin'.*
> *Yer ladyship be a grate teacher.*
> *Thank ye fer teachin' us brats.*

For some stupid reason her eyes welled. How maudlin she could be at times. It was not as if she hadn't received gratitude from the less fortunate in the county. Why, she and her sisters had been delivering food baskets to the needy for as long as she could remember.

But this was different, she realized with sudden clarity.

This was helping the less fortunate build a potential better life for them in the future versus pure charity.

"Are you crying?"

Verity looked up to find Lady Mary Haverty in the doorway. The former smiled. "Yes, I fear I am."

"But teachers aren't allowed to cry."

"I know. That's why I highly doubt I'll make it a week before I am either sacked or bundled up and placed in an asylum."

Mary laughed, and once again Verity was reminded that there was literally not another lady on Earth who was as strikingly lovely as she, with her gleaming dark russet locks, and impossibly elegant face and form, without a single defect.

"What are you doing here—" They both began the same sentence and then stopped to laugh. Verity rushed forward finally to grasp the other lady in her arms. There was a lovely sort of relief when in the presence of a confidante after a drought of companionship.

Verity took a long look at Mary. "Let me gather my things, and then shall we go to Boxwood? Do please say you will come for a visit. A good long one."

"Well, I am not too proud to admit it is precisely what I had hoped you might offer. You can imagine my surprise when I asked the smithy for confirmation that you were, indeed, at Boxwood as I had heard, but the man pointed to the schoolhouse."

Verity smiled. "I suspect I am the last of my sisters you would expect to find in a schoolroom."

Mary's laugh was a thing of feminine beauty. She shook her head. "Absolutely!"

That was the thing about Mary. She might be brutally honest, but she was so witty and kindhearted that no lady of good character could not help but like her.

"So," Verity began uncertainly, "I had thought

you were ensconced in Scotland." She dared not say more.

Mary's chin rose a fraction of an inch. "I would be delighted to accept your invitation to stay on. Just a dab of a visit. I'm not too proud to admit I am in a most perplexing state."

"Well, that makes two of us," Verity said ruefully.

Not a quarter hour later it was all arranged. Mary's affairs were sent on to the estate, while the ladies independently rode to Boxwood. They even raced the last furlong, which made Verity love Mary all the more. How could such grace and elegance also ride like a banshee? It simply was not fair.

Then again, was not life ever fair? How many times would she have to learn that lesson?

In a cozy study in front of a spare fire, meant only to chase the barest hint of coolness in the summer night's air, the two ladies reconvened after Mary had taken a race victory lie down.

"So, are you ever going to tell me why you are not in Scotland, Mary?"

"Of course. But first you must tell me news of your brother and the other members of the royal entourage. Where are they? The *Morning Post* was filled with . . . with drivel."

Verity bit her lip. "Well, the thing of it is . . ."

And within a quarter hour Mary was apprised of the details of James's catastrophic non-wedding morning. But Verity was just not ready to confide her own disaster-in-the-making.

"Well, I know it's not correct of me to allow this," Mary began. "But I think it was the unspoken thought of most of the ton that Candover's wedding of the century would have been the greatest *mistake* of the century. Although I will admit, quite selfishly, that it works out very well for me."

Verity stared at her. "Why?"

"All of London is so focused on the ruckus that the upper crust will be entirely uninterested in my sad story."

Verity waited patiently.

"The MacGregor is dead."

"*Dead*?"

"The day before I arrived."

"Lord, Mary . . . Was he murdered?"

"You always had the most vivid imagination, dearest." Mary shook her head. "Didn't you used to weave the most fantastic stories about jungle cats mating with zebras when you were a child?"

"Cheetahs and panthers," Verity replied with a sly look. "But they never mated. They merely flirted."

"Indeed," Mary added, nodding. "Quite provocative for a young lady."

"But what of MacGregor? Oh, I'm so sorry,

Mary. But we all understood him to be a virile man in his prime."

"He succumbed to a sudden lung fever the day before I arrived for our wedding in the Highlands."

"Oh, Mary."

The great beauty glanced toward the lengthening shadows reflected from the window. "It's all right, Verity. I've had a long carriage ride to reconcile myself to the fact. I believe he would have been a good husband, even if he was a stranger. But I seem to be walking under a cloud of ill luck. I was dreadfully sorry for his family, who adored him. I stayed for a week—for the burial, but no longer. I felt like an imposter in a house full of proper mourners. So now I'm eventually for London where I shall wear mourning gowns and decline invitations for the required period. It suits me perfectly, actually, as you can imagine."

"I have a far better idea," Verity began. "I'm positively begging you to remain here with me. You cannot go to Town. You know it would be unbearable for you. Lord and Lady Ha—" Verity stopped herself, horrified she had almost referred to Mary's recent deep heartache.

"It's all right, Verity. You can say the name." Mary's mouth formed a lovely smile but her emerald eyes did not show a hint of happiness.

"Lord and Lady Hadrien are in London, just returned from their honeymoon."

"I had guessed," Mary said stiffly, with that same determined smile. "But truly I am fully recovered, Verity."

Her stunning friend's visage spoke of the opposite.

"I refuse to be bitter. It's very simple really. What I thought we had formed was not genuine after all. It was mere illusion, nothing more. I know I'm lucky. And far better off without him. Hadrien sold himself for a price." She looked down at her hands pleated in her lap in front of her. "But eventually he will learn the cost. I pity him, really, Verity. I very much doubt he will find happiness as the lapdog of a very rich older lady. And her grand estate is far from the glittering lights of Town he prefers."

After a long silence, Verity asked her softly, "I never knew precisely what happened. Hope and Faith didn't breathe a word."

"I shall tell you, then," Mary continued, studying the hem of her simple black mourning gown. "Hadrien never formally announced our engagement as promised. Slowly, and painfully, but most assuredly, he disappeared from my life—still privately declaring his deep love for me on the rare occasion I would see him. I later heard rumors that all the while he was secretly corresponding with the widowed countess. You know the rest."

"I wish there was a word worse than 'devil' for that is what he is. I do hope you never question yourself for he duped us all." Verity reached for Mary's hand and squeezed it gently with affection.

"Don't worry, dearest, I refuse to become bitter, you see. And now I've had more than a week to take a decision and yet again a new path," Mary said, the barest hint of a smile forming on her face finally.

"Indeed. What is your plan, pray tell?"

"We both of us are in need of husbands, are we not?"

"And why would you suggest I am in need of . . ." Mary Haverty was usually the most brilliant schemer but—

"A letter from Hope reached me before I left the Highlands. She wrote that she and your sisters were leaving for a house party at the Duke of Kress's crumbling landmark in Cornwall—all ordered there by the Prince Regent. But she also noted cryptically that you alone returned to Derbyshire by direction of your brother. It made little sense to me. You and your sisters walk lock-step. And then I wondered"— Mary examined her closely—"why Abshire was not ordered south with the rest of the entourage, too. Surely this is some stupid misunderstanding. Your brother is more of a tyrant than my father used to be."

"He's on a fool's errand, I assure you."

Mary looked at her expectantly.

Verity hesitated.

"You're not going to violate the golden rule of intimate friendship, Verity, are you? Because truly I'm not certain I will hold up under the strain of the guilt I might feel, attempting to wheedle information you do not want to impart."

And with that, the veil of secrecy came crashing down, and for the first time in a very long time, Verity felt the relief of confiding that she had awakened to find Rory Lennox in her bed.

Mary looked at her transfixed. "But do you love him?"

"Of course not!"

Those sly green eyes, which were not at all spring pea in color, deduced otherwise. "How long have you been in love with him?"

Verity exhaled heavily. "Far before cheetahs began preying on panthers."

Mary chuckled. "Does he know?"

"Of course not. Look, the truth of the matter is that while I might have had a *tendre* for him when I was much younger, then I grew up. And I have seen enough of life to know that an on-the-shelf spinster will not find happiness with a charming rake."

"Thank the Lord you're so sensible, Verity. More sensible than I."

"All I know is that I cannot marry him. It would be unbearable to live the rest of my life beside a man who wed me against his will. And it's beside the point. I decided long ago that I would most likely never marry. And much as James blusters on and on about marrying his sisters off and offering staggering dowries as inducement, he has already agreed to Hope and Faith's request that they end their annual suffering through another Season. They are to remove to his estate in the Lake District this autumn."

"Your feelings are perfectly reasonable," Mary agreed.

Verity rushed from her seat and knelt on the hearth to accept the arms Mary offered. "Finally, someone who understands. I'm so tired of the false hope and encouragement offered by other females."

"You misunderstand, Verity. Your sensibilities are understandable, but you might have to reconsider. I know you would not ever do anything to hurt the future chances of any of your sisters. If a breath of scandal floats to your corner, you know very well it might tarnish their eligibility even with their immense dowries. Since we are in similar but different situations, I believe we must do what I suggested. We must find proper husbands in very short order despite your previous vow. And I have devised a strategy that will ensure that we find gentlemen who will fulfill all our requirements—love not being one of them. In your case, we will find someone who will offer you the protection of his name but not *intimate* presence in your life, if that is what you truly wish."

Verity sighed inwardly. She could not tell Mary Haverty why she had no desire to marry anyone in her lifetime. There was only one soul on earth who knew the most important reasons. Her brother.

But it was time to face facts. She should prepare for the worst. If gossip about that night in Carleton House began filtering into Derbyshire from Town, she should have a suitable gentleman willing to agree to a marriage of convenience—long on reserve and respect, and short on any sort of intimacy. Her dowry would go a long way as an enticement. And the search would be less awful if she did it with Mary. "You said you had a plan."

"I do indeed." Mary pulled a note from her black string reticule and unfolded it carefully. "It's so simple and brilliant I should have employed this method my first season. Memorize this list of questions. When is the next large social event in the neighborhood?"

Verity accepted the proffered list but didn't examine it. "Tomorrow night. The Talmadges' ball to honor the arrival of Abshire. What have you in mind?"

"Perfect," Mary replied, her eyes sparkling with humor. "We are going to query every gentleman we dance with or talk to tomorrow night and every day and night during the next fortnight. If any of them answer all these questions correctly, we will agree to marry them on the spot. Agreed?"

Verity shook her head. "You cannot be serious. Let me see." She read the first question and exploded with laughter.

1. Do you have a secret love child?

Chapter 5

Rory entered the Talmadge manor house near Dovedale Wednesday evening at precisely one-half hour past the appointed time. He would have arrived far later, if at all, had it not been for the matter at hand—forcing Verity's hand.

She was proving to be damnably difficult to govern. He should have known. Was there a Fitzroy in the last five hundred years who had not been stubborn? He very much doubted it.

But he wasn't used to the trait in a female. Coquetry, fickleness, a love of flattery, and everything that sparkled was what most ladies were made of. Verity appeared just the opposite. She was outspoken, honest, practical, and very amusing. He liked her.

For the first time in his life he wasn't certain

how to proceed even if he knew he would win in the end.

At least when she agreed to his proposal, his conscience would be less heavy and he could attend his appointment with death if Candover refused to accept his apology for harming his sister and . . . Catharine. Rory had meted out his own punishment for his unspeakable actions toward Catharine fourteen years ago; he had become a cog in the war between England and France. But he knew Candover would never forgive him. And so Rory had prepared himself to face death long ago. Who would have guessed it would take so many years to be served his dish . . . and that it would suddenly become far less appealing than it had been fourteen years ago?

He tugged at the neckcloth Towareq had spent so much bloody time arranging this evening. God, he just needed more air. At least he had managed to time it right. The Talmadges had stopped receiving and everyone was already in the ballroom when a liveried servant bowed and motioned him into the chamber he knew well from so long ago.

It was the same glittering scene of many a year gone by. Magnificent crystal chandeliers above shone reflected light from dozens of candles. The intricate gold leaf panels on the walls framed bucolic scenes from the last era of powdered and bewigged ladies and lords dancing, picnicking, and children swinging. The domed ceiling, painted by Laguerre, featured the Virtues and Vices in glorified battle. It captured the essence of the scene below perfectly.

Rory examined the people in the elegant chamber under hooded eyes. Conversation abruptly stopped and all eyes turned toward him.

He finally spotted Lady V. She had dared to refuse to see him yesterday when he came to call on her at Boxwood. He took one step toward her when Miss Phoebe Talmadge hurried to block his path.

"Your Grace," she said with a deep curtsy. "You are just in time. The music is about to begin and, let's see . . ." She glanced at the card attached at her wrist with a gold ribbon that matched her shimmering gown, which matched her gleaming hair held high with gold combs. "Yes, I remember. You are my first partner."

And this was merely the beginning of the evening designed in hell. The notes of a waltz wafted from the musicians perched in the balcony.

Lord, it was like holding Catharine. Phoebe Talmadge was the exact height as her dead sister. His arm fell on the same waist, and his gaze fell on the same intensely cornflower blue eyes filled with farouche mystery. "How old are you?"

She smiled and his gut clenched. There was the same sense of unruliness in her expression.

"How perfectly rude, Your Grace. I should like to tell you, but I shall have to do it in private for there are far too many people staring at us."

He looked away to negotiate the edge of the ballroom only to see his future bride—he winced at even thinking the word—yes, his *bride* entering the dance just ahead of him with a prematurely balding and bespectacled young gentleman. Why wasn't she dancing with young Talmadge? Rory increased the length of his stride to draw closer.

"Did your brother ask Lady Verity Fitzroy for the first set as we discussed?"

"Of course he did. My brother and I always honor our commitments, Your Grace."

"Good." His gaze tracked Verity and her partner.

She continued for his ears only, "I'm very unlike my sister in that way."

His attention swiveled to the beautiful Miss Talmadge. "Sorry?"

"I've been described as virtually identical to Catharine in figure, form, and every manner. I loved her, and still pine for her just like *everyone* who knew her," she whispered the last. "But where she was reckless and fickle, I'm quite the opposite, you see."

•

"I do see," he replied and pulled her closer. *Indecently closer.* "But the very thing most appealing about Catharine was her recklessness and her divine fickle nature. We were two of a kind, I fear."

Phoebe laughed. "I suppose this is the best moment to confess that while my brother did indeed request the first set with Lady Fitzroy, she replied that she was old enough to be his mother and that she did not want to start tongues wagging. She was very right in her thinking, I believe. But what do *you* think?"

He would not waste his time telling her what he thought. It required enough concentration just to follow the couple in front of them. He didn't even notice the babble coming from her pretty face until she disengaged her hand from his shoulder and grasped his chin to draw his attention toward her.

"You are quite provoking me, Your Grace."

"How so?"

"I will tell you if you take your eyes off the other guests and look at me."

It was what he least wanted to do. He reluctantly diverted his gaze from Verity and her very ordinary-looking partner in the dance and looked down at Phoebe's eyes, lips, upturned nose, and blond hair done up in the exact same fashion

Catharine had employed and he had memorized all those years ago.

"Thank you," she said coyly. "Now what I was saying . . ."

He had trained his eyes and ears to pick up conversations at great distances during his stint with Wellington. It had served him well. What in hell was Verity saying now?

"Lord Villiers, I'm so sorry to beleaguer you with so many questions, but I do believe it will expedite our acquaintance, you see. You are very free to ask me anything you like in return." She did not stop to see if he had anything to ask. Instead she plowed forward. "So, no mistresses or love children and no relations living with you. And did you love your mother while she lived?"

"Owwww!" Phoebe Talmadge cried out as Rory mistakenly put his full weight on her tiny foot.

She sounded like a cat in heat, was his first unkind thought. "Oh, my dear Miss Talmadge. Do allow me to apologize." He escorted her as she limped to the edge of the dance floor.

"You must carry me to the front salon." She pouted. "I do believe you've broken all of the toes on my left foot, Your Grace."

"Allow me to fetch your brother or a footman."

"No," she insisted. "It's only fair that you take me since it's your fault."

Catharine would never have behaved in such a wholly childish fashion. Surely, not. *Maybe.* He sighed heavily. "Oh, all right." He leaned down and captured her under her knees and her arms. She immediately placed her arms about his neck.

A hundred pair of eyes drifted in their direction along with a few calls of concern.

"Just a few bruised toes," he said loudly to anyone who would listen.

Not a moment after he deposited Phoebe Talmadge on the striped satin divan with a scrolled Egyptian arm on one side, Mary Haverty rushed inside.

"Oh my dearest Miss Talmadge. I've arranged for your maid. Shall we not call the apothecary? And you, Your Grace—"

He really could have kissed Mary for this. Her beauty was such that men lost their heads by the dozen, exhibiting advanced signs of lovesickness, penning atrocious odes to her eyes, and arranging deliveries of hothouse flowers by the carriage load. And yet? Rory had never been attracted to her. There was a sisterly quality to her.

"Yes, Lady Haverty?"

"Do find Lady Fitzroy for me. She always has smelling salts, and we might require them if the bones have to be reset."

Phoebe Talmadge nearly swooned in panic.

Perfect. "Back in a trace."

Nothing could have made Rory happier than to tap the shoulder of the gentleman who had stolen his rightful space on Verity's dance card, dangling from her slender wrist.

"I beg your pardon," she said, her nose rising in the air.

"No, I must beg yours," he retorted dryly. "You're needed in the salon. Or your smelling salts are needed."

"Oh." Her mouth made a small round O. "In that case, Mr. Findley, would you be offended if we resume our conversation between the—" She examined the card on her wrist. "Hmmm, shall we say between the third and the fourth set?"

"It would be an honor, Lady Fitzroy. And by the by, the answers to your questions are that I am neither a gambler nor a rake, and no, I am not in love with another female at this moment."

What in hell? He nearly dragged Verity out of the ballroom, amid much whispers all around. She wrenched away from him a few feet from the double doors leading out of the ballroom. He glared at her, before he realized she was merely fetching her reticule, which was as ugly as her singularly unappealing trio of ostrich feathers in a turban that made her appear twice as old as she was. Why did petite ladies mistakenly think that hideous, sneeze-inducing bird plumage would make them appear taller?

Beyond the doors, he pulled her into a private alcove, with two palms in front of it.

"What in hell are you doing?" The back of his neck itched and he scratched it.

"I can't imagine what you mean."

"Why were you asking that buffoon those provoking questions?"

"He didn't seem to find the questions provoking at all. In fact, he immediately agreed that my method of discerning a gentleman's true character was a capital idea." She tilted her head. "I find docility in a man quite novel and charming."

"And what method is this?"

"A series of questions designed to learn if a man would be an ideal candidate for a husband or not."

"This was Mary Haverty's idea, I'm sure."

"Perhaps," she said airily. "But, actually, I found the original questions a bit mild. The ones I added are far more interesting."

"Let me see the list."

She blinked. "I left it at Boxwood."

"Liar."

"Bully."

He reached for her reticule and before she could stop him he extracted a card and held it over his head as she reached for it. "Stop. The footman will think there are wild animals in here if you disturb the palm fronds any further. On second thought—" He withdrew her smelling salts and emerged from the alcove with his firm grip on her arm while he motioned to the liveried footman. "You there, young man. Deliver these salts to Lady Haverty in the salon across from the ballroom."

Rory then quickly led Verity through the main hall and past the gilded entrance toward the stand of birch trees threaded with lanterns on the side of the elegant stone mansion. "Now, then." He finally looked at her list of questions.

She pulled her arm from his grasp and snorted in frustration. "Go ahead. Read it. Why should I care a whit what you think?"

In the lantern light, he scanned the card and immediately almost choked. "You will be the laughingstock." He began to read the list aloud. "'Do you like children? How many children would you propose to have? What do you do with your time? Are you opposed to ladies riding astride? What do you suppose servants call you behind your back? Are you in love with anyone? Any mistress? Gambler? Rake? Which of your relations live with you? Do you love your mother? Have you ever tortured or killed small animals for pleasure? Do you believe in the superiority of the female mind?' And lastly—Oh, dear God," he paused to regain his breath. "Tell me you did not ask any gentleman this question."

"Which one?"

"The one that says: 'Would you be opposed to allowing me full control of my dowry with the understanding that your *pin money* would be at least five thousand a year?'"

"Of course. So far all the gentlemen I've queried thought the sum more than adequate."

"How do you know they're not all lying through their teeth?"

"Why, they're so shocked when I begin the rapid-fire questions that any fool could discern if they were lying. It's amazing how strong the male urge is to be polite toward a lady. You being the exception, of course."

He refrained from responding if only to prove her wrong. "And just how many gentlemen have you asked these questions of?"

"Hmmm, five or six I believe."

"But the ball only just started."

"You were late. Don't worry, rakes are always late. Then again, it means nothing to me as rakes are off my list, as you can see. But we can still be great friends, if you are feeling up to the challenge of friendship finally."

"This is not how the daughter and sister of a duke is supposed to behave."

"You would know given the number of these sorts of ladies you've seduced."

"Absolutely. Wait, how would you know anything about . . . Damnation, this is beyond idiotic. I am far more eligible than any of these country bumpkins."

"I don't know. The Earl of Lambton's heir is very nice. I happen to like nearsighted, balding gentlemen whose responses are within reason and whose only flaw appears to be an overbearing mother who refuses to live in a dowager cottage." She widened her knowing eyes for a moment. "And the vicar would have me. He is the best choice actually. With my dowry, I think we would do very well, don't you?"

He ground his molars. "Do be serious. It's settled. I have already offered and you must accept." Where was his famous wit and charm when he most needed it? For some blasted reason he could not seem to muzzle the prehistoric dominant male in him. It was probably the part of him that was beginning to be attracted to her molting hat.

She studied him beneath her eyelashes. And for the first time, Rory really noticed the elegant heart-shaped physiognomy of her face, and the plump nature of her lips. It was only too bad they were combined with her stubborn set jaw and intelligent high forehead.

"I've already given you my answer. And if you were a gentleman and possessed half a brain, you would thank me. But I fear that recent brush with absinthe has left you compromised in the upper stories, and so I suppose I shall have to explain it to you." She sighed. "I shall consider marriage if the gossip leaks from Carleton House. But I would marry someone other than you. So you can go on your merry way—with the added enticement that my brother won't have to kill you. But don't look so annoyed. It's highly doubtful I'd have the nerve to go through with it. I'd prefer life as a recluse in the Lake District if I can manage it without damaging my family's reputation."

He took a step closer toward her and she took a step backward, only to find herself backed into one of the white-barked trees.

He shook his head in exasperation.

"It's true and you know it. My brother only wanted me to have the protection of your name, but I think you know he certainly wasn't going to allow conjugal rights with his sister."

He went still at the thought of sexual congress with Lady V. He recovered only after a beat. "Especially his *favorite* sister."

"Precisely." Her gaze moved to some unseen object beyond his shoulder. "Look at it this way, Your Grace—"

"So we're back to formalities, are we?"

"I think it best since I might very well be on the verge of becoming engaged to someone else."

"You were saying?"

"Look at it this way. I'm saving your life." She sighed. "With very little effort on your part, I might add. The least you could do is thank me."

He was going to have to see the tooth drawer if he didn't stop grinding his back teeth. "Lady V?"

"Yes, Your Grace?"

"Stop that. I prefer you use my given name. You never used my title as a child. Why should you use it now?"

She paused. "All right, Rory. I admit there is something that grates when I'm forced to kowtow to you."

"Good. And if you don't want me to compromise your reputation for a second time, then I suggest we continue this conversation somewhere else. I've something of importance to relay to you. Tomorrow, say four o'clock, at the north end of the lake on your property?"

"But, there's no reason to—"

"Yes there is. And if you do not acquiesce with grace I will kiss you senseless right here and now in front of that footman who is now just exiting the front door."

"You would never—"

He ignored her and took her hand and tucked it under his arm to guide her toward the mansion. "And by the by, Findley was telling you the absolute truth. I can confirm he is neither a gambler nor a rake and he is not in love with another lady. However, you might want to rephrase the question in future, as Findley is indeed in love, but my last thread of decency prevents me from explaining the matter any further."

She suddenly halted and he almost stumbled. His agility was clearly going in his old age.

Verity's innocent face looked up at him in the moonlight. "I cannot imagine what you mean, but I'm certain I trust a gentleman whose passions in life include gardening and painting embroidery canvases instead of the practiced charm of an established rake."

He urged her to continue walking. "Of course you do. And that is further proof that this method of yours and Mary's is sheer madness."

"Actually, I had thought you would approve of my method. It would leave you the chance to wiggle off the hook."

"Perhaps I've chosen to accept the hook," he whispered in her ear.

"No one chooses the pain of the hook, Rory, if it can be avoided," she insisted softly.

He pulled his head back to examine her face. A pattern of the branches from the oak near the door reflected on her face in the night air. She had the most translucent complexion. And her eyes were ... extraordinarily guarded yet lovely. "What will it take for you to stop interviewing the gentlemen of Derbyshire?"

She smiled. "Nothing."

What was her game?

"I began to see the flaws of Mary's and my plan when one of the old goats began to question me!"

He grinned. "Even I know you don't like to answer to anyone, V."

"And that is why I have always desired your friendship, Rory."

Chapter 6

She was going to be late. Verity urged her mare harder. Lord, and after she had chastised him so for being tardy last evening for the Talmadges' ball. If there was one thing Verity despised, it was a hypocrite. And she might have to revise her stance on timeliness.

It was just that Timmy had needed an extra ten minutes to complete the set of arithmetic problems she had given him. And there had been the essays to correct from the three boys soon to go to Eton.

She approached the gap in the trees and made a sharp turn to the right, hoping he would be waiting for her at the north end instead of near the site of her formerly beloved tree. The last decade, she had refused to avoid the pine that had been the scene of her disillusionment, but that did not mean she had to torture herself by lingering. Thankfully, she spied Rory's beautiful dark gray horse a furlong away and sped to the prettiest vantage point of the lake.

She was tired. Last night after the ball she'd been unable to settle into her usual lovely deep sleep. Thoughts of Rory in all his splendid elegance whirled in her mind. Every lady, marriageable or not, had had their eyes glued on the long-lost prodigal son of Derbyshire. And she was the only one, aside from Mary, who had not one design on him.

She slowed to a sedate trot the last few feet before pulling to a halt and dismounting.

"You should walk your horse after a gallop like that," he suggested.

She rolled her eyes. "Have you always taken me for a fool?" She gathered her mare's reins and led her in a wide circle. Rory shadowed her other side. Out of the corner of her eye she spied him blatantly extracting his fob and examining his gold pocket watch.

She pretended to gaze at the vast beauty of the lake. Pine, poplar, and mountain ash skirted the water's edge, where wagtails and dippers swooped in to feed on the underwater mayfly and alderfly nymphs.

He returned his watch to his pocket and extracted a very formal-looking letter. She was determined not to ask what it was and so she bit her tongue yet again. At this rate she doubted she would be able to eat anything but mush in the near future.

"When you were a child I often thought that you fancied me in a fashion. And so now I am left to wonder if I have done something—apart from mistaking your bedchamber for mine, of course—to make you form such a violent dislike of me."

She finally darted a glance at his devastatingly handsome profile. "I can't possibly grasp what you mean."

"By the by, there is something powdery, almost chalk-like in your hair."

Her hands flew to her head. "Well, if you must know, I can't abide you because you're insufferable. And most notably toward me for some indefinable reason."

He laughed long and loud. "Of course I'm insufferable. But you should take it as a compliment, V. I'm only insufferable with people I like." He scratched his jaw. "And here I thought that becoming a duke would, at the very least, prevent anyone from pointing out my flaws to my face."

"Yet another reason we shall not marry, since dukes have never intimidated me."

The corners of his mouth rose, and the sun reflected off his beautiful smile.

"You know, V, your brother often remarked that one of his sisters required a new governess each season of the year. He wasn't talking about you, was he?"

"I can't imagine James ever suggesting I was unbear—"

He interrupted. "I find that when a person suggests someone has a flaw, it is actually a flaw they possess themselves. Do you agree?"

There were times that Verity wished she was a beautiful, sleek, and very lethal lioness. This was one of those times. "Do tell me if that note you so obviously withdrew from your pocket is a new list of questions for me to use in my pursuit to save your *arse*."

Amusement filled his eyes. "Are we agreed that your horse is cool now? Perhaps she would like to join mine?" He nodded toward his gray. "What is her name, by the by?"

"Captio."

"Hmmm. Latin for fallacy. Why would you give such a lovely creature a name like that?"

"I rather think it works perfectly. It is the opposite of my name."

"How so?"

"First, while she is lovely and dainty, unlike

me, she also has far more stamina, grit, and ability than any of the other magnificent creatures my brother has stabled at Boxwood."

He did not utter any ridiculous false flattery, which deep inside she rather liked. She couldn't stand it when people lied and suggested she was anything more than what she was: unoriginal and plain.

He disengaged the reins from her hands. She immediately dropped her fingers when they grazed his. He saw to her mare and then returned to Verity.

"You still haven't explained the chalk in your hair."

"And you still haven't explained the note."

He looked at her with an unreadable smile, waiting.

She gazed at the wild cloudberries dotting the defined pastures beyond the sparkling lake. Newly shorn ewes and lambs grazed near their folds. She wasn't sure why she was embarrassed to tell him. It was just that she didn't want him to mock her. "It's from teaching the children in the village while our teacher, Miss Woods, is away, tending her ill sister. It's only for a fortnight or so, I am certain."

He smiled down his approval but said not a word as they walked along the water's edge. She was glad he didn't make light of her efforts. It would have been so easy to do. Wavelets danced on the surface of the lake, where a flock of geese had settled for the warm season.

He finally stopped and she followed suit. "I received this express from a trusted acquaintance at Carleton House yesterday."

She glanced at the note in his gloved hand.

"There is much talk belowstairs in the royal residence. Of you and of me. My source warns that it is only a matter of time before Prinny and others catch wind of the gossip. And it will spread to the rest of London via the ruthlessly efficient network of the serving class."

The blood in her veins raced.

"And given the public's rabid reaction to the night of infamy, in addition to the *Morning Post's* incessant installments from a mysterious diary kept by a *raving lunatic* member of the ton, well, it will not be surprising if Prinny insists we marry. By summer's end. He has already arranged the marriages of one if not two dukes already."

The hair on her arms prickled. A mysterious *diary*? Kept by a *raving lunatic* of the ton? For the first time she could remember, she did not reach for her smelling salts. She was far too shocked to do anything but keep walking. In fact, she wanted to run like the wind, all the way to the exotic jungles of Africa and never return. Oh, it was ridiculous. She could not be that unlucky. Every pompous blowhard in London kept a diary. She refused to add another worry to her long list.

"And so, despite your efforts to save me from my own stupidity that night the devil ruled, I must beg you quite sincerely, V, to honor me with your hand in marriage."

Still in a dreamlike fog of shock over the mention of a diary, she watched in silence as the man with whom she had once been besotted before life had taken a turn, awkwardly got down on one knee and offered his hand.

She refused to take it. "Don't." She looked away. "Don't do this. Do get up. The letter makes no difference."

He didn't move. She turned in time to see a muscle in his jaw clench. It took every ounce of moral strength in her not to reach out and sooth it.

"Of course it makes no difference. I knew we would have to marry the moment I opened my bleary eyes and saw your adorable white lace sleeping bonnet and your brother, just beyond, with murder in his heart."

She stepped away from him. "Get up. I know it's not adorable, and it is a *cornette* not a bonnet. I only wear it to save myself and my maid the trouble of an endless bush of tangles in the morning."

He dropped his hand to his side. "I could do it far better and faster than your maid, I assure you."

"Oh, I'm sure you could. It's probably the hallmark of someone who womanizes."

A muscle in his mouth moved. "Actually that would be unhooking corsets."

"Thank you for your elucidation. Now please," she knew her tone was becoming a bit too high-pitched and unattractive, "please get up. You're ruining your breeches. Grass stains are impossible—"

"No," he interrupted without moving a muscle.

"'No' to what?"

He had stopped smiling. His face was alarmingly serious. He held out his hand again, palm up, urging her silently to accept it. "Verity, enough. I shall arrange for the first reading of the banns immediately. A Special License would only add to any gossip. I've had a word with the vicar, who said—"

"You told Mr. Armitage?" Her hand went to her throat.

He finally, slowly, regained his feet. The grass-colored cloth on his knees now matched the color of his eyes. Finally a better comparison than peas.

"I'm delighted to inform that that is how a marriage is done in England. One must go before a vicar unless one binds and drugs a female, crosses the border to Scotland, and pays an indecent amount to an unscrupulous smithy to perform a service over the anvil. I had hoped to save myself the trouble. But if you persist in this determination to ruin yours and your family's name, then I can be counted on to reconsider the other option." He paused. "Enough of this, V. Name the day."

"Of course. The seventeenth of July."

She almost laughed when she saw the odd combination of relief and fear mingling on his features.

"In the year of our Lord, *nineteen hundred and nine*," she added.

"That's what I thought," he replied dryly. "You are a hard woman, V. And here I was even prepared to give up your promised pin money to have you."

It was not often a person dumbfounded him. Indeed, it was this very quality—of reading people's character, way of thinking, and deciphering their moral code—that had earned him his nom de guerre, Chameleon, for the uncanny ability to adapt to any and all situations with astonishing ease. Prinny and a handful of people at the top of Wellington's food chain knew his true identity, to be sure, but they were determined to keep it secret in case the country's needs became too great, in which case he would be pressed into service again, despite his last mission, during which his identity had been compromised.

Rory surveyed the activity in the rear gardens of Rutledge from the vantage point of his north-facing library. He still could not fathom how he had mangled something that should have been the least complicated event of his life. And all this time he had been given the impression that the young ladies of good ton and their ambitious parents were willing to do just about anything to land an eligible duke.

Apparently Verity Fitzroy did not subscribe to this way of thinking. Perhaps it was that after having a ducal father and brother, she'd had her fill of the arrogant, domineering males.

And so, for his inept preparation to charm his future bride, Rory was reduced to this: overseeing the installation of a formidable feast outside, otherwise known as a *fête champêtre,* which was really nothing more than a blindingly extravagant *pique-nique* for what appeared to be every last inhabitant of Derbyshire. Not one person invited had declined the honor. And yet, there had been only one response to which he had paid any heed.

*Lady Verity Fitzroy and Lady Mary Haverty
accept with pleasure His Grace's kind invitation to
the entertainment Tuesday next.*

Well, at least she had not taken complete leave of her senses. Or more importantly, he still had a chance to make her see reason.

He scratched his jaw as he watched a parade of servants, bearing trays and platters, artfully arrange the fare on an endless series of elegantly appointed tables, dripping with mounds of grapes and oranges and lemons in etched crystal bowls.

All this to woo one petite, recalcitrant, dark flashing-eyed Fitzroy.

It was the most calculated bit of trickery since Welly had sent him behind French pickets in the middle of the night dressed as a replacement aide-de-camp for Napoleon.

There was really only one question far back in an unvisited corner of his mind. When had he become so ill-fired moral-minded that he felt it necessary to save someone? It was this thin air of the Peak District, it was.

Well.

He would successfully advance, subdue the enemy, use a bit of torture if necessary—he smiled to himself—enlist allies in the neighborhood if possible, and win the battle even if he had to eat every last grape in sight.

For the first time in a very long time, he had a mission. He hadn't known he'd longed for an aim in life other than obliterating the past through every known method possible, the number one being a concerted effort to get himself killed, an endeavor that had failed miserably.

It didn't matter that it involved winning the hand of a bride he did not want. He cleared away the cobwebs in that unused corner of his brain and reviewed the reasons:

1. She was the sister of the man he had betrayed.

2. She was a lady

3. She was in this fragile predicament due to his bloody error.

And 4. She was a female trying to elude, and he, being of the male persuasion, could not help but give chase.

There might be another reason lurking, he feared, but it was too hard to see. Point four was most likely the driving force. He'd seen a legion of gentlemen fall to that inherent jungle trait, and he should know better. And yet why could he not ignore that itch to conquer? It had been his undoing in the past.

And so it was with his natural black wit and charm, and unnatural trepidation, that the first Duke of Abshire opened his great house and vast gardens to a horde of two hundred eighty-six neighbors possessed of a curiosity that only a fourteen-year absence could foster. The chase was on.

"May I say, Your Grace, that Rutledge Hall is the very finest property in Derbyshire?" Baroness Littlefield inquired.

"You may, madam, however, I would not say it in Lady Fitzroy's hearing for I should like to impress her, and your comment may have the opposite effect."

The large-bosomed lady tittered, while her neighbor, the tall plain wife of Sir John continued. "Boxwood is extraordinary, Your Grace, but it is cold and imposing—especially that forbidding maze and lake of theirs. Rutledge Hall evokes romance and mystery."

"I'm delighted to hear it, madam." He smiled benevolently. "For there will be mystery and romance here today if I have anything to say about it."

The ladies' jaws dropped, and he suggested they help themselves to the wine and the duck canapés.

He did not have to say another word for he

knew it would take all of a quarter of an hour to get back to her. If there was one thing he had learned, the art of gossip in England was even more efficient than in France.

Precisely one hour later he bored through the crowds to pursue his main objective. And while the guests appeared to avert their gazes, he knew that every person within a five-mile radius had their beady eyes upon him.

Verity had fortified her position by protecting her buttresses with Lady Haverty on one side, and on the other, her cousin Esme, now the Duchess of Norwich. Norwich, himself, stood next to his new bride, looking much like a man who just discovered he had made a deal with the devil, and a lifetime spent with these ladies in Derbyshire was the price. It had been three weeks since Rory's fellow member of the royal entourage had mysteriously reappeared without a word of explanation for his hasty, hushed-up marriage.

"Delighted to see you again, madam, after all these years," Rory said to Esme, and then nodded to Norwich, using his moniker, "Seventeen."

The duchess curtsied while her gray eyes examined him in a way that made Rory feel as if she could read his every thought.

"Lady Fitzroy was just saying she is not impressed," Norwich stated.

"Nor is she interested in anything the guests here are circulating," Esme added, moving closer to Verity.

Rory bowed to the other two ladies. "Your servant, Lady Haverty, Lady Fitzroy."

He grasped V's hand before she could say a word and pressed his lips on the back of her gloved fingers. His nose touched her bare wrist and the unmistakable scent of violets flooded his senses. He immediately released her hand.

"Are you now," Verity began, a bit out of breath. "Since when does a *servant* inform guests there will be mystery and romance in the still of the afternoon?"

"Since today," he murmured. "You've forced me to up the ante, Lady Fitzroy."

Mary Haverty laughed, a deep, throaty melodic sound to most gentlemen's ears. To Rory, it was a sound reminiscent of disaster.

He offered his forearm to Verity. "I beg you to join me for a stroll to the water's edge. I've been given to understand that it is superior to Boxwood's. Less forbidding."

"And romantic," Mary inserted, still smiling.

"Romantically mysterious," he replied, looking only at Verity.

The Duke of Norwich sighed heavily. "Frankly, I don't care if it's where the eternal Lady of the

Lake lurks. Either way, we shall, *all of us*, play nursemaids to the both of you. Candover would demand it."

"Candover would not, I assure you," Rory retorted. "Mind your own debacle, Norwich. Pardon me, Lady Haverty, Esme—"

"No offense taken," Esme replied quickly.

He pointedly regarded Norwich. "I trust you will manage here well enough without us"—he offered his arm to Verity—"and in case you haven't noticed, there are *fowl* lurking in the shallows down there."

The odd comment drew a black glare from Norwich. Everyone in England knew his family had been cursed by a witch two centuries ago to die by duck—yes, *duck*. It had proven to be a most effective curse for the sixteen Norwich dukes who preceded Seventeen. The latter was known to avoid all bodies of water larger than a copper bathing tub—for good reason.

Verity cleared her throat and cut in before the fur on Norwich's back rose another inch. "Do remember our neighbors' talents at lip-reading. And, while I appreciate your effort, Your Grace"—she looked toward Norwich—"I assure you spinsters are perfectly capable of strolling with gentlemen without raising any alarm."

She refused to take Rory's arm, but moved forward to stroll down the wide lawn to the lake in the distance. Already, a bevy of energetic young ladies and gentlemen were rowing several small rowboats or strolling beside the willow trees edging the water.

"Rory?"

"Yes?"

"You are going to have to try a new tactic." She smiled up at him, to confuse anyone looking at them, he was certain.

"I beg your pardon?"

"I know your game, and it won't work."

"Game?"

"Yes. The one where you allow everyone in the neighborhood to think you have lost your mind and suddenly developed a *tendre* for me." She held her hands behind her back, her aristocratic profile tilted proudly despite yet another confirmation of her atrocious taste regarding hats. "But, you see, it won't play out that way, Rory. Instead, everyone will wonder why you are in such need of a dowry in excess of fifty thousand pounds since you were just lavished with a title and an extraordinary surplus of riches by the prince. Or it will positively confirm any possible future reports that you ruined me. This isn't the solution and you know it."

They came to a stop close to several beached

boats at the sandy edge of the lake. A small boat-house was adjacent.

"Let them wonder the former," he said, leaning closer. Under the brim of her hat, a tendril of her dark brown hair fluttered in the light breeze. "Do we really care what they think?" A part of him filled with ill-ease at his actions. He guided her toward the deeply shaded corner of the boat-house, nearest the lake's edge. She was hidden from the vast crowd on the rise behind them, but he was in plain view.

"I just don't understand why you are behaving so gallantly and against your nature," she insisted. "It isn't like you. Since when did you become so determined to play the knight in shining armor to the damsel in distress?"

Since when, indeed.

"It will all blow over, you'll see," she insisted. "You know it," she continued in a whisper.

Slowly, ever so slowly, he lowered his head until his forehead touched the rim of her hat. "Of course it *might* in time. Anything is possible, if not likely. But, you see, I find I cannot deprive myself of a chance to marry into the Fitzroy clan."

"I refuse to live a lie," she insisted, not meeting his eyes. Her dark lashes were fanned against the perfection of her smooth, even complexion.

"My dear V, everyone lives lies of some sort.

Until the day someone devises a way for others to see another's true thoughts, we will all of us only see truth in the privacy of our own minds."

"Thank God for that," she murmured.

It was the last thing he could have imagined she would utter. "We are of like mind, I see."

"Perhaps," she replied, turning serious. "More importantly, I've always believed the character of a person can only truly be discerned by their actions when no one is watching."

"Ah," he murmured, leaning his arm against the corner of the boathouse and moving even closer to her. "I don't need to spy on you or your thoughts to know you are a good and honest person."

"Not always." Her dark hard-to-read eyes finally met his. "I have many flaws—some more severe than others—like everyone else. Actually, I know of only one person whose flaws I've never been able to perceive."

"And who is this paragon?"

"A loyal friend who has more courage, character, intelligence, and innate good sense than anyone else in Christendom and beyond. She is also the most stunningly beautiful creature alive."

"Lady Mary Haverty?"

She shook her head. "But Mary is in some ways like her."

Lord, it was this way she had—of always saying

the unexpected—that surprised him. She would not behave as the other ladies he had known, who drew attention to their own sterling attributes. "She sounds like a product of your vivid imagination, V. No such lady exists." His smile belied his words. "So I don't believe you."

"Have you ever trusted anyone, Rory?" She tilted her head and gazed at his face. "Have you ever *loved* someone with all your heart . . . Unreservedly?"

"So serious, suddenly." Bold honesty never led to anything good. "By the by, the ribbon on that, ahem, *hat*, matches your eyes to perfection. But, why in the name of God of all bonnets are you wearing grapes and kumquats on one side and a trio of crows on the other side?"

"They are lovebirds, you idiot. And everyone knows fruits on hats are all the rage right now."

"But not an entire fruit stall. Are those violets tucked in back?"

She studied him silently for a moment. "I've never known anyone so capable of managing conversations via diversion, wit, or flattery. The last it has not been my privilege to ever hear from your lips, I might add. But, I would advise you to save your breath, for I think I've proven I'm quite immune to your ways. Now then, are you going to answer my question or not?"

"The love question?"

"Precisely."

"Why are ladies uniformly infatuated with the notion of love?"

She studied him without a word.

"Love does not promise happiness," he said, evading her question.

"I never suggested it did," she replied softly.

He pursed his lips. Today had obviously been a bloody waste of time, not to mention the cost of the food, and wine, and the effort to arrange the fruit artfully dripping from family crystal. He could have saved a lot of guineas by just using the elements on her hat.

Thank God the unmistakable sound of footsteps intruded.

"Coward," Verity whispered as he backed slightly away.

A cool breeze fluttered through the swirling leaves of the nearby weeping willow, and two ladies arm in arm approached. One of the females had an expression that promised a knife in the back during the dead of night, whilst the other had that seductive, bemused look he had tried to forget for so many long years. Well at least his effort to provide a show for his guests had worked. Verity would be one step closer to accepting the inevitable by the end of the day.

"Fancy that," Lady Mary Haverty said, stopping a few feet from them but addressing her walking companion. "I declare that now we've come all this distance, Miss Talmadge, I'm sorry to beg off rowing about in the heat of the afternoon with you. But perhaps . . ." She, of the daggers in her gaze, squarely looked at him.

He turned from the auburn-haired lady to the blond beauty.

Phoebe Talmadge smiled at him, her fine expression shimmering like a rose at the peak of bloom compared to Mary, who resembled a cross patch of nettles. Who was he to disappoint? He knew how to retreat, reassess, and regroup with the best of them.

"It would be my pleasure, Miss Talmadge." He extended his arm.

"Oh, but I am perfectly capable of going it alone, Your Grace," Phoebe purred. "No need to trouble yourself."

"I cannot allow it, my dear," he insisted, as he should. "I must assist you. Especially since I'm not furthering my cause here."

Phoebe exhibited the same coy smile Catharine had used expressly in his direction and lay her pale, thin arm along the top of his.

He didn't really want to go, but all his plans, schemes, and other ill-thought-out ideas, which had previously proved successful, needed time to simmer. "It's my pleasure. Oh, and Lady Fitzroy?" He turned slightly to address her.

"Yes," she replied, not lifting her head. All he could see was the brim of her atrocious bonnet.

"I was sad to learn from my steward that the signs we discussed are still not in evidence. Why, another collision with a ewe was very narrowly avoided just today."

She raised her brows. "I am to produce a sign that both people and sheep can read? How singular."

He winked at her. "I'm certain that superior Fitzroy brain of yours will figure it out. I do, however, pray you are the sort of person whose word once given is their bond."

She pursed her lips in annoyance. "My word, Your Grace? I rather think you would not care to hear what sort of vow I am making right now in the privacy of my mind." She turned on her heel and Lady Mary Haverty rushed after her, the dark green silk of her skirting trailed behind.

"I'm so sorry, Verity," Mary began, her long strides soon catching up to hers. "Norwich and Esme would not allow me to go to you. They said it would only draw further attention, which was not true."

"How ridiculous, Mary. No one in Derbyshire cares two sticks about a couple milling about a lake in plain view."

"Perhaps, but you were not in plain view. The only thing in partial view was Abshire's back, and his head was quite obviously tilted down to meet your own."

"What on earth are you suggesting?"

"Exactly what you are picturing in your mind this minute. If all those on the hill above us"— Mary gave a twirl to her pretty parasol and kept a wide smile planted on her face, to have all the world believe they were speaking of nothing more important than the beauty of the day—"had the same view I had, it appeared the duke was taking grave liberties with your person."

"Stop." Verity rolled her eyes. "Nothing of the sort took place. Indeed, I do believe I've successfully staved him off once again."

"How did you accomplish that?"

"It was quite simple." Verity tweaked her favorite new bonnet. "I spoke of the one thing sure to scare the scales off the most hardened bachelor— *love.*"

"Really?" Mary smiled and tapped the side of her temple conspiratorially. "I do believe I've underestimated your knowledge of the beastlier sex."

"Did you not see how fast he sped away to take

Phoebe Talmadge to the boat? Not an obvious gesture for a man in pursuit of marriage. Unless he is pursuing two targets with opposing designs." She had stopped and was now staring in the distance. Rory had pulled the small boat from the shoreline and had adeptly managed to enter it and escort Phoebe into the hull without so much as a drop of water ruining his immaculate appearance.

Phoebe and Rory looked so very handsome as a couple. A wave of déjà vu engulfed Verity and formed a hard ball in the pit of her stomach.

Life had a way of repeating itself.

Phoebe had the same even, beautiful profile as Catharine, and her gleaming main of thick blond hair was coiled in a vastly feminine sort of fashion. Rory could not take his eyes off her. Clearly, he was a man who appreciated and revered beauty—just like all others. A marriage with him, and a future filled with myriad similar moments, was one of the minor reasons she would never agree to this proposed match made in a spinsterish ape leader's hell.

"They shall do very well together, no?" Verity whispered, while keeping a smile plastered to her lips. She could do this even if it killed her.

"Oh, Verity," Mary murmured. "My dear, dear Verity . . ."

She forced her gaze away from the beautiful couple and trained it on the sweep of lawn on the hill where her more fashion-conscious neighbors went about the business of being entertained.

"Would you like to return to Boxwood?" Mary's eyes were filled with concern.

She wanted it more than she could express. "No."

Above them, Esme was walking toward the pea gravel path that led to the rose garden. Verity hesitated.

"Go to her," Mary urged. "I know you miss her friendship. She is your best friend."

This was why Verity adored Mary. She only wished she had seen beyond her beauty years ago. "Thank you, Mary."

As Verity negotiated her way toward Esme, under the combined secret glances of everyone on the hill, she pondered once again why Esme was evading her.

Twice Verity had ridden to her cousin's residence to try and pierce Esme's uncharacteristic veil of secrets, and twice she had failed.

It saddened her no end.

Her cousin was her best friend and she desperately needed her. And she very much feared Esme needed to confide in her, too, but was overwhelmed by the tumultuous events that had surrounded her hushed-up marriage to Norwich.

When Verity finally reached the rose garden, Esme was nowhere to be found.

Chapter 7

Verity trotted her mare toward the stile separating two pastures on Rory's estate. At the last
moment the animal broke into a canter and flew
over the obstacle with her front hooves well
tucked into position. Verity leaned forward, her
face in the wind, and patted Captio on her sleek
shoulder before urging her toward the base of the
ridge ahead.

She had rarely been so annoyed in her life.
Why was she doing something that was such a
monumental waste of time and would never serve
a purpose? Oh, she knew why all right. She had
never gone back on a single promise she had ever
made. The same could not be said of other people
who had trod the corridors of her life.

Furthermore, Rory's transgressions were far
graver than hers to him. *Botheration.* She had

merely galloped up a hill without taking proper care.

She was exhausted, truth be known. Oh, her work as mistress of Boxwood was not time-consuming, but it had never been combined with teaching children at every level of learning most days of the week. A small smile unconsciously crept onto her face. Little Tommy Redmund had finally read his first words today from the *Gentleman's Sporting Guide* she had borrowed from her brother's study. It had captured his interest greatly compared to the immensely boring primer. She had rewarded his efforts in a manner befitting her unusual teaching style. Tommy had regarded her with reverence the rest of the morning.

There. She would place the first sign on a tree at the base of the steep incline. She gently eased back on the reins and jumped off of the saddle with the same girlish movements she had employed her entire life.

Verity unlashed the bulky pieces of wood attached to her braided leather saddlebags. The handcrafted signs were not exactly as he had specified. The corners of her mouth curved slightly as she examined the words. Tommy Redmund's writing was not as advanced as his reading, she feared.

Withdrawing a hammer and nails, she affixed one large wooden plaque to the trunk. A quarter hour later found her in a similar pursuit beneath another tree on the other side of the ridge.

Her timing was well calculated. It was the hour Rory was known to return from the village. As if on cue, he appeared on the stony ridge—galloping as if he had no reason to follow any rule he set. Which of course was his prerogative, being the current owner of every square mile of the land and all.

He came to an abrupt halt near her but did not dismount. His horse mouthed the bit and then snorted. Loudly.

"My feelings precisely," Rory muttered, eyeing the sign.

~No Galloping~
Yield to sheep
(and His Graceless, the Duke of Abshire)
or ~~pay~~ paint the penalty

Methodically, Rory dismounted, but kept his distance. He glanced again between Verity and the sign.

She suddenly felt uncomfortable in her own skin. Oh, she didn't regret her actions, but perhaps she had taken things a bit too far. He was a duke, after all. Dukes considered themselves demigods. She should know.

Verity lifted her chin and crossed her arms. "As you requested."

He nodded. "Are you always like this?"

"I'm sorry?"

"So . . . reserved. Demure."

She had always appreciated his sense of humor. "Of course. According to my brother, our father used to blame our intractability on my mother." She paused. "Then again, according to my mother, it was all our father's fault, and his father before him."

He smiled. "How is your mother? I always considered her the grandest lady in all of Derbyshire."

A stab of pain lanced through her chest. She inhaled with difficulty. "She's dead."

Rory instantly sobered. "I had not heard." He'd rarely had access to newspapers during his war years.

She couldn't seem to open her mouth to reply. He immediately filled the awkward silence.

"I remember her well," he murmured. "I've never known another like her. As a boy, she enlisted me, your brother, and Sussex each fall to go into the wood to add to her astonishing collection of nests. And in spring, we were ordered to follow an elusive bird and steal one of its eggs, but only if there were more than three."

Verity nodded, her well of easy wit suddenly quite dry.

"And the hours she spent studying specimens, and sketching animals and plants of all sorts." Rory closed the distance between them.

His green, green eyes studied her, and she felt as if he could see the very edges of her soul the way he looked at her.

"I always considered her to be the greatest naturalist of the region, if not all of England, Verity. How long ago was she lost to you?"

Verity clenched her skirt with jerky fingers. "Ten years ago." When he did not respond, she knew he would not ask what he wanted to know. "Quite suddenly. She might have had an exuberant temperament, but her heart, it turned out, was not up to the demands of her disposition."

"I'm sorry, V," he said, simply.

She hated to think about her mother. She had loved her beyond measure and the pain of her premature death would never leave. It was always lurking whenever Verity was outside in nature. Just the trill of a songbird or the murmur of tree branches and leaves rustling with the breeze could trigger memories of her mother standing in the middle of her favored woods, breathing in its rich goodness.

Oh God. The back of her throat burned with emotion and she willed her eyes not to fill with tears. It was so maddening to not be in control of one's sensibilities. Especially in front of this particular male creature. Her head was spinning.

He grasped her shoulders and pulled her to his broad chest, which was as solid as an oak. That familiar scent of his clogged her senses and made her dizzy. She bit the inside of her cheek to keep from falling to pieces in the comfort of his arms. She had dreamt of this moment for a few brief years of her adolescence before she had grown up and learned the futility of a girl's dreams and altered her course. But she had never imagined his embrace could be like this . . . It was as if she could finally exhale and all her worries and fears would dissipate into the wild air of the peaks. She tried to pull slightly away. It was far too dangerous to let her emotions rule her head.

He ignored her feeble attempt to put distance between them. Instead he gently urged her deeper into his arms, and then he stroked her head. It was his touch that broke her and she wept silently for a few long moments before she regained control.

She released his shoulders when she became conscious of the fact that she was clenching them. Lord, where was her handkerchief when she needed it?

And then as if by magic a snowy white square was pressed into her palm and she ducked her face to quickly dry her eyes. "I don't know what came over me. I'm so sorry," she murmured. It was the first time she had cried again since that awful day her mother had died. Inexplicably, Verity felt her lip tremble, and despite the mountain of effort she exerted, she truly crumbled.

And just like that he grasped her and pulled her back into his arms. "Go on, then, V."

His words unleashed the torrent of tears that had refused to come for so long. A series of wretched sobs tore from her throat. She squeezed her eyes shut as his hands stroked her back over and over again. The storm lasted less than a minute but felt like a thousand years when she drew back to again press the wet handkerchief to her face, which would certainly be blotchy and as unattractive as it could be.

She shuddered as she regained control and attempted to speak. "I'm so sorry, Rory. How stupidly I'm behaving. And here I had little Tommy Redmund do these wretched signs. I shall remove them immediately and—"

"You'll do nothing of the sort. I like them," he said slowly, and then chuckled.

"Rory, really, I'm so very—"

"If you say you're sorry one more time," he murmured, taking the handkerchief from her fingers and dabbing her nose, "I will be forced to kiss you." He gazed at her, and suddenly the veneer of cool amusement and hauteur he usually sported dropped from his impossibly handsome face.

Then all at once she could not hold back her ancient desire. She had successfully held him at bay with wit and determination, but the fight was all gone out of her.

She wanted his kiss.

She wanted to *feel* again. And even more, she wanted to be desired. If she could not have love, she could at least have this, if only for a few precious moments. Even if it was this one and only one time.

She would never be certain whose head moved forward first, but in the blink of an eye his lips covered hers and again she was breathless. Her hands were so cold until they found their way up around his warm neck. She ran her fingers through his dark hair, which was shockingly soft.

He made a sound deep in his throat, which hummed with something very like pleasure, and she arched into him. Vaguely, as she was lost in the maelstrom of his kiss, she felt the heat of his powerful hands gripping her hips and shockingly pressing her form against his. She could not breathe.

His tongue traced the seam of her lips and she immediately opened her mouth to his demand. A rush of heat filled her as he toyed with her tongue with his own. A blaze of pure pleasure ricocheted through her and she held onto him for dear life.

Never had she experienced anything remotely like this. Oh, she had been kissed a long time ago, to be sure, but nothing so raw, so primal, so terrifyingly intimate.

He broke away from her lips to trail an uneven path to her temple. "My God," he whispered, and then dipped to lightly bite the delicate edge of her ear, which caused a shudder to race through her.

She didn't want it to end. She wanted, no, she desperately *needed* more.

He gripped her to him more tightly than she could have ever imagined and recommenced the exquisite torture. His classically sculpted nose rested against the hollow of her cheek and she could feel the heat of his breath cascading off her skin. He was all warm male, burning the frost off of her heart.

Verity knew it would end. Nothing so exquisite could last forever, as much as she craved. Reluctantly, they drew apart and stared into each other's eyes—green to brown, burning with intensity. Her breasts were still pressed against his hard chest as she tried to regain control of her racing thoughts and heart.

He stroked the side of her sensitive neck where a lock of her hair, which perpetually escaped the confines of her simple chignon, fluttered in the breeze.

"Verity?"

"Yes," she whispered.

"There is something of vital importance that I have forgotten to do since that fateful morning in Carleton House."

She averted her eyes from the intensity of his gaze. She studied a clump of wild gorse, not really seeing it.

"Can you not look at me? Are you now shy?"

Her eyes flew to his.

"I humbly ask your pardon for the horrid mistake I made that awful night—for entering your chambers and causing you to shoulder the burden of my outrageous actions. I did not then and I have not since behaved as a gentleman aught. Will you forgive me, Verity—even though I do not deserve it?"

She rushed to respond. "I forgave you that

morning. There's no reason for you to have such a crisis of conscience now."

"You are very wrong, Verity. I'm guiltier than you know and it's important to say it. But now I am going to have to beg for you to reconsider a far grander request. One that will right my wrong, and unfortunately for you, it will involve doing something I know you are loath to do, even if I feel just the opposite."

Her heart fell. "Rory, no," she pleaded softly. "Please."

"Shhhh," he hushed gently. "I know I do not have the right to ask. It is, what? The eighth or the ninth time?"

"Fourth," she said quietly.

"I can only promise I will not sink to yet another low tactic as I had planned."

"There is no need. I already told you I foresaw it."

"Foresaw what precisely?"

"Your efforts to have every last person in the Peak District presume our future nuptials. No less than five people winked and boldly asked me today when the 'lucky day' was to be."

He regarded her with care. "Verity . . . God, words fail me." He groaned and closed his eyes for a moment before continuing far more passionately. "I am begging you. I know I do not have the right. But, please, Verity, allow me the honor of your hand."

"I . . ." she began, but halted.

"Yes?" He encouraged her with his eyes.

"Rory," she began slowly, and then paused before rushing on, "I give up. You win."

He drew back and regarded her carefully. "Dare I hope? Or is this just a ploy to cruelly lead me astray—something I well deserve?"

"Stop, Rory. There will be no more charade between us. You owe me that much. But you have not heard the terms of my capitulation. And fear not, no matter how much you appear the reverse, I know deep in your heart you want this less than I."

"Verity—"

She held up one hand. "You have given me no choice. So yes, I shall live the lie of an engagement for the summer, but then it shall not come to the point. I shall end it—of that there is no question."

"I beg your pardon. But this would only cause an immense scandal and leave you even further ostracized from all of society and—"

She interrupted. "That is the point. A very long time ago I decided I would not marry. My brother knows this and even gave me his assent. I had intended to eventually retire to one of James's estates and live my own life."

He stared at her. "Is that possible?"

"I beg your pardon?"

"To live your own life. Do any of us really live our own lives, Verity?"

"Of course we—"

He interrupted. "And what of your sisters? Have you no concern for how this would affect your sisters' chances, indeed your entire family's good name?"

"Of course I do. But the fact of the matter is that my sisters have shown far less interest than even I regarding marriage. And we both know James's fortune and standing will not be affected by a sister gone astray."

He shook his head.

"If the truth be known, my brother is secretly delighted we have no suitors. No evil brothers-in-law to rescue from financial ruin. No hanger-on relations. And my sisters and I realized long ago that . . ."

"Yes?"

She gazed into his eyes and saw a flicker of sadness lurking. "We realized our enormous dowries were merely a device to weed out gentlemen courting us for the wrong reasons."

"I had not guessed your brother to be so soft. Marriage is nothing more than a uniting of two families—refilling coffers, strengthening influence, and acquiring land for future generations."

"Perhaps," she said quietly. "It's all that to be sure. But for one to be happy, marriage must feature a good deal more."

He raised his eyebrows.

"Kindness, respect, good humor, and above all . . . something I shall not say for I am in no mood to endure your disdain."

"Then I shall say it. You believe *love* is necessary."

"Yes, if one is to enjoy all the fruits of marriage—as my mother and father did. And before you change the subject by commenting on my excellent taste"—she nodded toward another of her collection of ancient bonnets tossed haphazardly in the tall grass—"I shall tell you why it's important."

He eyed her hat that was an amalgamation of three of her sisters's bonnets they had tried to lay to rest. "I can be persuaded to listen to you and to ignore your *exquisite* fashion sense if I'm allowed to liken your eyes to roasted December chestnuts."

She tried to ignore the pain of his wit, which he obviously used to retreat from the intimacy they had briefly shared. "If there is one thing I've learned, Rory, it's this: everyone wants and needs love, whether they have the courage to admit it or not."

"And? I sense an 'and' coming."

"And if one doesn't find it in their spouse, the person will either look for it outside the union or renounce love altogether. These two options promise nothing but heartache in the end."

"You are far more sensible than any woman I've ever known, V."

"Flattery?"

"You would prefer wit?"

"No. I would prefer brutal honesty. Something you are not prepared to give," she replied.

That gave him pause.

"Fear not, I don't expect it for the long term," she continued. "But I do expect it now. For this one instance, so we understand each other."

"I understand you more than you think," he replied softly. "But you have forgotten one thing, Verity."

"I doubt it."

"You have. You've forgotten that friendship and respect far outweighs the uncertainty of love."

Her gaze darted to his.

"How many people do you know who are happy five, ten, twenty years after a so-called love match? It is simply impossible. Love fades. Friendship stands a better chance. If we marry, I can promise you that I would always respect you, honor you, and endeavor to make you happy."

She could not figure the chess game he was

playing now. She had already promised to enter into an engagement to stave off the worst of the rumors yet ensure permanent freedom. "Rory?"

"Yes, my sweet?"

"I've promised to become your fiancée, but that is all. I've given you my reasons. You already know my stubborn nature, inherited from both sides of my family tree. I am offering the only thing I can. But do not misunderstand me. I will end this before vows are exchanged. This must erase any last remnants of your feelings of guilt. You will be helping me achieve what I have wanted for a very long time. And I will thank you. You will be relieving me from the burden of having to listen to an endless stream of people in the neighborhood clucking and asking if anyone has attempted to court me, while peering at me from pitying eyes. It is unbearable."

He was looking at her with those eyes she dreaded and knew far too well.

"Verity, I will not allow you to mire yourself in such muck to—"

"You heard me. Are we in agreement, then? No, I've changed my mind. You are not to agree. You are to consider yourself officially engaged to me from this moment on. I shall take care of the rest of it since you, as a gentleman, no matter how jaded, cannot possibly entertain the notion of a future rupture that would so wholly taint me."

"At such a cost," he murmured.

"I am more than willing to pay it."

"You know," he said with a sad smile, "if you keep going on like this, I might very well come to the conclusion that I've been blindly existing under the delusion that I am irresistible."

"Then," she finally allowed herself to smile, "all of this might be good for your soul."

Chapter 8

He did not dare to give her time to change her mind. Not that Verity was the sort to do so. Rory had recently deduced that her intellect worked in a fashion that was more orderly than most.

And so he took advantage of his elevated station, and did the unpardonably rude action of announcing their betrothal that very night—not at his own table—but rather at the long, well-polished rosewood antique of the Baron and Baroness Littlefield, where the established elite of the neighborhood dined regularly on a bounty of singularly inedible food.

He at least waited to speak until after the dessert course—a very dry, indiscernible fruit fool. Grasping his glass of watered-down wine, Rory abruptly stood, the legs of his chair squealing in distress. Three guests down and opposite him, Verity sat; her eyes had not met his once during the meal. He dared not look to her now while the clattering of knives and wagging tongues stilled.

"None of you can be at a loss for what I am to announce. I do beg your pardon, Baron, for snatching any of the good wishes during this celebration of the baroness's birthday, but I take heart for I do believe she will like being the first to know—"

Silver-haired Baroness Littlefield clapped her wrinkled hands in glee. "La! I fully anticipated this when the baron suggested—"

A chorus of hushes prevented her from continuing.

His eyes darted to Verity, only to encounter her bowed head. He inhaled. "As I was saying, you are all the first to know that Lady Verity Fitzroy has made me the happiest of men by consenting to be my bride."

A welling of excited sounds erupted all around. The baron exited his chair at the head of the table to personally pound him on the back with a great guffaw. "Oh, I say, Your Grace. This is famous." He turned to address the baroness. "My dear, do we have a bit of absinthe to toast the happy couple? It is the duke's favored brew, is it not?" Titters erupted all around.

"Oh, how delighted the Prince Regent will be!" The baroness continued coyly, "Has he given his blessing?"

So this was how the news was to be interpreted. An arranged marriage for a disgraced member of the royal entourage to save the monarchy. Well, at least it was better than what Verity had suggested. Rory glanced again toward her. Her face had finally regained an ounce of the color that had been lacking all evening.

"How kind you are, Baron," Verity finally said once the laughter had died down, "and all of you. His Grace and I thank you for your good wishes."

She was a proper lady through and through. Not that Rory did not know it. She instinctively knew how to endure the ribald ribbing while holding her head high. He made his way to stand behind her chair. Rory raised his glass and the rest of the occupants of the dining hall followed suit. "To the health and happiness of my future duchess."

"To Lady Fitzroy," the chorus of well-wishers echoed back.

Rory's gut was churning. No doubt due to the burnt quail with uncooked beets. But his heart was calm as he leaned down, kissed her cheek, and then whispered in her ear. "I have you now. No turning back."

She half turned in her chair and replied softly, "Say you. Everyone else thinks *I* caught *you*."

There was something about the moment. The way she looked up at him with her laughing brown eyes that made his soul expand just the slightest bit. He grasped her chin and in a wildly inappropriate fashion kissed her full on the lips, causing a roar of approval from everyone in the hall.

With the exception of one person, who had exited unnoticed many moments before.

Verity closed the last of the housekeeper's seven ledgers. She knew she'd put off what she had been avoiding all morning at her desk in the Great Chamber, the cavernous room she appropriated for herself many years ago when she discovered that no one had any use for it except on the rare occasion of a royal visit. Her sisters refused to set foot anywhere other than the beloved library filled with twenty thousand volumes dating back nine generations. And James presided over all in his walnut-paneled study.

And so Verity spent most of her late afternoons here, watched over by a veritable gallery of stern, brown-eyed ancestors staring at her from gilt frames. Limewood carvings on the polished dark walls, of birds, other wildlife, and the beauty of nature, surrounded the portraits. She glanced at the turbulent scene of archangels engaged in battle against Beelzebub's minions painted above her before she forced herself to examine the freshly ironed stack of newspapers just come from London.

It was the moment of truth. She had tried to ignore the growing tide of London gossip, deliciously whispered at every dinner, ball, and after church the last few days. But now that Rory had officially announced their engagement, she must begin the grand deception. If she had any last hope or impossible dream that the engagement would transform into a happy truth, these newspapers could effectively kill it. Verity had avoided all newspapers since arriving from Town but she had to forearm herself with the truth.

She turned the brittle pages to the only one that mattered. The delicately scrolled edges of "The Fashionable World" column framed the gossip of Christendom's center of the universe: London. Her gaze scanned and then came to rest on a strangely bolded series of paragraphs.

Excerpt No. 7. In which the high and mighty once again show the depths of their depravity courtesy of a delightful, mysterious author whose words continue to inform us of the sinful past of our soon-to-be-former aristocracy.

Her heart pounded erratically as the all too familiar words rushed at her.

I daresay that the very pages upon which I write will go up in flames from the shame of the actions witnessed this last night.

Fortunes were lost, fortunes were told, and a fortunate group of dukes made more than merry. Of course, they had little choice. A future king was in evidence and bade them to celebrate.

At half twelve, in the midst of a game of Vingt-et-un with stultifying stakes, the butler entered to inform that three Gypsies had been apprehended stealing chickens. It seemed they had not anticipated the viciousness of this particular duchy's hens. In a show of great condescension and, may I add, interference in what should have been the host duke's own business, Prinny demanded the "visitors" be brought forth for punishment. Their fine was to read all of the royal entourage's fortunes. They were then invited to go forth and raid all the surrounding neighbors' henhouses with impunity.

The game of Vingt-et-un recommenced, during which: seven horses, three pha-etons, four paintings by masters, twenty-two thousand gold guineas, and a small estate in Scotland changed hands.

Nine of England's finest woke at half past two in the afternoon the next day only to find chicken feathers covering every last square inch of the gilt State Bedchamber in which the Prince Regent snored.

Well.

Her head spinning for lack of oxygen, Verity finally gulped for air. Where were her smelling salts when she really, truly needed them?

Was there to be no end to the level of insanity overtaking her life at present?

Hands shaking, she forced herself to examine the next edition.

A quarter of an hour later Verity reached behind the portrait of the third Duke of Candover, he of the darkest stare of the bunch, and withdrew the key to the secret compartment of the burled wood desk. It was empty, of course, of her most recent diary as well as her favorite one from long ago. But beyond the other incriminating leather-bound volumes (soon to be burned), rested oblivion—the bottle of Armagnac her mother had secretly gifted to her from her great friend the Dowager Duchess of Helston.

Verity had only tasted the pungent, fruity spirits one other time in her life, and on that occasion swore she would never do anything so stupid again in her life. And one would think that the only other time she had dabbled with spirits—the night she tried absinthe—would have solidified her vow.

Then again, she could never have imagined her godforsaken life could drift into such unbearable darkness.

She halfheartedly searched the drawer for a glass. Not finding any, she uncorked the green bottle, the color so very like *his* eyes, and lifted it to her lips for a very long moment . . . for one bloody long evening of respite from this hell of her own making. And then she tipped the bottle again. And again.

Early the next morning, Rory placed two missives in the gleaming salver presented to him by the immaculately white-gloved hands of his butler. "The one to Candover is an Express, Cheever."

"Very good, Your Grace. And may I take this opportunity to extend the gracious good wishes of the entire staff here at Rutledge on the occasion of your betrothal?"

"You may." He bit back a smile. The old man was just as stiff as the day Rory had left.

"And may I add that we are all much honored you have chosen to return?"

"You may."

"And may I—"

He interrupted. "You may say whatever you please, Cheever. And you may also inform the staff that I shan't go away again for a long time."

The old man smiled. Beamed, actually. It was the first time Rory had ever seen the man's teeth.

"Now, run along, Cheever, I have far too many important things to do here than to spend the day flapping my gums with you." He made a show of glancing at a ledger. "Why, apparently, there are eggs to count, sheep to fleece, and horses to be shod if I have the right of it. I do assure you the army was far more amusing. But first, you may show the duchess in."

Cheever bowed and left one hell of a lot more amused than he had ever been in service to the last duke. Rory steepled his fingers. What had come over him? He could not remember the last time he had felt so lighthearted.

And now he had the pleasure of a visit from the

new Duchess of Norwich. Aside from his recent fete champêtre, the last time he had seen Esme was when he had gone fishing at the age of eighteen and she appeared at the same fishing hole. The mysterious young girl had put a serious dent in his manly pride by catching twelve fish to his one.

She had looked him up and down and announced, "Of course I have more fish. The females in my family know how to tickle trout onto a line far better than any silly boy." That this lady had somehow become Seventeen's duchess was not a surprise. There had always been something *fishy* about her.

"My dear Esme," he said, rising to greet her. "To what do I owe the pleasure?"

"Norwich doesn't fish."

"I see." He didn't want to see at all. His virility was about to be called into question again; he was certain.

She looked him over carefully from head to toe just exactly as she had done recently on his own lawn, and also all those years ago. "Can you still not tolerate defeat?"

She always had spoken her mind. Almost as much as Verity. Did the Peak District only produce this wild breed of females? He fervently hoped it was so.

"Correct," he replied.

"Good. Because if you allow Verity to beat you at this game she will not discuss with me, but of your own making I am certain, then I will be forced to cast a spell on you and it will involve something far more terrifying than a duck."

He scratched his chin. "You still haven't told him, have you?" He took pride in expertly diverting the conversation.

"Of course not," she murmured. "And you are not to tell Norwich either."

"Yes, ma'am," he said with false meekness. "But you are going to tell him one day, aren't you? I hate to think of the misery he is suffering not knowing your relation to the lady who cursed his line."

"You *love* to think of the misery he is suffering. You don't fool me, Rory Lennox. I'm glad you've finally come back, by the by."

"Are you going to sit down? Or are you going to keep me on my feet?"

"On your feet. My driver has the poles."

"I hadn't expected the pleasure. I'm afraid I have far too many ledgers to review to accept your very kind invitation."

She rolled her eyes. "Excuses, excuses."

"You are the most terrifying creature I know. Have you shown this side to Norwich?"

"Absolutely not. He can barely stand my painting alone."

He shook his head. "That does not bode well."

"Says a man whose engagement to my favorite cousin reeks of uncertainty."

A half hour later found the two of them standing on the west bank of his lake, with four plump trout in the grass to show for their effort. All hers, of course.

"And the real reason for your visit, Duchess?"

"Shhhh . . . I feel one, considering my choice morsel."

He sighed, removed his hat, and ran a hand through his hair to cool his head. "I really could have used your talents when a regiment of men were near to starving in Portugal."

"If you are going to talk, this is never going to work. You were much quieter last time." She paused. "Botheration. He's gone in search of a more lively water bug."

He replaced his hat. "Where?"

She pointed and a ripple marred the surface of the water. "There."

Counting eggs and sheep to fleece held far more appeal at this moment. "So?"

"So . . . what?"

"Your visit. Are you here to ask my advice or to offer advice?"

"Neither. I'm here to fish."

A moment later the corners of her mouth curled and she pulled the largest trout Rory had ever seen from the lake water. He calmly reeled in his line and placed the rod beside him.

"Already?" she asked, not looking at him as she moved the fish beside the others.

"A man can only take so much humiliation in one afternoon."

"Rory?"

"Yes?"

Her eyes were trained on the line she had cast again in an expert movement. "You must promise you will never hurt her."

That stopped him cold. "Pardon?"

"Verity. She is my cousin and best friend as you well know."

"Tell me something I don't know."

She finally allowed her huge, unearthly gray eyes to meet his. "She has more secrets than you."

He sat up straighter. "Whatever do you mean?"

She cast her fly upon the water with shocking speed. A moment later she reeled in another fish.

He would be damned if he would congratulate her or urge her to answer his question. He knew her well enough to know that she would choose her moment.

The minutes passed with maddening slowness, and his thoughts revolved around her words.

Secrets? Verity had secrets?

And what sort of secret did Esme know about him? Well, he could at least take comfort that he had not been forced to marry a female with a certifiable witch as a forebear.

"She doesn't know that I know," she whispered.

He whipped his head around, but Esme was so lost to the moment of reeling in another fish, he thought he might have imagined what she just said.

She quickly put all the fish in her wicker bag and gathered her affairs. "That should do it, then."

He took her pole and his, and they silently trudged up the hill toward her carriage, which was waiting.

The silence should have felt awkward, but it did not.

Halfway there she finally spoke. "You know, Rory, Verity is not at all like a fish. She is more like the birds her mother so loved."

He waited, patiently.

"And if you want to invite this little bird to live in your cage, you first have to make the place beautiful and inviting. But most importantly?"

"Yes?"

"You have to open the door."

A muscle constricted in his side and he couldn't speak. Instead, he nodded.

When they reached the elegant barouche, with the navy blue Norwich family crest emblazoned on the yellow paint, she turned to take the poles from him and handed them up to the driver, who stored them with reverence.

"Oh, I have a present for you," Esme said. "For your betrothal."

He raised his eyebrows. "A gift? For me?"

"Well, you did allow me to fish in peace. In the end at least."

"If you wanted to fish in peace, then why did you invite me to come along?"

"It's far more amusing when someone is there to bear witness." She handed him a rolled sheaf of paper tied with a red ribbon.

"May I?" He held one end of the ribbon with his fingers poised to pull it.

"Of course. It's my turn to bear witness."

He pulled and the paper unfurled to reveal the most beautiful charcoal drawing of Verity. Esme had captured her essence in the rendering. Honesty, painfully in evidence, mingled with just the slightest hint of sadness despite the bright smile.

He had seen that look on her face, but only once and very fleeting. He couldn't wrest his gaze from the compelling drawing. From somewhere far away he heard a whisper of a voice.

"You won't forget what I said?"

He looked up, only to see the door of the barouche shutting behind her.

The coachman snapped the reins and a matched pair of grays trotted on.

Chapter 9

Verity looked down at the wretched letter in her hands. Amelia's usually even lettering was off slightly. It was not surprising, given her abigail's impossible situation. She read the letter twice and then reread between the lines. Amelia would never ask for help. And the absence of any real news scared Verity more than anything else. She had to go to her. Within the week if possible.

Verity's head was splitting; the aftereffects of imbibing that fiery frog water last eve.

What was she doing with her life? More than a taste of absinthe at Carleton house after spying on the ducal party, dabbling in Armagnac last night . . . was cheap gin far behind? If the insanity that was her life did not change course for at least a short return to her prior dull days, she might very well have to consider a future stay in an asylum. That would be at least better than where dear Amelia might end up if she herself did not find a solution immediately.

Amelia's elegant scrawl of black ink filled two pages quite through. It seemed as if a twelve-month had passed since they had last spoke. But surely it was no more than a fortnight.

God.

She would have to go to London and then quite possibly to Cornwall. Verity wasn't sure how she would accomplish it, but then again, had she not done precisely what was required to end her banishment?

She was engaged.

She had done what was necessary even if it was only temporary. Now she must go to her faithful abigail and do what must be done to help her. And if there was a chance, she must recover her two missing diaries while in London or more likely find and pay someone to do it for her.

And it would be good to put distance between herself and Rory. She needed many miles to help her remember to stay the course, and end this properly. He had been far too attentive of late, and she could not waver for a moment. He was temptation personified.

Verity pulled a fresh sheet of paper from her

drawer and began the reply to Amelia, pausing only once to think of the earliest she could leave.

A knock sounded at the door of the State Chamber.

"Come," she called out.

Mary Haverty crossed the expanse of elaborate marquetry wood floor. "Dearest?"

Verity looked up to gaze at her beautiful friend. "Yes?"

Mary's brow furrowed and she tilted her head to examine Verity better. "You look a bit green. Your housekeeper said you had not breakfasted. Are you feeling all right?"

"Wretched, thank you."

"Ah." Mary looked at her knowingly. "The obvious mark of a happily engaged woman."

Verity shook her head and wished she hadn't. "No. It's not that." She couldn't bring herself to talk about the spirits of yester eve without fear of retching.

"Then, what is it?"

"I must go to London. And then quite possibly to Cornwall. And James will be furious if I show up unannounced at the Duke of Kress's house party in the latter place."

"When do we depart?"

Verity closed her eyes and rested her hot forehead in her hands. Esme still was avoiding her, and Verity was beginning to believe fate was ensuring she had a taste of her future state of loneliness in the Lake District. She looked toward Mary finally. "Whatever I did to deserve you for a friend, I would do it a hundred times over to ensure that you were here with me now."

"My dear," Mary replied, "we are both of us grateful. I was near to half mad with worry about the future when I found you here."

"Are you sure you don't mind coming with me? It's such a long way."

"I am certain you will tell me all about it as soon as we're in the carriage. What day?"

"If you truly do not mind, let's depart day after tomorrow."

Mary avoided looking at her while she shook out the folds of her gown. "Verity?"

"Yes, Mary?"

"When I feel like you look right now . . . I always go riding. For a great distance. A good gallop will cure what ails you—and don't accept any of the revolting concoctions most butlers would have you drink. They usually taste like tar and do not a lick of good."

Verity quietly bridled and saddled Captio in the shadows of Boxwood's immaculate stable.

As usual she wore tall boots and James's cast-off riding breeches from his boyhood. She waved away the stable boy's aid and saw to mounting the mare alone before setting out at a brisk trot toward her favorite path.

Entirely avoiding the estate's infamous box-wood maze, which had been the scene of the most humiliating moments of her past as well as numerous moments of panic for many other unfortunate victims of the deadly tall hedges, Verity finally loosed her horse's head and Captio broke into a canter.

She tried not to focus on the section of the woods ahead, her mother's favorite place in all the world. Her mother had once called these forested acres the true home of her heart.

Tears formed in the back of Verity's eyes. She swallowed hard. It was merely the wind, she told herself.

Lord, she longed for her mother. She would know what to do. She had always known what to do.

Oh, she was being so childish. There was no one to turn to. She had only herself to blame. In less than a month, once again, she had made a muck of her life, and probably the lives of a dozen others if she included her entire family. It was only a matter of time before the authoress of the diaries was found out.

She swiped at her face with the back of her arm and regrouped the reins. Captio took the hint and galloped toward the stile separating the lands of the two neighboring dukes. Her horse sailed over the jump with a foot to spare.

Verity tried to think of any good she had done—as her mother would always insist. There was the school in the village. She was finally beginning to see small signs of progress. And she liked teaching. Nothing could have surprised her more. Amelia would surely expire from the shock of it. Then again, Verity sobered, Amelia might very well expire from the shock of something far more serious if she did not take action immediately.

The least of her problems was her engagement. Then again, she had already told Rory her intention. She had only to see it through.

The green rolling hills and hollows of Rutledge Hall's lower pastures had always been Verity's favored places to ride. But her heart was heavy with worry, and she sought something less tame to break her frame of mind. She needed more wind in her face, more of a challenge to her ability, and so she turned Captio's fine head toward the little-used path with dense brush on each side. Around the small bend ahead lay a tricky stone wall. The one James had always forbidden her to jump. That had never stopped her in the past.

The muffled hoot of a barn owl, hiding somewhere in the trees ahead, lent an air of pungently pervasive wildness to the moment as Verity leaned into the blind turn. Captio negotiated the bend and she glued her thighs to the saddle as she faced the imposing obstacle just ahead. Instinctively, she measured the distance, and urged her mare to lengthen her stride so they would arrive at the perfect spot to begin the great leap.

Her mare's ears pricked forward and Verity's heart swelled when the mare soared into the air. At the peak of the arc time seemed to expand, and for that one exhilarating moment all Verity's worries and anxieties flew behind her and she was filled with the sheer joy of being one with nature.

Captio landed hard on the other side, jerking Verity forward. She regained her proper seat with ease.

A flash of movement caught her eye and she turned her head to the right at the same moment Captio shied in the opposite direction. She quickly brought the mare under control.

Rory. He was moving fast, his gait ungainly, and his face . . . why, it was so contorted, it almost didn't appear to be him at all. Instead, he was some grim, white-faced variation of a wild animal gone barmy.

"What in bloody hell are you doing?" His eyes were like hard emeralds, gleaming with fire.

Captio jigged in place, and Verity gave her

mare her full attention before her reply, which was given in as cool and calm a manner as she would address a lunatic. "I beg your pardon. I did not know you would take offense at my riding in your park. I am your betrothed, am I not?"

"As such I would expect less insane behavior. Have you no sound judgment in that Fitzroy head of yours?" His distorted words radiated pain.

Verity stared at him. Where was the dispassionate, jaded devil-may-care peer of the highest realm?

"Have you nothing to say for yourself? I expect not since no lady in her right mind would set her horse at that monstrosity. Unless, of course, she had a death wish."

Verity quickly snapped her jaw closed as soon as she realized it had dropped. No words could she form in her mind.

"Get off your horse, I tell you. You will walk home."

When she did not move a muscle, he approached.

"I'll snatch you off myself if you do not dismount this instant."

That released in her the torrent of words that had built up. "No. I don't think I will. I make it a habit to not freely give myself over to madmen."

He reached for her horse's reins and Verity

urged Captio away from his grasp. She narrowly evaded him and was about to gallop her mare away before she heard him call after her.

"Verity! Verity. Please . . . for the love of God. Please stop."

It was the tone of his words that scared her. Right down to her marrow. It was the sound of bleak despair. And she recognized it. She halted Captio abruptly and turned to look at his dejected form behind her.

His eyes were haunted, his posture that of an old man.

Verity dismounted and led her mare back to him. All the anger or fear, or whatever had caused him to behave like a heathen, had dissipated. "What is bloody wrong with you?"

It was his turn to remain silent.

"Well? What is going on here?"

His eyes glazed over and became remote as if he were not of this earth, but far, far away.

She grasped his shoulder with her free hand and shook him. Hard. He barely moved. "Answer me!"

His eyes looked beyond her shoulder in the distance.

She shook him again. "Rory . . . Rory, you're scaring me. Talk to me. What is it? Where are you?"

His Adam's apple bobbed.

She followed his gaze and swiveled her head only to find he was staring at the stone wall.

"The jump? Is that it? But I've taken my horse over it many a time. She's very capable, as you saw."

A tiny muscle in the hollow of his cheek beat a tattoo. "I—I . . ."

"Yes?" she encouraged gently now.

He shook his head.

"What is it you want? I will do whatever you ask—this is your property, after all—but please, Rory, tell me what is going on. I cannot bear to see you like this."

"Never . . . please . . ."

"Yes?"

"Please . . . don't ever go over that wall again."

"All right."

They stared at each other for a long time. Finally, Rory picked up her hand, his own shaking, and brought her fingers to his lips. He kissed them reverently. "Thank you," he whispered.

"There is no need to thank me. I was trespassing. It might be different if we were truly betrothed. And, oh, botheration, I know that jump is not the safest in the park. I shouldn't admit this, but James would have taken a horsewhip to me if he knew."

Rory's face, which had been taking on color, turned ashen again.

"Oh, no you don't," she began. "Come sit on this log." She led him to the fallen tree.

"No," he began. "You sit. I'll stand." He propped a foot against the log as she sat down.

She waited. She refused to hurry him.

Finally he opened his mouth. "Verity, I know you deserve an explanation. But, truly, I promise it will do no good—and has nothing to do with you."

The branches in the trees creaked as a rush of wind brought a sudden chill to her arms. The owl hooted again. "Look, this has nothing to do with curiosity or what I do or do not deserve in your eyes. Here is the thing of it. We are both of us at present in need of . . . of kindness and charity and, well, we *should* be of comfort to each other if nothing else. So I propose you tell me. I won't judge you—this I promise. I am the very last person to judge, but I can listen."

He rested his elbow on his bent knee and pressed his forehead against his hand. "I trust you, V. I trust you with my life, I think."

She waited.

"James had good reason to forbid you to jump this hellish—" He waved at the stone wall, unable to finish the phrase. "It's where *Catharine* broke her neck."

"I don't underst— *You mean Miss Talmadge?* But that's not right at all. James found her at the bottom of our north field, near the stream. Her horse slid on the muddy bank and she fell."

"That's what you were all supposed to think."

She watched a shudder race through Rory's body.

His body felt leaden. He knew it was fatigue after panic. It had happened only one other time in his life—and not on a battlefield.

She was alive . . . in front of him, sitting within reach. Verity's complexion was not waxen and white. But that is what he'd envisioned the moment he'd seen her racing toward that bloody wall. It had been a sodding reenactment down to the color of the horse. He squeezed his eyes shut. He could not escape the former haunting scene of fourteen years ago. Catharine's laugh, her flapping arms, the horse's refusal at the base of the wall . . . and the sound her body had made when she crashed into the stone wall.

"Does James know the truth?" Verity's whispered words floated to his brain.

"Yes. He was riding to Rutledge Hall. He saw me carrying her."

Silence reigned. Only crickets could be heard.

He finally continued. "I had planned to take her to her family, but your brother preferred that we make it appear that the accident happened on Boxwood land. He would not let me take the blame."

She touched his arm. "Of course you see it that way, but that is not why he insisted. You know why. If she had been found on your property there would have been a huge chance that people would have speculated about why she was here since her family's estate is next to ours, not yours. The gossip would have plagued James, possibly tainted Catharine, and haunted everyone," she stated quietly. "So you were with her when it happened?"

"Yes."

"Did your horse jump first, or did she . . ."

"It was my fault," he rushed on. "She was headstrong, to be sure, but she would not have gone if I had not told her of this jump. She was determined to prove she was fearless. I'll never know . . ."

"Never know what?"

"Why she was always trying to prove herself to me. She didn't need to prove herself."

"Rory . . ." she began.

"Yes?"

"I know why."

"You do?" He studied the grave face of the lady seated slightly below him.

"She was ashamed."

He started. "Why would you suggest that?" He leaned forward.

"She was obviously in love with you, but despite this she had agreed to marry my brother."

"You presume much." His heart raced. "Was this common knowledge in your family?"

"Not at all. But after hearing your story now, and what I alone observed in the past, it makes complete sense."

He watched his hand reach down and stroke the outside of her arm. She looked at him with such dark, fathomless eyes. Honest eyes.

"So you were both riding when this happened. I only ask because it's important to get it straight in my mind so I can give you my opinion as a friend would."

"No," he began. "I was walking. Just like I was walking when you came around the bend. I had told her the night before that only the bravest riders of Derbyshire had the daring to negotiate that wall."

"And?"

"She had laughed and insisted she could do it. I realized my mistake straight away and so I decided to dismantle it the next morning, to be certain she wouldn't do anything foolhardy. But I didn't do it soon enough."

"And so you blame yourself." It was not a question.

"No," he said.

"Yes," she said softly. "You shouldn't, but you do. It's your nature."

"How would you know my nature?"

She shook her head. "I have one last question."

His eye twitched with tension. "Yes?"

"Why is this sodding thing still here?" She stood up and marched toward the wall, leaving her horse behind to munch on a tuft of grass. She reached as high as she could and wriggled a topmost stone until it fell into her hand. She immediately tossed it into a dense patch of the woods and grasped another.

"What are you doing?" He couldn't let her destroy this. Not this.

"Dismantling this monument to your guilt."

He rushed to her side and stilled her hands. "Don't, Verity."

"I will," she insisted. "Even if you stop me now I swear to God I will return in the dead of night and take it apart. And I don't care if you come here and lie in wait for me every day and night. I'll see it done. It was *her* own fault, not yours. She never sat a horse well. And I'm guessing she was stupid enough to attempt it in a sidesaddle."

He could not draw his breath properly. "It never would have happened if I had turned my back on her once she was engaged. I should have let her go—wished her truly happy with James. But I was selfish. I wanted her for myself."

Verity rolled her eyes, and he, given the tension of the moment, nearly laughed. He was pouring out such revolting soggy sentiments, and this was her response?

"I only have one question," Verity said dryly. "Did you love her before James loved her?"

"I don't know. But I'm not certain it was love. It was more that I was entranced by her wild exuberance for life."

"When did James deduce there was something between you?"

"I haven't the faintest. Gentlemen don't speak of such things."

She rolled her eyes again. "This is precisely why you need me for a friend. Ladies are not nearly as reticent. Oh, and by the by, James knew Catharine revered you."

"What? He told you that?"

"Are you sure you're a rake? We sound like two twits at the Pump Room in Bath mulling over thirdhand gossip. Look, I always observed my brother watching Miss Talmadge who was always watching you." She shrugged. "He knew."

She was the most peculiar female he had ever known. And she made him feel . . . like their roles were reversed. And worst of all? He hated this entire revolting conversation. He had to end it to regain a measure of virility before someone caught wind of this brazen brush with *feelings* and booted him from the royal entourage.

He reached above her and removed a stone and threw it into the woods. And then he reached for another. For some blasted reason he took enormous joy throwing each stone as far as he could. With each one, he felt lighter.

Despite his efforts to stop Verity from helping him, she refused. Three-quarters of an hour later, the wall half its original size, Verity reached for a jagged rock and . . . well, it was a good thing that while watching females jump fences terrified him, bloodied limbs—even the hand of his betrothed—left him unmoved.

That did not mean he did not inspect her cut with more care than he had ever taken with anything in his life.

Chapter 10

He bandaged her hand with his neckcloth as best he could, despite her protestations. Then Rory insisted that she go with him to Rutledge Hall, which was closer than Boxwood.

His housekeeper flurried about when they arrived and instantly went in search of a salve while Rory made her comfortable on the chaise lounge in the far corner of what had been his mother's small salon, which adjoined his father's favorite chamber of the great house: the billiard room. Forever with cards in his hands or a billiard cue balanced on his shoulders between shots, it was in this room that the last Earl of Rutledge had spent the majority of the short periods of his life he'd been forced to endure at his country seat instead of in Town.

Rory felt guilt drip from every pore of his body.

Guilt for Catharine's death, guilt for ruining Candover's future happiness, and now guilt for admitting everything to Verity, who should not know of such sordid affairs.

The housekeeper finally returned with the salve and a parlor maid, who carried a tea tray with chocolate biscuits balanced on a plate.

After the servant laid everything out, Rory herded them away so he could tend to Verity himself.

She deserved as much, despite her steady stream of assurances that she was perfectly fine. He didn't feel the need to insist that a maid stay for propriety's sake. She was his betrothed, temporary or not.

"The tea is all I really need and you know it," she said calmly, trying to reach behind him.

He sighed and stopped unwinding his neckcloth from her hand to prepare her tea as she liked it.

"How did you know how I take my tea?" Her brow was furrowed in confusion.

"It's important to always remember how a lady takes her tea," he replied, handing her the cup and saucer.

"Anything else I should know about rakes?"

"Yes. A bona fide rake also remembers food preferences and dislikes, special occasions, comments on new apparel, or in your case—your, um, extraordinary hats."

"Then I must inform that you are slipping."

He finished unwinding the bloodied neckcloth and closely examined the nasty gash on her palm. "Am I?"

"I suspect, indeed I shall wager a small fortune, that you cannot name my favorite delicacy or what I consider the most loathsome food in Creation." She took a sip from her steaming tea.

He glanced up at her for but a moment before he dabbed a large amount of salve on her wound. At least she didn't complain or jump about like most ladies. "I'll admit I've been a bit lax in your case. I suspect this is due to your easy capitulation to making me the happiest—"

She interrupted. "Your happiness will come much later I assure you."

He studied her carefully. He had never known a woman so determined to distance herself from him. It reminded him of . . . himself, albeit his manner of doing so was far different. He had learned the art of wit and charm to bridge unbreachable gulfs in the past. "Well, I shall confide that in my book—peas are the most vile legumes ever created." He stopped short when he spied her shocked reaction.

"I thought I was the only one." Her expression was that of a young girl.

He smiled as he took her empty teacup from her still fingers and returned to bandaging her hand with a clean cloth. "There you have it, V. We are, indeed, made for each other. Just think of the signs you—or more likely little Tommy Redmund— shall paint for our vegetable garden." He tucked the ends inside her palm, but would not release her hand. It felt so comforting to touch her.

She was staring at their joined hands. "I know you mean well, Rory. But I must ask a favor of you."

"So serious," he said, stroking the back of her hand with his thumb. "Anything, my dear V."

"I'm tired of playing this game."

"What game is that?"

"Where you pretend this betrothal is real, and that your sensibilities go further than friendship." Her eyes were huge and dark in her face. "I know you must do this in public, but in private I would ask you to be genuine. You owe me that, Rory."

His neck itched but he would not remove his hand from hers. It was so warm. "So we are to be serious then. No more teasing."

"No. I like teasing just as much as you. And I'm used to it. It comes with having five siblings. But there are times there is an awkwardness between us and I would prefer us to be true."

He stared at her. Never in all his days had he known a lady who spoke her mind without reservation. She simply refused to dissemble or be cunning and artificial.

"Do you have much pain?"

"No."

"I am certain the housekeeper has laudanum stashed away somewhere."

"No thank you."

He stifled the urge to fill the silence.

"I should go," she said softly. "I should really—"

"No," he interrupted.

She looked down at her hand, which he was squeezing, unthinking. He immediately released it. She refused to meet his eyes, and her dark lashes against her delicate complexion was suddenly everything feminine and beautiful to him. Half of her dark hair had escaped the confines of her coiffure, and his fingers, unbidden, reached to touch the loose ends.

Still she did not look at him.

Her hair was so very soft. Slowly, ever so slowly, he stroked her head, still warm from the sun. And then he was on his knees, gathering her to him, wordlessly.

She rested her head against the top of his shoulder. Soon her arms slid up the taut fabric of his coat and he could finally exhale.

He eased onto the long, wide chaise and took her more properly in his arms. She fit there so very perfectly, naturally. He dropped a kiss on her head and she finally raised her eyes to his. It was then he noticed the dark circles.

"You haven't been sleeping well?"

She looked away. "Not last night, no."

"And why is that?"

"I would rather not say."

"I see." He could so easily tease her, but the urge was gone. "So rest your eyes now."

"No. I really should go back—"

"Humor me as I humored you by obeying your every demand earlier today." He brushed a lock of her hair from her face.

Without another word she closed her eyes. Oh, he knew she did not sleep. Her breathing was not even and deep, but he took such comfort, holding her, and stroking her head and arms and back. Her riding ensemble—voluminous white shirt and breeches and ancient, scratched up boots— was boyish and practical; the least feminine articles of clothing he had ever seen a lady sport. And yet they were uniquely her.

When she moved restlessly, he tilted her chin and lowered his lips to hers. She responded with a small sound and pressed herself closer. Enfolded in his arms, she tasted of goodness and passion and woman.

Rory could not stop himself from lowering his

hand to cup her breast over the thin fabric. But he wanted more. He wanted to touch that shimmering flesh of hers below the frantic pulse at the base of her neck. He released a few buttons from their holes and delved beyond the fine edges of the shirt. The shock of her bare flesh against his hand nearly undid him.

The bud of her breast instantly tightened between his fingers, and he caressed her, valiantly struggling against his desire to crush her to him.

He wanted so much to taste her. He didn't want to stop even though his mind was screaming its refusal. He lowered his lips to hers, all rational thought deserting him.

Through the roar of sensation of her kiss, he felt her touch his chest. She had unbuttoned his own shirt and her hand was cool on his hot flesh.

This was madness, surely. And yet it was not. He could have stopped if she had paused for one moment. But he did not want to. He wanted to give her anything and everything she would accept. But he would not take from her.

"V . . ." He spoke softly. "Is this what you want? Tell me."

"Yes," she whispered. "And you?"

"Of this there is no question."

Oh, he would not truly take her, but he would

give her all the pleasure she could stand. And then some.

"Do you trust me?" He echoed the same words she had so recently said to him.

"Of course."

"Then wait here." He closed his eyes for a moment to gain the strength to leave her for but a moment. He then carefully disengaged her from his arms and rose, keeping his back to her. Desire was heavy upon him and the evidence was a bit too obvious. He crossed the small chamber and locked the door. And then crossed to the adjacent wall, where the door to the billiards room was ajar. He entered his father's favorite room, took care to lock its main door to the hall and returned to the small salon. He closed that door and set a chair under the lever. Finally, he walked to the two windows, checked the sashes and unleashed the dark amber velvet curtains.

She was watching his movements silently until he returned to her side. "You are worried the servants will intrude?"

He regarded her small form on the chaise. "No. They know never to enter unless they announce their presence and are invited to enter."

"I see."

"I'm sorry," he replied. "I just don't like open doors."

"I know," she whispered.

"Whatever do you mean?"

"Nothing," she murmured. "It's not important. It's just something I observed many times."

He extended his hand and she placed hers in it. He urged her to her feet and drew her into his embrace once again.

It would be so easy to lose herself in his arms, Verity thought. She had once longed for it. For so many years of her girlhood he had filled the romantic corners of her mind until she had witnessed him with Catharine beneath the old pine tree.

Even after he went away to war a few months later so abruptly, she had dreamed of him. And now she finally understood why he had gone without a word. In her naïveté, she had never imagined Catharine Talmadge's death had been anything different than the story her brother presented to the family.

Her diary entries had changed a few years after he had gone away. A new name cropped up in her ramblings one summer. She pushed the thought away, when Rory whispered something incoherent in her ear. She didn't want to remember the past or the future. She only wanted to feel this moment. To drink it to the dregs.

Rory pulled her deeper into his arms, and she could not resist him. He was so warm in the coolness of the darkened room. She wanted him desperately. All she could hear was his breathing and the rustle of their clothes as he stroked her.

She lifted her head and tugged his to hers. He kissed her once again, his lips easing hers open and twining his tongue with her own. He smelled of dark spices and shaving soap. Irresistible.

And all at once she knew. She was going to fully experience the feelings he had awakened in her and allow herself to make love to him. For that is what it would be, at least for her . . . showing and giving her love to him, a man who deserved it more than anyone she had ever known. Oh, she harbored no hope at all for marriage now that her diaries had been stolen and published for all the world to see. She gave herself one chance in a hundred that her identity would not be discovered, which would very well taint the reputation of anyone and everyone associated with her.

But there was something vitally important she suddenly longed to do despite her ruined future. And it would harm no one.

She wanted desperately to grab onto the one chance she would ever have to conquer her fear. She could only do it by giving and receiving from the only man she could trust . . . Rory. Just once, she wanted to have the courage to experience physical love with someone who truly cared for her on a genuine level. She knew he would be gentle, and kind, and she would show Rory all of the secret love she possessed for him in return. Then she would forget her past of ten years ago and know, once and for all, what she might have had.

His breath was uneven along her jaw as he traced his mouth down her neck.

"Rory?" she whispered.

He didn't lift his head from his ministrations. "Yes, V?"

"I have a great favor to ask."

"Anything," he breathed.

"Make love to me."

He stiffened.

"I should not have said make 'love,' Rory," she murmured. "What I mean is that I want to lie with you. Have—"

He interrupted gently. "I know what you're trying to say, V." He straightened slowly, grasped her shoulders with his large hands and gazed at her.

"Well?" She hardly dared to breathe.

"May I ask why?" His eyes were a dark, still green in the light of the afternoon.

"Of course," she replied softly. "It's just that

I will go away eventually as I said. I will never marry. No one will ever know except you and me. We have another secret between us, and I'd like to have this one too. It will hurt no one, will it? And I would like to have this as a memory. Would you?"

"Verity . . ." He raked back his dark hair with one hand. "It's not so simple. And I would not hurt you for the world. I just don't think—"

"I understand," she interrupted. "Really I do." She broke away and put distance between them.

"You don't understand," he replied. "Having relations can create serious attachment for many fe-ahem, I mean for people such as me."

"You're lying, and I'm not all you think. But I understand." She rebuttoned the top two buttons of her shirt and headed toward the door, determined for him not to see the hot swell of sadness. "Thank you for tea and for bandaging—"

The air left her lungs as he came up behind her and spun her back into his embrace, all gentleness gone.

"I want you," he said roughly into her ear. "Don't you dare go."

A moment later he gathered her in his arms, and for the first time in her life she felt extremely fragile and feminine.

Her heart was beating so loudly she could almost hear it. He deposited her at the foot of the chaise and with a few, deft, fast, and furious movements had divested her of her old boots and breeches. His eyes never wavered from her face as he slowed to carefully unbutton her shirt. She was certain a blush extended to her toes. He grasped the bottom of the shirt and eased it over her head.

He sucked in a breath. "Oh, V . . . you are perfection," he murmured in a dark, gravelly voice she had never heard.

She was too shy to glance at him as he removed his own clothes. But she felt his eyes studying her, watching her.

His shirt was still in place, but she very much feared and was equally delighted that all the other articles of his clothing were not. He took her hand and she finally gazed into his eyes.

"I have not told you what we were doing when I woke up beside you at Carleton House," he said as he eased her onto the chaise lounge.

She could not form a word in her mouth.

He stood in front of her and grasped the ends of his shirt to pull it over his head in a supremely masculine fashion. Lord above, he was all sinew and muscle. Hard planes of flesh jutted in a beautiful picture of everything virile. She would not allow her eyes to drift lower. He kneeled onto the chaise and stretched out beside her.

"Are you certain, V?"

"Continue with your story," she returned.

"Not until you are in my arms," he murmured. He opened his arms and she moved into his embrace.

Something so primal and elemental happened the moment they were skin-to-skin. It was a hot, thick, pungent desire that took her breath away. She felt him swallow.

"V . . . oh, V." He grasped her neck and pulled her closer.

"The story," she whispered, barely able to concentrate while his flesh caressed hers.

"When I began to wake I felt the most astounding sensation. I looked down and my hand was entwined with yours." He grasped her uninjured hand with his. "Like this," he murmured, and then kissed her with parted lips.

She wanted him to touch her breast again. It had set her aflame. She arched her back and he immediately broke free of her lips and lowered his head to the very place she wanted.

Oh my Lord . . . his mouth hovered over her breast and then descended. His tongue swirled the tip of her and she entered paradise.

Her body surged with pleasure and she instinctively ran her injured hand up the deep indentation of his spine to where his hair dovetailed.

He exhaled roughly as she brought her other fingers to his flexed hip.

"Not yet, V," he ground out, bowing down to

minister to her other breast. His hands fanned out and grasped her ribs, forcing her to endure the torture he rained down on her with his tongue.

And then she could not wait another moment. She had to touch him. Her curiosity would not be denied; she just had to know. So much for any remnants of maidenly virtue.

Her fingers closed the distance and she grasped the hard, massive jut of him. She could never have imagined what his manhood would feel like. It was very like an iron rod covered in silk satin. She stroked his full length and he pulsed. She had not known it would grow to this size. The idea of it made her shiver. She caressed him again.

He groaned as if in pain and she released him.

"God. Please . . . please, do that again," he groaned.

She complied, taking confidence in the pleasure pain she surely was inflicting.

And all of a sudden he became a madman. He swept her body under his. His forehead dropped down until it touched hers and he went still.

She could sense his trepidation. "Hey . . . are you all right?"

He looked at her; his eyes were glassy with guarded mystery. "I should be asking you that."

"I'm perfectly fine."

He shook his head. "I don't want to hurt you, V," he said with pain radiating from his eyes.

"This is my decision, not yours."

His eyes were old, the harsh planes of his face grim as he gazed down the length of her figure. "You are so damn beautiful."

She knew it wasn't true. Never in her life had she felt beautiful . . . but this one instant in time she suddenly did. Here with him on this soft chaise.

Verity knew what would come next. She released the tight grip of her knees and allowed him to slip between her thighs.

A vein in his neck pulsed with tension as long moments passed without a word from him, his head slightly above her own. For a moment she feared he had changed his mind and would leave her. Instead he finally moved his strong hands to push her legs still wider and came up on his forearms to stare at her below him. She never ever wanted to forget this moment. It was the pinnacle of her every dream . . . only so much more poignant than she had ever imagined.

She was with him, and he with her. And for just this one moment out of time nothing else mattered.

The cool air in the darkened chamber made her shiver. And then he was stroking the side of her body and running his hand to the dark nest of curls between her thighs. With his strong, deft fingers, he parted her folds and it was all she could do not to shout from the wicked sensation he released from her. His touch was so shocking and sure over her soft flesh. A moment later she felt her body's molten response. She became hotter, wetter. She raised her head, only to see his own move ever lower.

A curl of the most irresistible heat swirled over her. God. He was kissing her. *There*. Where his hand and fingers had been. She would have objected if not for the intense pleasure that left a silent scream in her throat.

Oh, she should not have suggested this. How could she live without it? There was a reason this was forbidden to unmarried ladies. Ecstasy like this—once tasted could never be forgotten.

And then she felt his finger enter her. A dark passion overtook her when he moved within her passage. The thrust and release was a sweet pleasure pain that was immeasurable in time and place. The intensity was almost too much to bear, and she forgot to breathe.

She closed her eyes for a moment and regretted it. She suddenly remembered another time, another very different place. She forced her eyes open. She only wanted to remember today. With Rory. It was burning away all the old, horrid, humiliating memories.

He looked up from below her, his eyes burning

with intensity. "It's me, Verity . . . and I want you."

It was as if he could read her every need. She nearly cried for the sweetness of it.

And then he entered her again gently with his finger, and took a long taste of her at the same time. It unfurled a great need deep inside of her. She pulsed with some unknown longing, which was terrifyingly intense. She wanted to speak, but she could not. Something was growing louder in her mind and in her body. And suddenly she reached some unknown zenith, and a white burning pleasure gripped her as she balanced on the edge of an invisible precipice. A massive series of pulses raced through her core so deeply she cried out, which only served to make the pulses echo throughout her again.

As reason returned to her, she felt him inch up and lay his head on her belly. He turned to kiss her navel. He seemed to caress her ribs with something very near reverence. But surely in her daze she was imagining it.

Without a word his body moved fully over her and his whole weight pressed down on her. She felt almost suffocated by the strength surrounding her. And for a moment, just the briefest moment, she had the urge to stop him.

But this was Rory. He would not hurt her. He would stop if she asked.

And yet now he would not move. He would not raise up on his arms and kiss her. He was like a statue, and she could imagine his thoughts churning wildly.

"Don't you dare stop," she whispered. She parted her knees once again and raised her legs, inviting him, almost daring him not to possess her.

He finally raised his head and she saw a look of raw need in a dark expression he wore like a mask. The heavy length of him pressed against her thigh. He moved slightly and his hardness was now at the entrance to her, still radiating sensations. And once again she couldn't breathe for the intensity of the moment . . . and the small fear growing in the pit of her stomach. His body was solid and sinewed with strength. Her apprehension grew when he did not move.

He finally rose to look at her with such an expression of worry on his face. His hand pushed a lock of her hair from her cheek. "Breathe, Verity."

She exhaled roughly.

"Shall I stop, then?"

She shook her head with force, unable to speak.

"Are you sure? I can't bear to hurt you."

"Oh, Rory," she said finally. "I can't stand this waiting. Please . . ."

And then he was testing the edges of her. She

angled her hips and then he seemed to make a decision. He slid an inch inside of her and withdrew. And then again, slowly going carefully deeper. She tensed as he withdrew. She could feel how intensely he was holding himself in check. He paused and studied her for a moment and then dropped his face to gently kiss her brow. She relaxed instantly. At that moment he arched and drove deep inside her.

She closed her eyes and almost groaned with relief that there was none of the searing pain of so long ago. Instead there was his fullness pulsing deep within her when he stopped. She had never felt such intimate communion. She finally opened her eyes and found him studying her, his eyes dark and remote.

She knew what would come next. A few jerky, painful movements and then he would withdraw and get dressed, cough, and apologize.

She prepared herself, only wishing this could last far longer. She almost begged for him not to stop again. She wanted this to be more binding; everlasting.

He withdrew, breathing deeply, and then slowly plunged deeper than before, and deeper still until she felt so full, so vulnerable, that she would burst.

The edges of her burned with pleasure-pain.

He slowly withdrew yet again only to begin a long tumble into a steady rhythm meant to draw from within her a maddening desire that would only build. And again she felt herself on the edge of something wild and reckless. She would not let go again. She could not.

But he would not leave her there. He alternated between looking at her, watching what he did to her, and then losing himself in the ageless rhythm. He seemed transfixed in agonized pleasure as he thrust the great root of himself into her again and again.

"Open yourself to me," he demanded with a groan. "Yes, that's it. Even more. Don't be afraid. I have you, Verity. I won't go without you." His hands suddenly slid to grip her bottom and he pulled her ever closer to him.

She couldn't speak, couldn't think. But she listened to him.

"Close your eyes."

She shook her head. She had to look at his beautiful body covering hers. She had to know it was him.

"Let it come, then," he ground out. "Oh God." He closed his dark green eyes and strained his head back, giving her as much of him as she could take.

She could not have breathed if she had wanted

to. The air within her swirled wildly into a vortex that spun out of control, and finally, teetering, she felt her cleft constrict and she shattered into a thousand incandescent filaments of pulsing light.

He let himself follow her, pumping and pumping, until with another groan he swiftly withdrew from her and spilled his seed on her body.

With an unsteady hand, he carefully stroked her belly clean with the discarded neckcloth he had used as a makeshift bandage. And then he slowly collapsed his great weight on her, his exhaustion finally evident. Great emotion welled inside her and she didn't dare move for she feared it might jar the sudden tears in her eyes.

Oh dear Lord. She should not have done this. She knew she should not. She had held herself so rigidly in check. And this was the reason. She had instinctively and unconsciously known it would be like this with him. And it was hopeless. It could never happen again. It *would* never happen again.

And so her punishment would be knowing for the rest of her life what she had given up to keep her sanity.

She knew with all her heart and soul that she could not marry him. He could never love her as she loved him. And he had even warned her of this effect. Of the ungovernable feminine emotions that followed an event of this magnitude.

She fought valiantly to keep her emotions in check. She would not allow him to see how deeply these moments with him had affected her. She could not let him see. It would only lead to guilt on his side. And it would be unbearable to see that in his expression. She knew without one doubt that he had a great conscience. And she would not let him suffer regret again. She loved him too much to allow it.

But above all, there was one other reason she could never marry Rory. It trumped all. When someone finally figured out she was the author of the Duke Diaries—and she had no doubt her identity would eventually come to light—she had no intention of dragging the man she loved down with her.

At that moment one of Rory's hands found hers and grasped it gently with a squeeze that promised comfort. She shivered.

Chapter 11

In the final throes of passion, Rory had fought to ignore the familiar tightening in his lower back. He had concentrated on her happiness, on her pleasure. He wanted more than anything to bring her to completion again. He would have shot himself if he hadn't. He had focused on slowing and deepening the even rhythm of thrusts. She had been so soft and inviting. It was an exquisite torture he could not remember ever experiencing.

Rory had never been more surprised in his life. He'd expected her to show fear. And where had been the resistance, pain, blood, and all the rest that came part and parcel with a virgin?

He had lain with only one before—the widow of a gentleman too elderly to exercise his marital rights. The entire experience had been so unpleasant, had involved so many tears, and so much obvious pain, that he had sworn off virgins altogether.

But Verity had asked him to make love to her and he could not deny her. And in equal measure, he had not been able to deny himself.

And so he had not.

But she had been everything sweet. Her body was like an impossibly delicious fruit, ready to be savored and revered. He simply could not get enough of her. He was insatiable at the sight and scent of every inch of her.

But at the moment of truth, the moment where there should have been an impossibly tight impasse, there had been only intense pleasure as he slowly penetrated her narrow passage.

He closed his eyes and rested his forehead against the back of the chaise. He could not understand. He had heard that riding astride could damage a lady physically, but there had been something more to it.

When he entered her and discovered there was no barrier, he had studied her face for a moment and seen the unmistakable signs of fear and . . . *guilt*. That was the word. There was absolutely no shock or surprise in her expression.

"Rory?" she whispered.

He released her hand and raised himself up on his forearms. "I'm squashing you."

"No," she replied evenly.

He was certain he saw uncertainty and the remnants of sorrow in her eyes. "Are you in pain?"

"No," she said quietly.

He could see the hesitancy in her dark eyes. It was the first time she was not saying what was on her mind.

He had left her reputation in tatters in London, and had no doubt the whispers would soon reach Derbyshire. Yet she was determined not to force him into marriage. Little did she know, he would never allow it, even if he could not yet tell her since he knew she would refuse. But he sensed he had learned the reason for her refusal. He had also finally learned that winning her hand would prove to be the most complex and important mission of his life. He would never again make the mistake of thinking that surmounting her reservations would be an easy task.

But finally, he could do something for her. He could open a path for her to confide in him.

He stroked her head and gazed into her lovely face. "You know, V, you can say or tell me anything, don't you? You did say we are to be the best of friends."

Her anxious eyes roamed his face.

"You showed me not two hours ago that you would not judge me," he began. "I would hope you know that I am the last person to ever judge you." He rolled slowly to the inside of the chaise and pulled her into his arms to cradle her and nuzzle her nose. "And everyone knows rakes make the very best confidants."

She bit her lower lip. "I suppose you know, then."

"That you are extraordinary?"

She whispered, "You can say the truth."

He pondered his words. "You were not a virgin." He paused. "There's no need for an explanation. If you start, then I'll feel compelled to tell you about my past indiscretions, which I am sorry to say will surely shock you, and then where will we be?"

"But I want to tell you, even if I really *don't* want to." Her smile was wan.

Levity was clearly not giving her ease. He gathered his thoughts. "I gather it is something more serious than riding astride." He pressed a kiss on the top of her warm head.

"I wish I could say it was riding. I hadn't thought that was a possibility."

"You know it doesn't matter to me. It only matters to you. You can still tell me it was due to riding, V."

She closed her eyes and shook her head slightly. "I cannot."

He waited to see if she really wanted to tell him more or not.

"I—I . . . did something unpardonably imprudent the summer I was seventeen."

He felt a slight chill. Seventeen was such a dangerous age. The same age Catharine had been. Females were usually not quite out at that momentous time, but desperate to begin life. He should know. "What did you do?"

"I fell in love. Or I thought I fell in love. I cannot be certain. I was so young and foolish."

"You fell in love," he said with certainty. "Love does not pay attention to age."

"And so . . . against everything I knew or believed to be right or true, I entered into a secret engagement."

He raised his brows. "And who was this lucky fellow, may I ask?" He had the oddest sensation in the pit of his gut. He simply had to know who it was. He tried to relax without success.

"Mr. Battswell," she whispered. "You probably remember that my cousin Esme's father was a great artist. Well, he invited three of the most promising students from Hillwood's Fine Arts School to spend a month on his estate—painting, and sketching the vast beauty of the peaks. Theo was one of the three."

"And?" He asked the question casually, taking

care to keep every trace of ill ease from his voice.

"And I was always there. Visiting Esme as usual. And . . . and, well, I became infatuated. Mr. Battswell possessed an extraordinary talent. He was witty and charming, and he was . . ."

"I don't like him already."

"He was very handsome."

Rory could feel her growing sadness, and tried to cheer her. "But not as handsome as I, one could hope."

"No, of course not," she said, biting her lower lip.

He wanted to kiss her lip, tell her not to worry so, but he did not. Speaking was more important. "And yet you did not marry him," he continued. The gentleman must have died. They must have yielded to the wild passions of youth, anticipated the wedding night, and then this ill-behaved young man had probably succumbed to a sudden, violent illness. That's how it always went in romantic cases such as these.

"No, we did not marry."

Her legs were restless and so Rory carefully spread a deep green velvet throw over them both. "You don't have to go on, V."

"I want to." She rushed her words. "When he went to my brother to ask for my hand, James agreed, but then added a proviso."

"Yes?"

"He explained to Mr. Battswell that there would be no immediate dowry due to our father's wishes. That James had been instructed to provide one thousand pounds a year should any of his sisters marry, but any dowry would be left in a trust until we were five and twenty."

"And how old was this Mr. Battswell?"

"Eight and twenty."

God. She had been eleven years his junior. James Fitzroy, the premier duke of England, was no fool. "I assume Mr. Battswell had pockets to let, then?"

"He had a very modest sum from his family. James understood he was a second son of a vicar."

"I've never trusted vicars," he murmured.

Her eyes cheered a bit. "Of course you don't. You're clearly not one for sermonizing."

"Or promises of hell or heaven. I already know where St. Peter will send me when I clang on his gates. At least I won't have to endure any more of these blasted wretched English winters."

"I've always admired your ability to see the positive in any situation," she replied softly, her eyes finally taking on a gleam of humor.

"You should always smile like that, V. It's very becoming."

She didn't respond. Instead her grin disappeared. "And so, Mr. Battswell agreed. He said he didn't care about my dowry, that we would live modestly and very quietly in a tiny cottage in the country somewhere. He would paint, I would keep house, and have children, and eventually all would fall into place. He said eight years was nothing to wait. Everyone knows money did not bring happiness, he insisted." She was studying the tips of her fingers as she spoke.

"And then he took advantage of you." He was careful to keep the anger threatening to break into his voice.

"No. It wasn't like that, and yet—" Her voice caught. "—it was in the end."

"When?" His word was more curt than he meant it to be. "Verity, tell me."

"Does it really matter? It was ten years ago," she whispered. "The day before the summer solstice."

"Where?" he asked, his voice more even.

She stared at him mutely, uncertainty on her face. Finally she answered. "At the heart of Boxwood's maze. Where I knew no one would find us."

He waited, his body tense.

"I am the only one who knows how to find the garden in the center without getting impossibly lost."

He would not let himself speak.

"Oh, I shall tell you all, what does it matter?

We picnicked in secret after his meeting with my brother. He said he would return to Town, make all the arrangements for us to marry there, and also secure a cottage as close to London as we could afford." One of her hands was so tightly clenched her knuckles showed points of white. "And I told him I loved him, and he said something very like it in return. I cannot remember precisely what he said, but he told me to wait for him, and then, well . . . you can imagine the rest."

He replied evenly without emotion. "The heartless bastard took advantage of your generous young heart, ruined you, and never returned."

"Actually," she murmured, "he disappeared. Esme's father learned that Mr. Battswell's father was not a vicar, but rather a tooth-drawer who went from village to village to ply his trade."

Rory's eyes never left hers. "And James tracked him down and extracted all of the son's teeth, followed by all of his limbs."

"No," she replied calmly. "James doesn't know what happened in the maze. I never told anyone. Except one other person and now you, and, well, I'm certain my—my mother guessed, although she never said a word." The last was said in a whisper that Rory had to bend his head to hear.

"And that is when you decided you would never marry anyone," he replied.

"I suppose my decision formed then," she said slowly. "But, you see, it never really mattered. My older sisters, Faith and Hope, and I had decided long before that we would never marry. So it was not such a grave tragedy as you obviously think by the look on your face."

"Ah, there you are wrong. Very wrong." Suddenly he envisioned a handsome, black-hearted devil of a bastard taking the innocence of the lady. The first icy cold taste for revenge flooded his senses. He narrowed his eyes as he stared at her.

And he could do it.

If there was anything he had learned as Wellington's wily, chameleon henchman, it was deception, tracking, and murder.

She looked at him steadily. "But Rory, please don't misunderstand. That is merely one of the reasons I decided long ago that I would not marry."

He lay back on the chaise again and closed his eyes. Of course that was only one of the reasons. Had he not just figured out that nothing would ever come easily regarding Verity?

The next morning, Verity handed Captio's reins to the stable boy with carrot-colored hair in the tidy stables bordering one side of the village green. She tousled his thick hair and he dimpled.

"My lady," he said, bobbing his head. "I saved the best alfalfa for Captio."

"Perfect," Verity replied with a wink and a smile. "And I saved the best ha'penny for you."

His eyes shone as she pressed the coin into his hand.

"So are you ever going to visit the school?" she asked. "You remember what I promised."

He looked away, sheepish to the nth degree.

"What? You've heard I'm an ogre at a chalkboard, have you?"

"Not at all, Lady Fitzroy. It's jus' me pa, he needs me here."

"Don't you worry. I shall have a word with your pa. I'm very good with fathers."

She gathered her books and papers from her saddlebags and marched out of the dark stable into the bright sunlight of a Wednesday morning. The air was fresh, and a few small clouds slowly drifted high above. She would rather be riding or . . .

And in a moment she was right back with Rory, and the shock at what she had instigated and what had transpired between them. She never would have imagined something could be so mesmerizing, so elemental, so wildly, heartbreakingly beautiful. And yet, it would never happen again.

It could not for she knew he would never love her as deeply as she loved him. She had already experienced that sort of pain with Theo Battswell. She had survived by promising herself never to make that same mistake twice.

Brushing aside Mary Haverty's words of concern during the evening meal, Verity had tossed and turned in her bed in her elegant, cozy bedchamber, desperate for sleep but then desperate to wake when the terrible dreams began.

She inhaled sharply the scent of the freshly cut lawn of the green. She'd had the horrible dreams of so long ago. Of Theo and his laughing brown eyes. But then they had changed to green and then turned serious and hard. Just like Rory's eyes had changed as she confided her story yesterday afternoon.

He had taken great care not to show his disgust of what she had allowed to happen with Theo Battswell all those years ago. But she had felt the tension in his body next to hers as she revealed all. And his carefully phrased questions, oh-so-casually spoken, had shown the truth of his thoughts.

For years she had determinedly fought her memories to gain a measure of peace. She hadn't even told Rory the entire sad truth of it. His eyes had begged her not to say another blasted word.

And so she had not. It was far easier this way. Besides, she never allowed herself to dwell on the last event of that same summer.

Her poignant moments with Rory had turned awkward in the end. When he had become silent, she became discomfited and insisted she had to depart. And so she had taken her leave of Rutledge Hall—unlocking the connecting door to the other chamber, where she quickly dressed, while he did the same and then unlocked the chamber's door to the hall.

And when he had insisted on riding beside her during her return to Boxwood, she urged Captio into a canter, as it was obvious any intimacy that had developed between them was at an end.

There had been less than a dozen words exchanged when they arrived at Boxwood's immaculate stables. She had marched toward the avenue of tulip trees, which was the main approach to Boxwood's sweeping entrance, and refused to look back at him as he departed.

What did it all matter? They would never marry. Why should she care what he thought of her? Oh, but in the recesses of her heart, she knew she cared a great deal. She had bared her most private secret to him and been found as guilty as she felt. His every kindness to her afterward had reeked of insincerity.

Now, Verity forced back her regrets and entered the small clapboard structure she had come to love. None of the students had arrived yet and so she quickly glanced through her lesson plans and organized her ideas. She was so grateful for the distraction.

The boys heading off to Eton in the fall entered the school first, with shy grins. They bowed and found their desks as the other children crossed the threshold. Verity approached the older boys and with a hushed voice pointed out the sections of the books she wanted them to read and discuss later. And then there was the mathematics she had to suffer through.

She loathed mathematics. Numbers gave her hives—unless they were in a ledger and involved simple addition or subtraction. Anything involving more than three letters in equations made her cross. Numbers mixed with letters reminded her of inedible legumes attempting to mix with lovely mashed potatoes.

The hours and minutes in the quiet schoolhouse ticked by. Tommy Redmund shocked all by reading aloud a poem he had written. It was about a lighthouse and a shipwreck, and a duke who appeared to save the day. His schoolmates were mesmerized, just like she. Verity looked at the young boy with pride. She was certain he would eventually follow the other three to Eton one day in the distant future. Not that she would be there to witness it. She would be in her family's ancient abbey, lost somewhere in the northern-most portion of the Lake District.

"Excuse me, Lady Fitzroy," a booming voice called from the doorway. It was the village baker. "I has the loaves you ordered."

"Very good, Mr. Terrel. You may leave them over there"—she indicated a long side table —"And Mr. Felton?"

"Is coming, ma'am."

The room had gone silent as twenty-odd pairs of eyes watched the bread being laid out on the table.

Mr. Felton, the butcher, entered on the heels of Mr. Terrel's departure, carrying so many parcels that his knees nearly buckled under the weight.

"I knews I shoulda bring the cart. But 'twas silly, you're jus' across the green, you are!"

"Oh, thank you, Mr. Felton. Please deposit it all over there, beside the bread."

She said not another word while the tradesmen arranged all the foodstuffs on the long table.

As soon as they departed, leaving the door open to allow a breeze to enter, she looked at the sea of thin faces in front of her. Their huge eyes, a sea of brown, blue, hazel, and green, stared back at her.

She smiled and felt slightly embarrassed.

"Well, let's see, how do I explain this? I know. You all have been the most perfectly wretched students since I've replaced Miss Woods, the greatest teacher this village has ever had the pleasure to have. And I expect she will return any day now, so I decided you all deserved a gift from me."

Not one of them moved a muscle.

"So here it is, in all its simplicity. You are each to take two loaves of bread and a parcel of meat and give it to your parents to thank them for allowing me to teach you. I shall also bring a few things from Boxwood's vegetable gardens tomorrow, before I leave you."

"Leave us?" a small voice called out.

"Yes, for a short while. I must go away for a very little while—but I shall return if Miss Woods is still away. But I expect you all to read at least three books apiece and write brilliant essays on each. But . . . well, we shall not worry about your mathematics until I return."

"No mathematics?" a deep voice echoed from the open door.

Verity turned her head only to find Rory leaning casually in the doorjamb. He had not a hair out of place. His immaculate dark green superfine coat fit him to perfection. His eyes matched it. His buff breeches molded his thighs and ended where his gleaming, spit-polished boots began.

Not a sound could be heard in the schoolroom as the boys gaped at their exalted visitor.

She could feel a blush creeping from her bodice toward her collarbone. In a few more moments the unbecoming color was sure to rise to her face.

"Your Grace." She curtsied. "May I help you in some way?"

"Not at all. Please don't let me interrupt you. I merely came to watch our village's newest teacher. My position in the parish requires supervision of schoolteachers."

A few small giggles escaped from one of the boys' lips before another hushed him and sent an elbow to his ribs.

She took her decision in a rush. "All right, you are all dismissed. Please, once again, tell your parents how grateful I am that they spare you each day. I shall have word sent when I am returned. It will be less than a fortnight."

They filed past the long table, in wonder at the bounty. Arms full, they each bobbed their youthful heads in awe of the Duke of Abshire, who had entered and stood to one side.

Tommy Redmund was the last and he stopped in front of Rory.

"Yes?" Rory asked with great hauteur. "What is your name, sir?"

"Tommy. Tommy Redmund, yer highness."

Verity worried her lower lip.

"Delighted to make your acquaintance, sir. Did you have something to say, then, for I am a very, very busy man."

"Yes, yer honor. Dids ye like them signs I made fer ye?"

"Indeed, Mr. Redmund. Excellent. I may have to commission you for a few more."

"I don'ts know about missionin' me fer anything, yer graceness. Me da won' let me follow the drum till I'm grown. I'm sorry."

Rory tipped his hat. "Well, then, we shall just have to negotiate with your father. I'm certain we will come to an agreement. I could use a man of your intelligence in my regiment."

Tommy's eyes widened with excitement. "Me da said he wagered you be Wellington's Chameleon. Is it true then, yer lordness?"

"Tommy?"

"Yes, sir?"

"I promise you I will eat that, uh, confection on Lady Fitzroy's head if someone can prove it."

Verity did not know if she wanted more to laugh or cry. The awkwardness between them was still there. It was palatable. She valiantly attempted to maintain the fixed smile on her face.

She came behind Tommy and whispered in his

ear, "Bow and tell His Grace that you would be honored to paint any sign he needs."

Tommy's eyes lit up. He tapped Rory on his hand. "No problem, yer sirliness, I'll paint any ol' sign ye want. Good-bye, then."

They watched Tommy run off, his feet kicking up a trail of dust from the road before he hit the grass of the Green.

She wanted to fill the uncomfortable silence but could find no words.

"I see why you love it," he said finally, still looking at Tommy trotting off.

"Love what?"

"Teaching these children. Are they all so amusing?"

"No. Most are very serious."

"You're good with them," he said in a brisk tone, still not meeting her eye. "You are to be commended."

Her heart fell to her toes. He really had cooled to her. She could feel the ill-ease creeping between them and she wanted to cry.

But she did not. Guilt she might possess, but pride she had in abundance. It was the one thing that had sustained her all these years.

He finally turned to her, his eyes remote. "Where are you going?"

"To Boxwood, of course."

"I heard you telling the children that you were leaving for a fortnight."

"Actually less than a fortnight. I'm departing for London in the morning."

His chin rose and he looked down his perfect aquiline nose at her. "Really?"

"Yes. Really."

"What's in London?"

"Affairs to attend to."

"I see," he said.

By his tone, Verity believed he didn't see so much as the end of his nose.

"And what of your brother's order to remain in Derbyshire?"

"He only demanded that I remain here unless I agreed to marry you. We are betrothed, and now, as you suggested when you first arrived, the incarceration is over. I'm free to go. But fear not, I know appearances must be maintained. I shall return very soon."

"So I am to remain in the hellish boredom of the country while you trample off to London?" His eyes darkened. "I thought most betrothals or marriages work the other way 'round. While the females are languishing or breeding in the country, the gentlemen go to Town to gamble, drink, and attend to other *affairs*—Parliamentary in nature, of course."

Now he was being vulgar and there was an edge to his tone. She didn't have to stand for his contempt. He might be a duke, but she was the daughter and sister of the premier duke in the land. She might be ruined twice over, but she was his equal on the gilded ladder of English aristocracy.

She brushed against his arms folded one over the other as she swept out of the school. The anger began to build—at herself. She was such a stupid, stupid woman.

Why had she opened herself to him—of all people? She had sworn she would never speak of her past to anyone, gentlemen in particular, and she had committed a far greater sin—sharing her body. *Again*.

Well, she was through with all of it.

Today.

She would go to London, find the diaries, solve Amelia's pressing delicate situation, possibly descend to Cornwall, and then return to Derbyshire, ready to end the engagement from hell. And then she would immediately depart for the Lake District and begin life anew even if Faith and Hope were not with her yet. And pray for her soul. A lot.

And in that moment, she envisioned a school of some sort. She was going to change the course of her life and never, ever look back.

She swished her skirts around to face him as he stood in the door frame. "Good day to you, Your Grace. I wish you only the best, as a good friend would."

She turned back toward the Green and marched as fast as she dared toward the stables to recuperate her beloved mare. She only wished she could move faster. And she prayed he would not follow her and stop her to torment her any longer.

"Lady Fitzroy!" a kind, familiar voice called behind her.

She turned. It was the vicar, waving a letter at her.

"Oh, Lady Fitzroy! So glad I found you." He was out of breath from chasing her down. "I have a most important communication from our dear Miss Woods."

"Yes?" she asked, refusing to see if Rory had followed her.

"Miss Woods is not returning. Her sister is recovered somewhat, but remains in a fragile state," Robert Armitage stated, glancing at the letter he held in his hands. "Miss Woods has decided to remain with her indefinitely to care for her."

Verity felt rather than saw Rory Lennox, the reminder of newest great folly, come to stand near her.

The vicar bowed. "Your Grace."

"Mr. Armitage."

"Pardon me. I was just informing Lady Fitzroy that—"

"Yes, I heard."

The vicar nodded, uncertainty obvious in his expression and stature.

Rory stepped into her side view. "So it appears Lady Fitzroy's presence is very much needed here."

"Oh, yes, Your Grace. She is the most marvelous teacher. We are very lucky she has stepped in to oversee the school."

Verity steadied her nerves by breathing deeply. "Thank you, Mr. Armitage. I am happy to continue for the short term, but for the moment I am needed in London. When I return, we shall discuss the search for a new teacher to head the school."

The vicar stared at her and then darted a glance toward Rory, whose eyes she would not meet.

Mr. Armitage spoke quickly. "I do believe I should take my leave, Your Grace, Lady Fitzroy. Pray, offer my respects to His Grace, the Duke of Candover, should you see him. Lady Fitzroy." He bowed deeply to both of them.

"I shall," Verity replied.

A moment after the vicar departed, Verity turned to Rory. "I don't believe in dancing about a subject, and so I shall tell you plainly. I am needed in Town. I am not going to tell you why—we owe each other no explanation for anything we choose to do, despite everything. I am asking you to allow me to pass. I have things to do before I take my leave."

He narrowed his eyes, which appeared extraordinarily green in the heat of the afternoon. "So yesterday meant nothing." It was not a question, but a statement.

"We offered each other solace and friendship, but that is all."

"Solace and friendship, was it?"

"Yes."

He took a step closer to her, and she held her ground. "I suppose then that I only need to thank you for your warm camaraderie."

"Precisely," she snapped. In an effort to push a stray lock of hair under her black straw bonnet with a novel shape, she inadvertently knocked the wilting huge cluster of purple asters attached to one side. He immediately retrieved the sad bouquet and handed it to her as if it were a rotting carcass. "Good day, sir," she said peevishly. As she walked to retrieve Captio, she wasn't sure if she was more irritated with herself or with him.

If there had not been Mrs. Greer, the jolliest, kindhearted, but loquacious gossip from here to the Scottish border, heading toward her, Verity might have turned around and not stopped quarreling with him until she could figure out precisely what they were arguing about, and more importantly, why.

She didn't even have a desire to dissect why she was so annoyed and out of sorts on so many levels. She feared she might for the first time in her life be displaying that feminine trait she abhorred known as pouting. And it might be caused by another even more juvenile trait of wanting not to appear like a pathetic fool by demanding what in hell was going on in that fat brain box of his. But now was a time of action, not reflection.

Reflection had never solved any of her problems.

Chapter 12

Rory watched her depart. She had jammed the disintegrating bouquet of hideous flowers back onto that wretched concoction of hers that even people in the dark ages would not have considered suitable. If he had not been so infuriated by her confounding behavior, he would have found the sight of her atrocious hat impossibly amusing.

She was obviously perturbed, but of what he did not know. Had they not given the best of themselves to each other yesterday?

But today? What in hell was going on? He tapped his hand, unthinking, on the side of his thigh. He knew women. He knew how they thought—in an abnormal tangle of sensibilities tied to mysterious, ofttimes perceived slights. But V wasn't like that. Except right now she was not acting in her normal forthright manner.

He had not a clue what was swirling in that petite, intelligent head of hers.

But he was going to find out. Oh, of that there was no question.

He would follow her to London. And find out precisely in what sort of cock-up *affair* she was engaged.

It did not take long to arrange. Even his Egyptian batman was delirious to learn they would leave this cricket-infested land of peaks and hollows.

He really made only one mistake in his hurried plan to depart. He should not have taken the blasted ornate carriage that Prinny had gifted him. It was too well-sprung, and too easy to get lost in one's own thoughts. He needed wind in his face to chase the memories of Verity's petite form madly grabbing the stones off the top of that hideous wall and throwing them into the woods, of her with her hands on her hips telling him it was a monument to his guilt. But most of all he remembered her on the dark green chaise at Rutledge— her translucent flesh, her dark mysterious eyes, and that luxurious hair that was the color of exotic coffee beans from faraway lands.

He poured another slosh of brandy into his glass. His fourth. The amber liquid barely moved, despite the brisk pace of the carriage horses. Well, there was one good thing about this moving palace. He could drink in peace.

It was only too bad he couldn't enjoy it.

Hell. And the way she had looked at him when he told her the truth about Catharine Talmadge. Her utter acceptance of the god-awfulness of the murderous incident he had caused.

But now Verity was running away. He wasn't certain if she was running away from him or if she was running away from herself. Most likely it was the former.

That was a novel experience. It was bloody infuriating to have a female take her leave of him.

By God, if she were a man, he would have called her a bloody *rake*. He winced at the thought; he was so tired of that sneering term. Rakes belonged in garden sheds. Libertine was a far more appropriate label. Either case, he would refute it the next time someone tossed *rake* in his dish. A low but quite satisfying belch erupted from someone he suspected very much was himself.

The carriage was suddenly swaying much more than before. It was actually quite lovely.

As his head met the dark velvet of the padded squabs in the carriage, Rory remembered the first lesson he had learned when going to war.

Put your heart on the shelf and your head on straight when going into battle.

And yes, he was going to fight for her.

Whether she liked it or not.

There was no one on this green Earth that was like Amelia Primrose. That had been what fifteen-year-old Verity determined within a week of meeting her new governess. It was also, more importantly, what her mother had also thought. Her sisters had declared her a saint.

But Verity had called her ninth victim—ahem, governess—something far different when Miss Primrose first arrived. James, then the newest Duke of Candover, had called Miss Primrose her final chance.

Miss Amelia Primrose, who had become Miss Amelia, and finally just Amelia when Verity had reached her majority, was far more than a governess. She was like the older sister of her heart and soul. Amelia knew how to laugh, how to make work amusing, how to build character and moral fortitude, and most importantly, how to scold. And when not to scold.

She had also been the only person who could comfort her on the day Verity's mother died.

And so, when the well-lacquered door of one of the fleet of Candover barouches opened in front of the Fitzroy family's magnificent townhouse in the most prized square in London, it was not surprising that Verity almost leapt from the vehicle and dashed up the white marble stairs, only pausing at the top to wait for Mary Haverty to catch up.

Mary laughed at her eagerness. "Go on, then, Verity. Have your tea with Amelia. I'm exhausted, to be honest. I shall join you both after a lie-down."

Verity kissed her, instructed the housekeeper to escort Mary to the chambers across from Verity's own apartments, and watched her dearest new friend ascend the house's famed winding staircase. A footman informed her that Miss Amelia Primrose of Scotland was in the library, awaiting her.

The very pale blond head of Amelia was bent over a large embroidery panel—the sort that caused mice to go blind, Verity always insisted. Her beloved abigail glanced up upon her entrance. Her ethereal pale blue eyes were shadowed. It was so unlike her.

"And so," Amelia finally spoke, as she rose with the grace of a queen, "you are come to see if I am wasting away with worry."

"Not at all," Verity said, trying to resist rushing to her side, and failing.

The two ladies embraced, and Amelia pulled away first. "Let me look at you, dearest. Yes, it's as I thought. You are grown even more lovely despite what I am sure is the trial of a lifetime, is it not?"

Verity shook her head with a small smile. "No, Amelia. We are not going to talk about me. I forbid it."

"Ah. Now that you are betrothed to a duke, you think our roles reversed and I will finally begin to take orders from you?"

"Well, yes," Verity retorted with little hope of success.

"All right, then. You know I'm always willing to experiment."

"And that is why I never put a newt in your bed," Verity retorted. "Which by the by, I have recently concluded, might in truth be a mark of respect from the giver to the givee."

"Which means you've brought a lizard from Derbyshire for me?"

This was the lady Verity knew. Albeit a thinner and paler version than the one she had left a mere month ago.

"No," Verity replied. "I've brought something far less promising. A plan."

Amelia raised her brows. "A tricky business . . . plans. They usually don't go according to, if past experience is any indication. Our recent overly hasty and atrociously ill thought out plan at Carleton House is an excellent example, no? I should have never agreed. In fact, I would not have if—" Amelia interrupted herself. "No, I refuse to offer any excuse for my actions."

Verity sighed and glanced at Amelia's embroidery. "Don't we have enough cushions yet?" She could always hope to put off the worst of the discussion for a bit of light diversion.

"No, and since you refuse to lift a needle to help me, I'll be one hundred and five before my work is done. Although . . ."

"Yes?"

"It looks as if I might have a lot more time on my hands if things continue unchecked." Amelia nodded to the bay window, and they both crossed to their favorite view of St. James's Square. "And you might, too," Amelia finished quietly. "Have you seen the papers?"

"Only the two from last week," Verity answered. "Could it get any worse?"

Her beautiful, angelic abigail and friend licked her lips. "Indeed, yes."

"Do you know who took my diaries?"

"No. I couldn't find them the morning I hurriedly packed your affairs for your trip to Derbyshire. I thought you already had them when you entered your brother's carriage."

"So someone stole them the night before my brother's botched wedding."

"I believe so. I fear we left them in the prince's library after that . . . awful interlude." Amelia's face lost all color.

"So it could have been a servant, or a guest, or anyone who had access to Carleton House," Verity said with concern for her Abigail.

"There's nothing to be done about it now," Amelia murmured.

"You're right of course," Verity said, suddenly deciding she could not ask Amelia to help her recover her diaries. Verity was through with asking others to help her out of disasters of her own making. She continued smoothly, "And . . . don't think I don't appreciate that you are not ringing a peal over my head. Once again I find I should have taken your excellent advice to burn them."

"I never said to burn them. I suggested you hide them very well, and never remove them from Boxwood. There, I've said my piece. Again, a useless effort."

Verity stared out the window, her eyes unblinking. "Is the Duke of Sussex still in Cornwall with my brother?"

"Yes."

"Then I will go to him. Inform Sussex what occurred that night, since he obviously remembers nothing. And then I'll kindly insist he return to London."

"No," Amelia rushed on. "You will not."

"Amelia, we have no choice."

"That is not what we agreed that night."

Verity took her abigail's hand in her own. "It might not be what we agreed, but sometimes events alter the course. And this one is off the map. Trust me. He is the kindest duke of the entire royal entourage as we both know. He will help you and know what to do."

The lovely, even profile of Amelia Primrose finally turned to face her. "Just like the Duke of Abshire knew what to do?"

Verity had the familiar sinking sensation that her abigail knew exactly what had transpired in Derbyshire. Every last moment.

"No. The opposite. You should know by now that I am incapable of learning my lesson."

Later that afternoon Verity managed to escape her brother's townhouse by way of a little-used side door. She only hoped four quarters' worth of pin money would be enough to secure the services of a Bow Street Runner with lax morals. Now, where she would find this dazzling specimen of sin and agility was another question altogether. The last thing she was worried about was her safety. There was no possible hope for redemption now. She had everything to lose, and only her drive to protect the people she most loved fueled her courage and resolve.

Rory Lennox, His Grace, the Duke of Abshire, first and only holder of the new duchy, entered the august royal bedchamber of His Highness, the Prince Regent for his father, King George III.

It was still dark, but then, it mattered not a whit, as Prinny had privately decreed that for his service to the Crown, Rory was permitted to wake him anytime day or night, preferably day, if convenient.

Well, it was almost dawn. The birds were already chirping in the pear trees outside Carleton House.

The first thought Rory had after he was ushered into the future king's chambers was that Prinny's shorn hair on the left half of his head was going to take a long time to grow in properly. Not one of the other dukes of the entourage had been able to remember how the royal head had become suddenly quite bald on one side. It was a good thing wigs were still in fashion.

But if it had happened to Rory, he would have shaved the other side, if only to avoid the snickers of the servants. But then again, he was not the future monarch of Christendom, and so, who was he to give advice? And princes had the unattractive habit of thinking themselves above humankind, and definite trendsetters of the first order.

Prinny's trends unfortunately included eating to excess, drinking to excess, cavorting in excess, gambling to excess, attempting to rid himself of an excess wife, spending in excess, and excessively annoying Parliament due to the latter three vices, and infuriating his subjects due to all of the above. Yes, the monarchy was ripe for revolution.

"Your Highness." He showed a leg when the prince opened one eye.

"Abshire," Prinny croaked. "To what do I owe the displeasure?" He paused. "Are you married?"

"No, sire."

"Candover will kill you if you don't go through with it. You know that. You could at least try a bit harder. Do you know how difficult it will be to explain away a duel?"

"I beg your pardon, sire, but since it's merely a question of whether he will kill me before or after the wedding, I find it difficult to worry, even if I should pretend to care."

The prince barked a laugh. "That's why I've always liked you far and away the best of the lot of those spoiled prigs."

"Happy to play the court jester."

The Prince Regent's lids were low on his eyes. Despite this royal's inability to spend his subject's pennies wisely, and do anything moderately, Rory was in no doubt of his intelligence. Hundreds of years of royal inbreeding had somehow come full circle in that area.

"I'm glad you've come, whatever the reason. I miss your bloody hide."

"The feeling is almost mutual, sire."

The Prince Regent chuckled. "And your timing could not be better. Since you're here, I require your services. It's perhaps a bit more enterprising than a jester, C."

Rory nearly balked at the euphemism for the name the prince had assigned him more than a decade ago.

"Have you seen the *Morning Post* of this morning?"

Rory shook his head. God, he should have foreseen this. The prince was never more jovial than when he tried to coax a chameleon from well-deserved rest in his natural habitat.

Prinny nodded toward the marble-topped gilded table beside his massive bolstered bed. A stack of newspapers—the *Morning Post*—resided there. Each was folded to show the infamous column.

"Go on, then," Prinny insisted. "Read the first one. Very *fashionable for you*, indeed, today. You will like it, I assure you."

He quickly scanned "The Fashionable World" column.

Bloody, bloody hell.

As it is not Tuesday or a Thursday, this column will not feature an excerpt from the Duke Diaries today. Instead we shall give our loyal readers our initial impression of who might be the extraordinary author of this compelling read after having completed a thorough perusal.

It should be noted that in not one instance does the name Rory Lennox, Earl of Rutledge, more notably the new Duke of Abshire, appear on any of the incriminating pages.

In light of this, and the ceaseless whispers by the ton—wondering why the Prince Regent conferred a duchy on this *notorious rake*. Oh, yes, he fought for the Crown, and was occasionally in our dear Wellington's circle of officers, but still . . . is that all it takes to earn a dukedom? Why, surely Wellington must be secretly offended, as he should.

These diaries hint at an answer: blackmail. Abshire's talent is obviously chronicling his betters' misdeeds, and using them to his advantage.

To further the argument, I shall confirm that these diaries were found in Carleton House the evening before the Duke of Candover's failed wedding.

So I ask you all to watch very carefully the Prince Regent's behavior toward Abshire in future. Will he ask the Prime

Minister to rescind this new duke's ministerial position, of which he has absolutely no expertise? Will Abshire soon be escorted to Newgate prison on trumped-up charges? Or will the Prince Regent stand by this rakehelly blackmailer? You be the judge.

And by the by, dear readers, take note: I am forced to resign my position since the Prince Regent has threatened the publisher of this fine paper with charges of sedition and libel should he continue to publish this column. So I have decided to go the way of so many others, who demand proper behavior by their rulers—underground. But I shall persevere with your aid. Look for my Tuesday and Thursday column on street corners and posting houses! Until then, remember this: while we may be at war with our French neighbor, their Declaration of the Rights of Man, which details the universal natural rights of all mankind, as well as government by elected representatives, is based on the Age of Enlightenment and resistance to oppression.

Citizens unite!

Rory returned the paper to the ornate table. *The goddamned Frenchified traitor wanted to see a rake, did he? Why, he would take great pleasure in placing the coward on the British common soldier's front line and would face him and pull the trigger himself, while wearing his best counterfeit French uniform.*

He examined his fingernails as Prinny examined him. "You were about to suggest simple breaking and entering, I suppose?"

"I leave it to you, as always, my dear," Prinny replied, while scratching the shorn half of his head, which featured a half inch of graying stubble. "But you are not to destroy that bloody diary. I insist on the pleasure of reading it before I burn it."

Rory sighed and was suddenly tired. "God rest the soul of the poor sod who wrote them. A disgruntled servant, most likely, no?"

"I really don't care who it is, Abshire. But I shall personally draw and quarter him myself." The prince sniffed. "Of course, I shall require you to hold him down."

"And then you'll gift me with . . ."

"Hmmm . . . perhaps a small country? Well, we don't want to draw too much more attention your way, given that column, do we? Perhaps a nice large island somewhere exotic, where you can cool your heels until this dies down." The prince chuckled.

Rory shook his head. "I admire your cool, sire, as always. But perhaps you should consider joining me under this promised coconut palm if you cannot contrive a way out of this revolution in the making."

"Never fear, my dear," the prince replied. "My ancestors have withstood far greater evils than published recriminations over royal excess made public. I've told all of you—reform your reputations, cast off your mistresses, marry within your class, and that will be the end of it. Once you've all accomplished that, the fickle public will become bored with this evil little man's tirade and cast their eyes toward new gossip."

"Of course, you are right, sire."

"So after you bring me the diaries, I command you to marry Candover's sister, the name someone here whispered in my ear. What is it, again?"

"Lady Verity Fitzroy."

The prince rubbed his hands together. "What a delightfully prim name. I almost feel guilty delivering a peaceful little dove to a hawk such as you. Almost."

"Oh, she's little, all right. Peaceful and dovelike? Of that there is considerable doubt."

"How divine," Prinny continued. "I sense a true reformation in your future. Ah, well . . . everyone knows reformed rakes make the best husb—"

"Murderous traitors?" he cut in loudly.

Prinny chuckled. "One would hope not. Especially when a small country or large island is in the offing."

The problem was, Rory thought, as he carried out preparations for what he hoped would be his last mission (something he considered for the very first time after two hundred forty-seven sorties for the Crown in the last decade), that he didn't want to live on a tropical island paradise.

He wanted to figure out why the not so very prim, un-dove-like, unpeaceful lady he had wanted to throttle the last time he'd seen her was running away, and then he wanted to haul her back to the wild beauty of the windswept peaks of their youth and open the door to the promise of happiness.

He would consider it an added bonus if he could also manage to replace all of her ghastly, miserable hats in the process.

Chapter 13

It took Verity Fitzroy one day less than a fortnight to travel to hell and back. Or rather from hell to a different sort of Hades in Cornwall before a return to the cold realm of the devil in the Peak District she had once known and loved until recently.

At least she'd had Mary Haverty to keep her company from Derbyshire to London, and then from London to Cornwall. Of course, the delightful composition of her carriage's occupants had changed during the last leg of the endless carriage ride. And it was her own fault.

Verity had felt she had no choice but to offer a place in the carriage to the Archbishop of Canterbury when he came to call at St. James's Square. The poor man was so flustered after an apparent dressing down by the Prince Regent that he had misunderstood the prince's command to personally deliver an urgent missive to the Duke of Candover.

Verity was not surprised at the dressing down. From what she had witnessed that awful night, the archbishop had been the most sodden drunk of the lot of them.

"But my dear Lady Fitzroy, I simply must see His Grace, immediately," the archbishop had said, his old wrinkled hands shaking visibly. "The Prince Regent demanded it."

"But he's in Penzance, at the Duke of Kress's house party on St. Michael's Mount. The Duke of Barry and the Duke of Sussex are there as well. The Prince Regent ordered them away from London. My brother informed me in a letter that Prinny insisted he oversee a house party where Kress was supposed to select a bride to help quell the public's outrage."

The elderly gentleman mopped his brow with a black handkerchief. "But I had thought your brother was to remain here to try to convince his former fiancée to forgive and marry him."

Verity shook her head. "There was never any chance of that."

"But the prince gave me three days to deliver this or else . . . or else, I don't know what. I will not have enough time." His neck wobbled as he spoke. "Oh, the Prince Regent will be most displeased."

"Archbishop," she could not withhold a small sigh, "Lady Mary Haverty and I are just leaving for Penzance. I should be very happy to deliver the royal letter for you."

"Oh, no, no, no. I must do it myself." He looked at her with such hope.

He was an elderly gentleman and it would obviously take him half a day to return to his elegant residence and arrange for his carriage, and his affairs to be packed before he would leave.

"Well, then, sir, you are invited to join us straightaway. We would be, um, delighted by your company."

"You are very kind, my dear," the man said with a blinding smile, which nearly transformed his face into that of a much younger man. "I shall just give your footman a note to deliver to my chambers to have my affairs sent on to Kress's castle there. Always wanted to see the place. A former Benedictine monastery, don't you know?"

Well, there went any chance of an exchange of confidence and of deepening the already great bond between Mary and herself.

Verity had never subscribed to the notion of

confession to a man of the cloth. She preferred the privacy of tormented pleadings and apologies to her Maker directly.

And so Mary and she had sat up straight, kept on their toes, and all other clichéd phrases that indicated pious behavior. That did not include hiding a novel between *Johnson's Sermons.* But they had some luck, the archbishop finally fell asleep the last hour of the journey, and could not be roused, even with Verity's smelling salts.

Verity had to laugh. She had finally met her snoring match. Of course he was eighty-seven and smelled like yellowing parchment.

It was Mary who snatched the royal missive from the archbishop's fingers and suggested a way for Verity to have a private interview with the charming Duke of Sussex, who was the only one who could save Miss Amelia Primrose.

If he didn't kill Verity first.

Ah, but that was another story.

It was good to be back in London, Rory had to admit as he remounted the white marble steps of Carleton House the next afternoon. A little intrigue and a little lock picking was good for the soul from time to time. It would have been an excellent prescription for keeping the mind alert, if the high probability of death during one of these escapades wasn't a negating factor.

And for the first time, he had very much wanted to cheat death. He didn't want to examine the feeling too closely. It was just that he knew he had to finish this business with Verity Fitzroy. He owed her that, he told himself, refusing to add that perhaps, just perhaps, he owed it to himself as well.

He quickly forced away the thought by remembering the events of yesterday in detail. With a disguise in place, and a modicum of gold guineas placed in the furtive hands of the working man who cleaned the offices of the *Morning Post*, Rory had gained the address of the former author of "The Fashionable World" column before it had been discontinued. When the columnist departed his residence with a jaunty bounce to his step, Rory gained entrance and recovered the diary under the bed mattress within minutes. Why were people so uniformly uncreative in their hiding places? His last discovery, one of Kress's bottles of French absinthe, confirmed the obvious. The damned ink-stained tattletale was the original thief who had somehow entered Carleton House and ferreted out Verity's diaries. But despite the momentary thrill of the find, these working hours were becoming tiresome.

While walking toward Prinny's royal bedchambers for the second time in two days, Rory quickly scanned the purloined red leather-bound volume that was at the heart of London's hysteria.

The bold black scrawl was not the typical handwriting of the serving class. More likely it was that of a bitter gentleman who due to reduced circumstances had been forced into serving his equals who were now his betters. It was the only likely scenario, as Rory refused to believe one of the royal entourage would have been stupid enough or *sober* enough to remember and document years of debauchery with such clarity and wit.

He had woken the Prince Regent mid-snore, which was a wicked good imitation of Verity's adorable gurgle. The future king snapped awake with the alertness of a royal on the verge of losing his crown. The prince had been near to tears in happiness when Rory delivered the diary into his beringed fingers.

Rory hadn't received a small country in return, or even a large island. Instead he had asked Prinny to give him the name of the best Bow Street Runner in London. Prinny provided it and then handed him Crown jewels fit for a queen—a diamond-encrusted ring in whose center nested a ruby the size of a quail egg, and a bracelet and necklace made in the same style. Rory immediately thought of how all of it would look on the dark beauty of Verity.

Well.

Now as he sat high in his phaeton, driving his matched set of gleaming dark bays through the hot, crowded streets where the fashionable shopped, he reflected that he was almost finished with all he had meant to accomplish in London, and more.

He had saved the prince's hide once again, and had, in addition, achieved his main objective. He had interviewed and engaged the services of the finest Bow Street Runner in Town, and supplied the man with every detail he possessed concerning one Mr. Theo Battswell, charlatan son of a vicar turned tooth-drawer.

Rory turned his horses onto the side street leading to St. James's Square. Candover's pile was, of course, the largest of the magnificent townhouses. Only Welly's Number One, London, bested it.

He tossed the reins to the footman permanently stationed outside, then leapt from his perch and took the marble stairs two at a time.

He wanted to see her. He wanted to force aside the distance that had somehow crept between them the day after that terrifying but glorious afternoon of intimacy. He raised the large brass knocker of Candover's townhouse and realized he was not dreading any moment of this confrontation with her. Even when they sparred or misunderstood one another, he still liked her. And after he ferreted out what had obviously been some sort of misunderstanding, they would return to Derbyshire to resume where they had left off.

He merely had to convince Verity to truly agree to marry him—whether she liked it or not. He was actually starting to warm to the idea. If he was honest with himself, it was far more than that.

He could not let her go.

The austere butler of Candover House did not smile when Rory was received. Then again, butlers rarely smiled. He reflected that it must in part be a gentleman's gentleman code of conduct.

"Your Grace." The elderly man bowed—not as low as he would have had it been the master of the house, but not as slight as if Rory had still been merely an earl.

"Sir." Rory nodded. "Is Lady Verity Fitzroy receiving?"

"No, Your Grace."

"Is she at home or not?"

The butler eyed him balefully and sighed. One was not supposed to ask such things so baldly.

"Just tell me, man. I'm her betrothed." His demand was rudeness personified. Rory just didn't care. He had to see her. Straighten out this mess.

The butler's single bushy hedgerow for eyebrows rose a notch. "Yes, as stated by Your Grace's announcement a week ago in the *Morning Post*, in the exact place where 'The Fashionable World' column once resided."

Rory resisted the urge to grind his teeth. The old tic in his left eye returned. "If—and only if—one hazarded a guess that Lady Verity Fitzroy is not at home, or perhaps not receiving me alone, or everyone else included, would you be kind enough to inform me when the lady in question will change her status? Of receiving, or returning, or both?"

The man didn't bat an eye. "I have not been apprised of Lady Verity Fitzroy's future plans."

Rory sighed deeply. "What is your name, sir?"

The man blinked. "Wharton. William Wharton, Your Grace."

"Mr. Wharton." Rory bowed slightly. "We can do this the hard way or the easy way. I would rather the latter if only because I am guessing you have been long in service to His Grace and his family—Lady Verity Fitzroy, in particular. I particularly do not want to cause an incident that might displeasure my intended." He exhaled sharply. "But if you do not immediately tell me where Lady Fitzroy is, I shall shake it out of you." Where in bloody hell was his cool reserve and diplomatic wit?

The butler's gaze traveled from the top of his hat to the tip of Rory's white-tasseled Hessian boots. "If Your Grace had asked me where her ladyship was upon arrival, knowing she is engaged to Your Grace, I would have been happy to impart her location."

"My eye."

"Lady Fitzroy departed London this morning with Lady Mary Haverty. I understood their destination was Cornwall."

The tic now moved to his right eye. "And why is Lady Fitzroy on her way to Cornwall? I assume it is to see her brother?"

"I'm not at liberty to say, Your Grace." The elderly man puffed out his chest in fine form.

A staring down commenced in which neither party won.

Only a blond vision of beauty, who appeared from some otherearthly place, snapped the two men out of their praying-mantas-like state.

"Did I hear you ask for Lady Verity Fitzroy, sir?"

Rory nearly growled when he looked away from the butler. "Indeed, ma'am."

A smile broke out on the woman's face, which illuminated her purity of spirit from within. And yet there was something about her that was mischievous. He couldn't put his finger on her character.

"Ah," she finally replied, "you must be the Duke of Abshire."

He bowed. "And you must be an angel from paradise."

She chuckled. "Is that how a libertine plies his trade these days? Very unoriginal, in my humble opinion, if you will pardon my forwardness, Your Grace."

Who was this presumptuous beauty? He rather liked her nerve and wondered how Candover dealt with such impertinence. "I will pardon anything you like. Especially if you will tell me why Lady Fitzroy is on her way to Cornwall, ma'am."

"Honored to make your acquaintance, Your Grace." She did not curtsy as she aught. "I'm Miss Primrose, Verity's companion, formerly her governess and abigail." It was the sudden pause in her next sentence, and the slight glance to the side, which put Rory on alert.

"I cannot say, Your Grace, but as Mr. Wharton *kindly* informed, Lady Verity Fitzroy was traveling with Lady Mary Haverty," the angelic beauty stated with just the slightest Scottish accent in her dulcet voice. "And the Archbishop of Canterbury accompanied the ladies, so both are very properly chaperoned."

He sighed in exasperation. "Delighted to hear

it. Will either of you be *kind* enough to tell me when they will return?"

"Oh, of course, Your Grace. But Lady Fitzroy is not to return here, she made known to me. I do believe she made a promise to Mr. Armitage—do you know the vicar in Derbyshire, Your Grace?"

"Doesn't everyone?" He was careful to keep the sarcasm in his mind alone.

"Yes, well, she promised she would return to Derbyshire as soon as she sees the delights of Cornwall. She must return to teach the children in the wonderful school she and her brother started last year. But then you must know all about her promise. I believe I remember her telling me you were there when she told Mr. Armitage. She didn't lie about that to you, did she, Your Grace? Verity never lies. All her true friends know that about her."

"Yes, I know."

The butler, in his boredom, and sudden decision that Rory was not going to steal anything in the cavernous front hall, strode off to attend to a silent query from an elegantly liveried footman.

Rory lowered his voice. "Has she always been this confounding?"

"Confounding?"

"Yes," he continued. "So astonishingly courageous, and everything kind, and good, altruistic even, and then she becomes distracted, and distant, and mysteriously behaves as if one has moved to the bottom of her long list of friends, just when one is merely trying to help her."

She interrupted him. "Verity doesn't need anyone's help, Your Grace."

"I realize that. She is the strongest damn— Pardon me, Miss Primrose, but she is . . . Oh, I'm not going to continue. I have a reputation *not* to maintain, and I might as well, go forth and do what all exceedingly tedious good men are expected to do: allow their actions to speak to their character instead of words."

"I don't know, Your Grace, I know Verity would insist that words are just as important as actions."

"Of course she would. She would expect nothing less than perfection in a gentleman."

Miss Primrose arched an angelic blond brow. "Would you expect anything less in a lady, sir?"

He studied the beauty before him. Something bothered the corner of his mind that was always working, filing away facts whether he was aware of it or not. "You're she," he finally murmured.

"I beg your pardon?"

"You're she," he said louder. "You're the one held as a perfect model of a lady."

A beatific smile slowly spread across her face.

"How lovely." She raised one brow again with the barest hint of mockery in her glance. "You have now made my life complete." Her tone spoke of cool irony.

"Those were Verity's words, madam."

"Ah, that's different. She has already made my life complete."

He liked this female. And Verity was most probably right. On first acquaintance, Miss Primrose did not exhibit a single imperfection. But that was the thing of it.

Perfection held no appeal to him.

And that's when he knew.

That's precisely when he knew what he liked about Verity: she possessed all the important traits of a lady—true words, true actions, but confounding imperfection nonetheless. Her hats were a prime example. And Verity had intelligence and wit to spare. She would never, ever bore him, and he instinctively knew she would never let him down.

A lethal combination.

That meant only one thing. He was going back to Derbyshire.

To do what he most detested—but she would most like.

To wait for her.

Verity missed Mary's company on the long return ride to Derbyshire. Her friend had decided to remain at the Duke of Kress's mad house party, which might have been ordered by the Prince Regent to marry off at least one of the royal entourage, but did not appear to be proceeding very smoothly in that direction. Indeed, it appeared to be careening wildly out of control, just like all events where the royal entourage could be found.

James had been furious at her for arriving unannounced, and even more so for defying his order to remain at Boxwood. Only Mary's distracting beauty had allowed Verity to achieve her purpose. The next morning she had departed without even the archbishop to sermonize during the endless journey to the Peak District.

She had tried everything to distract herself from the hell of her own mind. She might have made two steps forward in her effort to resolve Amelia's disastrous affair of which she again was responsible, but one glance at the suddenly popular pamphlets, written by the author of the currently defunct "Fashionable World" column, which were now available at every posting inn on the Royal Mail route, caused her to fall 101 steps back in her own catastrophic world.

There were no words to describe the depth of her despair. She had single-handedly:

1. Let down her brother, indeed her entire family, on two counts. Most likely when she was found out as the authoress of the diaries, she would forever tarnish the Fitzroy name for generations to come. Not to mention the whispers (which would soon become shouts) concerning her ruination after the revelation concerning the diaries.

2. Imperiled her most beloved Amelia the night at Carleton House.

3. Fallen in love once again with a man who did not love her.

4. Shown no moral fiber or the pride she *prided* herself with possessing when she had given into temptation to experience passion before banishing herself to the oblivion of the Lake District.

5. Asked a Bow Street Runner to locate the former author of "The Fashionable World" and then steal the diaries for her. Of course she had revealed that the diaries were hers,

so it was not technically stealing, but the man took great offense at her request before he suddenly squinted at her and asked if she was Lady Verity Fitzroy. When she denied it, he laughed and told her he was already doing something for her so she had best be on her way. She refused to argue with a man who was clearly affected in his upper stories. Then near injury soon followed insult when a ruffian picked her pocket as she walked back to Mayfair.

6. Worst of all, she had pushed the entire country to the brink of anarchy, with all daggers raised toward the monarchy.

7. And finally, she had caused the gentleman who did not love her to be publicly accused of not only authoring her own treasonous ramblings, but even worse, of also blackmailing the Crown for a duchy. The most ironic part was that the columnist was correct. For some reason, aside from the day she had witnessed Rory's encounter with Catharine Talmadge, she had never recorded any of his dissipated actions when she'd had the opportunity to spy on her brother's friends.

In the middle of the third sleepless night, swaying with the rhythm of the well-sprung barouche, Verity suddenly sat up straight.

My God.

She had never written about Rory for one simple reason. He might have been present during many of the events described in detail in her diaries, and he might have made comments during the occasions, but . . .

He had never been the instigator of any foul play.

And . . .

He had never made a fool of himself.

Indeed, if anything, he had deftly managed to steer the oft-imes deep-in-their-cups members of the royal entourage from financial ruin or physical harm by way of his self-deprecating wit.

And yet all this time . . . everyone, herself included, had considered him the worst of the lot.

It was that perpetual way of his—that dark, forbidding, mysterious look he sported, along with a slight smile that made him appear dangerous and . . . *guilty.*

Verity's hands began to shake violently. The tremors raced up her arms, and soon her entire body was trembling.

She had not only misunderstood him, along with the rest of the world, but she, who was so careful not to judge anyone, had misjudged him.

In her own selfish desire to protect herself from again loving a man who would never love her, she had not loved him unconditionally for himself. And she had even forced him to let down his guard, probably for the one and only time, regarding the love of his life—Catharine Talmadge.

While she might have eased some of the irrational guilt that he'd carried for twice as long as she, she had only added to it by forcing him to lay with her. And he had done so because, despite his dark wit, he was a giver.

Not a taker. She could not name a single person he had ever harmed.

She suddenly knew that Rory had loved Catharine long before James had ever allowed the wild beauty to claim his heart. And Rory would never have revealed to anyone Catharine's and his attachment unless he could have offered for her.

And . . . oh God . . . it all fell into place.

At that time, everyone in Derbyshire knew that Rory's father, the former Earl of Rutledge and his wife, lived to wager, and had gambled away nearly everything that was not nailed down or entailed.

Verity even remembered overhearing the old earl selling Rory's horse to James, who had immediately agreed on the condition that it never be revealed to Rory and that the horse was to remain at Rutledge with future feed costs to be absorbed by James.

And so that was why Rory had pushed Catharine toward his best friend's gilded cage. He didn't want the lady he loved to live in straitened, shabby circumstances.

Rory Lennox, fourth Earl of Rutledge, first Duke of Abshire, was a sacrificial lamb in wolf's clothing. He was not a—

The carriage rounded a corner, someone sounded a horn, and the barouche jerked to a stop. The tired driver's muffled voice called out his apologies, and an ostler opened the carriage's door.

Verity stumbled into darkness, exiting the vehicle.

And in that instant she righted herself.

Righted herself within the world of wrongs of her own making.

She might very well destroy herself in making everything right, but she was going to do what needed to be done, taking the least number of innocent bystanders down the rabbit hole with her.

And it would begin tonight.

"Mr. Jenkins?"

The faithful carriage driver of Boxwood had driven most of the way south and north, allowing his younger driver-in-training little time with the reins, because, Verity knew, he was always overly concerned with her safety.

He reached her side and tipped his hat. "My apologies again, Lady Fitzroy. There is no excuse for my error in—"

"Mr. Jenkins," she interrupted, reaching for his cramped hand. His eyes widened.

"Yes, ma'am?"

"Tend to your needs while the horses are changed. We are a mere ten miles from Boxwood, are we not?"

"Yes, Lady Fitzroy."

"Go on, then. I will see you here in a quarter of an hour."

"Of course, ma'am."

Ten minutes later Verity mounted the barouche's driving seat, with the aid of a very startled ostler, who was too in awe to stammer a word.

A moment later Mr. Jenkins returned with his bleary-eyed underling.

"I order you to not say a word, Mr. Jenkins. If you have an ounce of respect for me, then you and Tim will get in that stuffy velvet box behind me and go to sleep. You know very well I know how to drive." She stared him down. "*You* taught me."

Her old teacher of everything equine knew a madwoman when he saw one, and he complied without a sound. His apprentice followed meekly behind.

As the first true rays of daylight crept into the

edges of the eastern sky, Verity expertly turned the final corner onto Boxwood's manicured drive. The vast lawn and fields beyond, separated by a patchwork of hedgerows, shimmered with morning dew.

Each time she returned here, it was more beautiful than she remembered. Her heart filled with purpose, she prayed it would not be her last return.

Chapter 14

Verity mounted the outer stairs to the north front hall, touching the head of one of the stone nymphs along the way. Sunlight filtered through the woodland of the park.

A footman opened the mammoth carved oak door. She nodded, and after a word of greeting headed toward the stair. She would finally sleep in peace.

"Begging your pardon, my lady," the footman began. "But you have a visitor."

She halted and half turned. "At this hour?" The young man was anxious, she could see.

"Yes, ma'am."

"Who?"

"He's been here from dawn until midnight the last five days, my lady," he said in a rush. "His Grace, the Duke of Abshire."

She nodded. "I see. And where is he, then?"

"In the library. I just escorted him there." He looked at her expectantly.

"Very good."

No wonder the stable hands and footman had greeted her with trepidation. Nothing could provoke anxiety among servants like unexplained odd behavior by the upper class.

As she walked along the east corridor, past the Oak Room with its forbidding, dark-paneled interior, her pace never altered.

He raised his head from a book he held in his lap. A small fire in the grate chased the chill in the long chamber.

She curtsied.

Rory rose from his seat, his movements elegant and precise. He placed the tome beside the Egyptian urn on the round table covered in moss-colored silk. "You've arrived," he said simply.

"Yes. Just."

The urge to run to him was strong, but she held back.

He crossed the space between them with slow, even strides.

He bowed and took up her gloved hand in his own. He turned her fingers and examined her soiled palm. "What happened?"

She finally exhaled, only to realize she had been

holding her breath. She shrugged. "I love to drive from time to time." She waited for a dry retort.

He looked at her with those green eyes of his that were so dearly familiar now. "So do I," he said softly. "And how are you?"

She desperately did not want to ruin the apparent truce. "Well enough."

"You are tired. I'm going to take my leave of you now so you can rest."

He still held her hand in his own, and the warmth of them seeped into her numb fingers. "But why are you here?" She wouldn't sleep unless she knew.

"To have the earliest possible news of your safe arrival."

It hurt her heart to raise any hopes for a possible happy future. But she could not stop it. No one had ever done anything remotely so kind. "I thank you, Rory, for your concern. I'm deeply sorry if I caused you any worry."

"Say no more"—he squeezed her hand gently—"I would only suggest that you write to Miss Primrose after you rest. She holds her cards close to her breast, but I believe she wishes to hear from you." He paused. "I liked her. Very much. Your dear butler, the formidable Mr. Wharton, on the other hand, can go to the devil."

Verity had feared she might never laugh again.

But on the heels of his words, she let loose a flood of laughter. "You will not like it, but I cannot help but tell you that you sometimes remind me of him. And I like him. Very much."

He refused to smile, but a muscle on the corner of his handsome mouth twitched. "Well, then. I shall take my leave of you."

He dropped her hand. But just after turning to depart, he stopped in his tracks, then quickly turned back and closed the gap.

She swallowed as he stared down at her from his great height.

In a rush, he leaned down to press a kiss on her cheek. "I'm very glad to see you safe, V."

She chastely kissed his other cheek, and just like that the awkwardness between them dissolved.

The only problem was . . . she needed the awkwardness, as that would make it easier for her to put to rights all her grave wrongs.

With a grave look, he bowed once and was gone.

Verity fell into a slumber like no other not a quarter hour after his departure.

She slept through her maid's valiant attempt to wake her eight hours later, as Verity had requested. Four hours after, at six in the afternoon, her maid attempted again, armed with water and smelling salts. To no avail.

Another three hours passed before someone else attempted the impossible.

There was something about touching her skin that ignited a place within him with which Rory was not familiar. The flesh of the top of her hand was so soft, and yet her palm spoke of untold hours of handling a bridle's reins.

He could not stop the grin he could feel spreading on his face. She was on her back, her mouth slightly open, and every once in a while she emitted a gurgling snore.

Her maid behind him cleared her throat in a most unpleasant manner. "I've tried everything to wake her, Your Grace."

He brushed a stray lock of her warm, dark hair from her face and kept his gaze on her. "She is exhausted."

"But it's been more than fifteen hours. It's nearly half ten at night!"

He finally turned and headed for the open door. "Madam, I don't care if it's half past never. Let her sleep." He stopped at the door. "Uh, that's an order, by the by."

The maid appeared suitably chastened. "Of course, Your Grace."

"Don't look so forlorn. You can blame me when

she wakes. Tell her I will be waiting for her in the library." He sighed. "Forever the library, it appears."

Her maid bobbed a curtsy and informed in a whisper, "His Grace, the Duke of Candover, keeps the racing journals in the upper west corner."

"Lovely," he whispered back. "Why are we whispering?"

She nodded toward her mistress. "She doesn't approve of racing."

"Why, that's unpatriotic."

"Not according to the horses, Lady Verity insists. And so her brother hides the journals so as to not offend her sensibilities."

"His Grace is not very manly, is he?"

The maid giggled.

The night in the library passed with surprising swiftness as soon as Rory pushed together the two sofas that faced each other in front of the fire. Only his booted heels hung over the edge of one side of the strange contraption he had devised.

But it was not as secure as he had hoped, for when someone entered the great chamber and cleared her throat—Lord, would that maid ever just cough like normal servants?—he sat up and his posterior fell between the two sofas, which had chosen that moment to separate.

But it was not the maid with the annoying phlegm.

Verity rushed forward, placed a tray on a nearby table and rushed to help him to his feet.

"Thank you," he said, rearranging his rumpled shirt. "Ah. Breakfast." He squinted toward the daylight flooding from the windows. "Or is it nuncheon?"

"Both," she replied. "You must be famished. You slept for hours and hours."

"Your wit has taken a turn for the better, I see."

"It is only natural. If I had only known what a solid eighteen hours could do for one's spirits."

When had her face become so dear to him? He had to physically restrain himself from going to her and taking her in his arms. Instead he rearranged the furniture to the original order, with the table between the two sofas. Silently, she moved the overburdened tray to the low table.

She sunk into the plush center cushion of one of the sofas, looked at him, and gently tapped the cushion beside her. He immediately complied like the lapdog he was meant to be.

They fell into an easy rhythm, with each of them taking turns at placing morsels of the delicacies on each other's plates.

He was just on the point of dabbing a crumb from the corner of her lovely lips, as the initial action before kissing her senseless—as he should have when she had first returned—when the maid with the throat irritation (that he should insist required a three-month cure in the Swiss alps) intruded once again. Did no one knock before entering in this crumbling monstrosity?

"Excuse me. I've brought the *Morning Post* as soon as it arrived, as you requested, my lady. And the ostler, who returned the team from the posting inn, also brought a pamphlet."

He stilled, before casually reaching for another hot bun. This should be interesting. Of late, the *Morning Post* had returned to its original purpose, that of advertisements on most of its pages. And the pamphlet? Probably a lot of blubbering, gnashing of teeth and wailing at thieves in the night and the unfairness of it all. The little knacker should be jailed for sedition.

Verity reluctantly handed him the pamphlet as she silently spread the pages of the paper. Her index finger traveled over the page until it slowed to a halt.

"Read it aloud, if you will?" he asked.

Her eyes filled with shock. "You first."

"Of course," he replied, opening the pamphlet.

He scanned it quickly and stood up suddenly without a word. Balling it into a wad, he tossed it into the fire.

"What did it say?" She stared at the burning mass.

"Nothing of importance."

"That bad?"

"Not if you speak French like a native, and are good friends with the owner of a charming house in the Pays Basque . . . which I do and I am."

She bowed her head. "So if I understood, you were in London recently."

He nodded. The words of the pamphlet, *Prinny's henchman might have stolen one of the diaries in my possession, but not the one I gave to my loyal employer at the* Morning Post *before I resigned,* were still hot points of light in his brain. The little bugger had probably sold the other diary to gain enough capital to begin publishing the pamphlets. May all scavengers go to hell.

He was losing his touch in the game. And Prinny would be furious.

"I assume you saw the recent column, which suggested you were the author of the diaries," she continued.

He glanced at her. "Yes." Would she ask him straight out if he was the infamous scribbler? Would she doubt him if he told her he was not? He waited.

"I know you're not the author," she whispered.

"And why is that?"

He was an expert at reading faces. As the creeping flush above her lace fichu began to rise to her cheeks, so did his instincts whisper to him that something was gravely amiss.

"Why did you follow me to London?" She twisted a napkin in her lap and then released it when she realized he was looking at her hands.

She had turned the subject. Ah, she learned quickly.

"Why did *you* go to London?" He kept his tone easy and neutral.

She glanced at her hands, which now covered her knees. "My abigail, well, she's really a companion now—"

"Miss Primrose?"

"Yes . . ." She paused. "Right. You met her."

"And dear Mr. Wharton."

"Yes, I remember. I was a bit tired when I arrived last night. My memory is not serving me well."

"So?"

"Of course." She hesitated. "Miss Primrose has been unwell, and I was worried, so I decided to see firsthand how she was faring."

"This is the female you consider the finest in Creation. The one your brother threatened to relieve the night at Carleton House, is it not? The archangel who was apparently tasked with keeping your bed free of marauders like me, I suppose?"

She shook her head. "How silly. James didn't mean it."

God. Rory's heart sank. She was protecting that beautiful devil of a servant. Miss Amelia Primrose was the author of the scandalous diaries.

Why hadn't he pieced it together sooner? It made perfect sense.

He took up Verity's hands again, which had begun to feel as if they belonged there. "Verity, listen to me. I am going to help you. I know who is the author of the diaries."

She blanched. "You do?"

"Yes. And I can offer protection." He stroked the back of one of her hands.

Her dark eyes turned serious. She shook her head.

"I promise I will see Miss Primrose safely out of the country. I know she is dear to you."

Verity's brow wrinkled. "You could do that if necessary?"

"Of course. I know you care for her like a sister."

She closed her eyes and a shiver ran through her, before she reopened them. "Rory?"

"Yes, my love?"

She stared at him. "Who are you suggesting is the author of the diaries?"

He sighed. "You don't have to protect her any longer by yourself. I already told you I will spirit your Amelia to safety, even if it costs me Prinny's favor. I will do it," he emphasized, "for *you*."

"So you think Miss Primrose is the diarist?"

Perhaps he had been a bit too hasty in his conclusions about his beloved's quickness of mind.

"Of course."

Verity blinked. "You're completely wrong."

"Prove it."

She pushed the *Morning Post* into his hands, which were still warm from the soft touch of her fingers, and stood up. The blush had disappeared from her face.

"Amelia was in Kent the month that entry was penned. She was not with me in London."

Her expression was off. He gazed at her steadily. His sixth sense told him she had something more to say. She finally looked away.

"It's me," she murmured. "I'm the idiot who authored that rubbish."

Verity had never seen someone struck dumb. But there was a first for everything, and she was obviously cursed with having to experience everything and more. The last six weeks were proof of that.

She hoped never to see that look on anyone's

face ever again. But she rather feared her brother's and sisters' expressions would mimic his.

She did not wait to see more of the same or worse while Rory read the newest column in the paper. While the infamous "Fashionable World" column was gone, the publisher of the newspaper had filled the space with a new column entitled . . . "The Unfashionable World." Gone was the biting commentary by the former columnist. Instead, the publisher used the space to include a larger excerpt from Verity's diaries.

And that day's excerpt? Oh, the events described were just another string of spectacularly unimportant examples of excess just like the earlier columns. But the excerpt lent support again to the conclusion that Rory was the author, as again his name was not included.

Fine print at the conclusion of the excerpt stated: *The publisher of this fine newspaper does not necessarily endorse the free-spirited thinking of the anonymous author of this important and inspiring report. This is not gossip, it is not revolutionary in nature, it is merely news, which this newspaper has a duty to report.*

Verity raced down the burgundy carpet runner covering the centuries-old stone corridors of Boxwood. She had to get to her room. She should have finished her letter to the vicar about how none of the teachers she interviewed would do, and the other letters to Amelia, her brother, and the Prince Regent before she had woken Rory. She should have already finished packing two valises with her maid, and given instructions to the housekeeper and butler. She should have called for a carriage to take her directly to London, since hopes for permanent banishment to the family's cold abbey in the Lake District were fast fading.

She never should have allowed herself another look at his face. When would she learn to think first and act later instead of the opposite?

But in her heart she knew why she had gone to him.

She'd just *had* to know.

Did he truly love her?

Or was she again imagining it?

Chapter 15

It felt like he was really getting old. It took Rory a good twenty seconds for his brain box to start sparking again after her declaration. By then it was too late.

She was gone.

His heart stuttered in his chest, and his lungs constricted as he leapt from the blasted overly soft sofa, and nearly broke his knee crashing over the table, on the way to the door. At least he knew where her chambers were. She would be too distraught to think of going anywhere else.

He hoped.

He ran down the carpeted corridors—what was Candover thinking, covering the perfectly acceptable stones of this place with such slippery runners?

At the end of one corner, that maid with the

obvious symptoms of a throat plague stood her ground. Without a word, she giggled and pointed in the direction of Verity's apartments.

He almost kissed the woman.

In fact, he turned around and did kiss her. Right on the lips. He *wanted* the damn plague, if it would lead him to her, the one and only person who had insisted—without question—that he was not guilty. And then she had destroyed the stone evidence.

And damn it all. Cliché that it was, turnabout was fair play. He would not let her make the same mistake he'd made so very long ago.

She should not feel guilty for writing a diary that had fallen into the wrong hands. He might have thought the diarist was an idiot in the past, but now that he knew it was she, he thought the writing brilliant. He *loved* the dry humor of them.

He nearly raced past her door, before skidding to a halt. He pounded on it with force, then stopped and leaned against the wood to listen.

Nothing.

"Verity, let me in. I need to talk to you." He paused. "Please. Look, I'm not angry with you. At all." God, he was allowing his stupid sensibilities to cloud his speech. Even he knew his words sounded false.

He cleared his throat. Lord, the plague was

already upon him. "Verity, damn it, open this bloody door. I mean it. If you don't, then I will."

He placed his ear to the door and concentrated. Crickets.

"All right. We'll do it your brother's way at Carleton House. I'm sure he would side with me in this matter. So stand aside, I'm coming in."

This would be child's play. He had kicked in so many doors during his war years that Welly had nicknamed him "Rory the Doory." It was part of the reason he preferred double-locked and reinforced doors at his own houses.

The other part of the reason was that doors were like love. Once opened, reason fled and emotions entered—never a comfortable or good combination. It only had ever led to death or disaster in his case.

Rory took two steps back, concentrated on the sweet spot in front of him, and fired off a kick that would have pulverized Prinny's three-inch-thick doors.

The door did not budge.

He made a second attempt and then a third. God, he *really* was getting too old for this.

On the fourth attempt he changed tactics, and legs.

He swung back his boot, and Verity opened the door.

He stopped in mid-kick. "It was unlocked all this time, wasn't it?"

She nodded, her face still filled with fear.

He opened his arms, and after a second's hesitation she walked into them.

Moments later, without even knowing it, he'd backed her into her chamber, locked the door with one hand while still holding her, and then lowered his head to kiss her in earnest.

God. He had forgotten the sweetness of her lips. He was like a half-starved castaway finally found.

He could spend hours just kissing her, holding her, breathing in the mysterious scent of her that drew him to explore the nape of her neck, her lovely ear, and the starkly defined hairline above her aristocratic forehead.

She had been made for him.

He suddenly imagined hundreds of her ancestors behind her and hundreds more of his behind him, and after a thousand years of history, they had been born to get to this moment—a meeting of two souls destined for one another.

"Rory," she whispered as he stroked her chilled arms.

"Yes, my love?"

"You know this is impossible."

He brushed aside the fabric of her bodice at her

shoulder. "I know nothing of the sort." He kissed the delicate flesh.

She pushed away from him, creating space he didn't want.

"Rory, it might have taken me a long time to understand who you are. In fact, I'm beginning to think I'm the worst judge of character of all time. It took me nearly fifteen years of watching you and all the members of the entourage to finally understand that you are nothing more than a fraud. An angel masquerading as the devil's spawn."

He closed the space she had created, enfolded her into his arms and breathed in the scent of her warm, beautiful dark head again. "You are obviously a bit biased, I'm afraid," he murmured.

She wiggled out of his arms and stalked to the other side of a large round table in the center of her bedchamber. "No. I will have my say."

"You know, I've been looking forward to this."

"To what?" Her eyes were haunted and old beyond her years.

"To taking off our gloves and fighting properly, unlike the last time."

"You're not supposed to look forward to fighting," she said, misery still in her expression.

"Well, that first time, both of us exhibited a lackluster performance. And by the by, what in hell were we arguing about then?"

"I have no idea what you're talking about. We didn't argue about anything."

"Precisely. That was the problem. It was all cold distance, misunderstandings, and each of us dancing some strange minuet of which neither of us knew the steps. This time, I say let's enjoy ourselves. Let's waltz and squash each other's toes."

He had finally coaxed the very faint beginnings of a smile to her face.

"I know what you're trying to do, Rory, and it isn't going to change my mind no matter what you say or do."

He rubbed his palms together and strode to the table, inching around the glass top toward her.

She inched to keep the table between them. Her smile disappeared. "Please."

He immediately stopped. "All right. Let's try your way."

"Thank you," she murmured.

"Shall we sit across from each other?" He indicated the Aubusson carpet in front of her elegant marble fire grate.

She nodded and crossed to the place with him. Each sank down, Verity gripping her knees tightly to her chest, Rory more casually sprawled in every direction after he tugged off his boots and wiggled his toes.

"Go on then. I won't say a word," he promised.

She extracted a rumpled sheet of paper from her gown's pocket, her signature bold handwriting covering every inch on both sides. Lord, this was going to take forever, and all he wanted was to take her in his arms.

He waited patiently.

"There are several important things I must do before I go away."

He straightened. He opened his mouth but then quickly shut it. He had promised to listen. And he would listen even if she began to sing an epic opera where a female heroine died in the end.

She smiled when she realized he would not say a word. "Thank you. But first I will explain why I am going away." She spread the sheet again with her long, delicate fingers. "I've let my entire family down and have tarnished the Fitzroy name. Worse, I've caused someone I love to be in terrible peril."

Lord, he hoped that last part was about him and not someone else.

"I've—I've, no, I think I'll skip the next part."

Oh, thank God. The full letter was going to take forever to read.

"I revealed that I possess no moral fiber when I asked you to make lo— Well, this is too long anyway, let me be brief . . ."

There was a God. He resisted the urge to hum

to distract himself from pondering if her breasts were as beautiful as he remembered. One might be able to take the gentleman out of the primate, but one could never extract the primate out of a gentleman.

"Yes, here it is." She pushed aside that adorable lock of hair that always tumbled into her face. "I've single-handedly pushed the entire country to the brink of anarchy and revolution." She glanced up from the paper. "Are you listening to me?"

"May I answer?"

"Of course."

"Just checking," he said. "Yes, I'm listening very carefully."

"Then why are you staring at my—my bodice?"

How he managed to keep a smile from his lips, he would never know. "It's a lovely bodice."

"Keep you eyes right here, please." She made a V with two fingers and pointed them at her own eyes.

He stayed silent but his eyes did not obey his mind and traveled to her exposed trim ankles.

"Pardon me," she said crossly, "but did you hear me?"

"Is this how you treat the boys in the school? It's a wonder they like you so much."

"Fine," she said. "I see how it's going to be. I will finish now before I lose your attention completely."

Oh sweet happiness, it was almost over.

"Hmmm . . . I've caused the, uh, person who does not love— Right, yes, what I mean to say is that you now stand publicly accused of not only authoring my own treasonous ramblings, but even worse, of also blackmailing the Crown for a duchy."

She finally put down that blasted litany of hers and looked at him. Writers were always so damn *wordy*.

"Rory, I just need you to understand that you will be fully vindicated by the time I correct all of my unpardonable mistakes. You are the only one I can make that promise to. After I reveal myself, you will be proven not only innocent, but also you will never be vilified since your name was never in the diaries." Her expression darkened with worry. "But my family and anyone connected to us will be forever tainted via association. Sadly, there is nothing I can do to truly fix that."

"May I speak now?"

"Yes, of course."

"First, I want to know why you never mentioned me in those diaries."

She stared him in the face. "It took me until a day ago to figure that out. You never did anything stupid. You were always there to pick up the pieces."

"Except the night I woke up in your bed."

"Yes, but that was not your fault."

"And whose fault was it?"

"It was the Duke of Kress who provided the absinthe."

"Did he force the bottle to my lips?"

"No, but—"

"Verity, don't you realize what you're doing?"

"I'm listening," she murmured.

"The French call this type of discussion 'pondering the sex of angels' or 'considering the fragility of pipes.'"

"The first description is far more interesting."

He smiled. "I know. But the point is that dissecting blame, regretting the past, and endless contemplation that will not change anything is absolutely useless." He picked up her hand, and she allowed it. He turned it and pressed a gentle kiss on her palm.

She shook her head. "Well, this is no fun. You promised this would be more satisfying than the last time we *didn't* argue."

"Well, at least we learned silence is not the answer."

"Agreed," she replied softly. "So to continue, before I go to the Prince Regent and—"

"Verity?"

"Yes?"

"I've patiently listened to you, but now I think it's my turn."

She smiled. "Almost every duke I know insists dukes don't have to take turns."

"Sounds like Kress and Helston to me."

"Precisely." Her expression willed him to continue.

"I could utter a dozen hideously romantic words to you, or patiently explain everything I will do to make all your worries disappear." He slowly pulled her into his arms, and she did not resist. He settled her in the cradle of his lap. "But what I really want to do is hold you, comfort you, do a few wildly wicked things with you, and then afterward I will promise you a few things that will ease your heart and your mind. Will you allow me to do all this?"

"But you cannot fix this."

"I can and I will."

She looked at him, trust coloring every inch of her expression. Never had anyone ever looked at him like that.

Verity finally replied, "Do I get to do a few wicked things to you, too?"

"I'm counting on it." He traced a finger along her collarbone, and when he encountered the edge of her gown his fingers reversed course to the back of her gown to undo the small buttons. Her corset was a simple affair, and beyond the translucent shift lay what he had dreamed of forever.

She inhaled sharply when his hand touched her skin. He felt her inexperienced fingers attempt to unknot his neckcloth when he dipped down to kiss her. He brushed away her fingers in un-characteristic impatience and nearly tore off his bloody neckcloth, soon followed by his coat and shirt.

And then Rory gathered her in his arms once again and nimbly regained his feet to carry her to her bed. She refused to let go of his neck when he placed her in the center of the heavily mono-grammed white linens covering an eider-down duvet.

Rory dragged his knees across the covers to fully join her, nearly ripping his breeches in the process of removing the rest of his garments.

He couldn't wait another moment. He had to have her in his arms. Skin-to-skin, breathing to-gether the same air, and gazing into each other's eyes as if there was no one else in this world.

And finally he was covering her, but he was struck stock-still when a truth hit him: she was someone he had been missing his entire life.

Her hands stroked his back and caressed his derriere until he thought he would go mad. No lady's touch had ever affected him like this.

He could not hold himself in check to take the time necessary to bring her slowly to the peak of pleasure and then methodically push her over the edge to fly in relentless waves of a release.

"Are you ready?" He could barely breathe; the need to have her was too great.

Her legs parted beneath his and he shifted so she could bend and raise her knees. He gripped one of her thighs and moved it higher still.

Heavy with a primal desire to possess her, he flexed his hips, now cradled between her thighs. When the tip of his sex touched hers, a sensation seared his mind with white hot intensity.

"Why is it like this?" He bit out the words as his body took over his mind. He pushed himself into the depths of her being, each time driving her higher on the bed.

Her hands were still caressing his flesh, and she had found the sensitive dimples at the base of his back. When he looked down at her face, he found a woman flushed with passion. She was already on the brink of ecstasy.

He eased his upper body weight onto her breasts and cupped her bottom with his hands.

Tilting her a fraction of an inch higher, he drove into her in one long thrust, filling her fully. Her breath caught and then she turned her head and shouted into the pillow.

And then shouted again.

He covered her lips with his own and flexed his hips again. Slowly.

She was lost in a whirlpool of pleasure; her muffled cries echoed in his ears, driving him to near madness.

She could not seem to stop, and he would not let her. While he had thought he would explode as soon as he entered her, the opposite happened.

Each time he reached the end of the tightrope to release, he had only to look at the passion in her face, and that sight brought him back under control—to a level of intimacy that left him perpetually hanging on the precipice.

Verity suddenly clenched him closer to her, and all chance of halting the unraveling of his desire was gone.

He could not move.

He did not want to leave her.

And so he released his seed into Verity's body, choosing a true future for the first time in his life.

Verity was lost in a stark wild world of vivid sensations and overwhelming emotions coursing through her veins. But each time she felt herself getting lost in the tangle of sensibilities, she refocused on his green unblinking eyes.

When Rory shifted above her and gripped her with his powerful hands, she'd lost all sense of time and space. A sensation, not to be denied, gathered force and her flesh suddenly constricted.

His breathing became harsh, his rhythm uneven as he swelled inside her. Every muscle in his body hardened and he shook from the effort to possess her.

And for one thrilling moment she felt truly desired. He had become a wild animal; out of control instead of the practiced seducer.

When he shouted her name, and stilled inside of her, her heart sang with joy. She knew what it meant.

Immediately.

He might have gotten her with child.

She should have been worried but could not suppress the sheer joy flooding her spirit.

It was odd how when one faced a mountain of impossible mistakes of irreversible consequences, all of it could fade away for a few moments by just the idea of the smallest possibility of nurturing the child of the man she loved. It brought her a joy she had never imagined.

Oh, but it would not happen.

While Rory had suggested he could save her, deep inside, she had not a prayer of a chance.

When his breathing evened, he carefully rearranged her in his arms as if she were made of fine porcelain.

He gently kissed her. "You yell," he murmured, his voice like hot whiskey on a cold night.

"So do you," she whispered back.

"I do not."

"You do. You yelled like a *girl*." She laughed at the expression on his face. "This is what you meant when you said we'd fight with the gloves off, right?"

He gazed at her with reverence she didn't deserve. "Not exactly. This is when I admit that I'm not sure I'm done having my wicked way with you," he murmured, and bent his head to kiss her again. He stayed there to nibble her lips. "I'm too heavy," he finally suggested.

She steadied his hips. "No, you're not. I like you here."

"The feeling is entirely mutual."

Verity could not get her fill of gazing at him. It felt like she was part of a living, breathing dream.

Until he spoke.

"I'm going to withdraw from you now." He disengaged himself, fell on his back and drew her with him, into his arms, her head resting on his hard shoulder.

"Verity," he said, gazing at the ceiling as she studied his even profile. "Listen to me. I am your betrothed, whether you think it temporary or not. For me it is real and true."

She opened her mouth to interrupt but then closed it again.

"Look, you told me once we were great friends. And I told you that was even more important than love. Do you remember?"

She nodded mutely.

"All right, then. As your friend, I am asking you to trust the truth of what I say." He paused. "You are a good person."

She bit her lower lip.

"And as your friend, I am going to help you make this right."

"I'm not asking you—"

"You're right, you're not. This is my own decision."

"But—"

"No, it's still my turn," he said.

"Your turn has been infernally long."

"Well, according to you, you should be grateful that I even agree to allow turns."

"True, but—"

He brought a finger to her lips. And she stilled.

"It's very simple, I—" His voice gave out.

He tried again, but again nothing came out.

She held her breath.

"Verity . . . I need you."

She exhaled, and murmured softly, "You don't need anybo—"

He finally turned his head to look at her. "You are not listening, my love."

She gazed at him mutely.

"Good. Now then. It's like this." He muttered an oath. "The thing is, I don't *want* you."

It was like getting the wind knocked out of her when she had once fallen awkwardly from a horse. She simply could not breathe.

"No," he continued, "hear me out," he insisted, passion rising in his voice. "Verity, I'm not a man who has ever *needed* anyone. I might have *wanted* women in the past, but I never *needed* one. Do you understand the difference?"

She refused to allow the hot prick of tears to take hold.

"I need you," he repeated. "You are part of me now and I am part of you."

Chapter 16

A silence had taken hold after his simple, yet powerful words that made her heart sing despite the darkness that lay ahead. She had stopped the words by kissing him without pause.

His breathing had evened and she knew he finally slept. She would not follow him to sweet oblivion. She wanted to make a careful impression in her mind of every detail of these moments.

For the first time in over a decade, or maybe ever in her life, she felt lucky. Blessed, even.

She pondered what he had told her. The poor, deluded, wildly wonderful man of her dreams thought he knew her. He seemed to have overlooked the massive streak of stubbornness that ran in her blue-blooded veins. Only her brother bested her in the universal Fitzroy trait.

And because she was willful to the core, and

knew he might very well attempt to sacrifice himself to save her, she had to beat him to it. But first she had to try to protect her family's name if she could, and she also wanted to ensure Amelia's safety if Sussex had not managed it.

Yes, sleep would have to come later. Much later.

He had tried to pamper her with words that were half truth and half fiction. He could not fix the problems she had made, and he did not have the power he suggested. Prinny listened to no one, especially members of the royal entourage at this particular moment.

Someone was going to have to go up in flames to end this grand disaster. And Verity was certain that full and complete honesty was the only answer.

Rory woke with a start and a feeling that something vastly important was missing.

He turned his head abruptly only to find her gone. Since when had he stopped sleeping like the cat that he was—one eye open all night?

He went still and listened. Only the wind rushing through a tree's creaking branches beyond the open window made a sound. He glanced toward her door and gaped.

It was open.

He was starkers and she had left the door open?

What was she thinking? Had she not enough worries on her dish to add yet another round of whispers among the servants of Boxwood this time?

Something on the Aubusson carpet near the fire grate caught the edge of his vision.

A note. He squinted. Lord, he was going to have to get spectacles soon.

And then he remembered. Verity's list of sins.

He grabbed his breeches, which had fallen to the floor, and tugged them on. Next, he pulled his shirt over his head, and hastily fashioned some sort of knot after winding his neckcloth into position. He gathered his stockings and boots in one hand, snatched the note from the floor, and stopped at the door.

He peeked out like a regular thief in the night, instead of with the practiced moves of a seasoned spy. Looking both ways, he quickly sprinted down the hall to the east corridor, past the spot where the cheeky maid had accepted his kiss. He continued through the south's narrow passage filled with all sorts of odd artifacts, such as a gigantic foot in marble beside what appeared to be African tribal headdresses on the walls.

So this is where his beloved gathered inspiration for her bonnets.

He stumbled over a bronze serpent and fell into a gloomy chamber he remembered from his youth as being the Oak Room.

Picking himself up, he hopped on one foot as he rolled his stocking onto the other foot and calf and then switched to accomplish the same on the other side. He was finally wiggling into his second boot when he heard the scratch of match to flint.

Rory turned his head to find . . . James Fitzroy, the infamous Duke of Candover, sitting on a padded leather chair, one leg crossed over the other, not a hair out of place, his eyes narrowed to slits as he puffed on a cheroot.

For a few moments the face of the man Rory had once considered a brother was obscured by a cloud of smoke.

"Still writing, I see." James coolly glanced toward Verity's note, which Rory held in his hand. "One would have thought you would quit by now."

"I could say the same to you regarding that filthy thing between your fingers." Rory stood his ground. It was the only way.

The silence grew deafening. Now he knew where Verity had learned that silent way of hers. James was far better at it than she.

He finally strode to where her brother reclined and stood a few inches from his knees.

James inhaled from the cheroot, examined the butt before tossing it in the grate, and then slowly stood up. Then, as slowly, he exhaled the pungent smoke in Rory's face.

Rory didn't bat an eye.

"There is only one reason I'm not tossing your rutting arse in after that cheroot," James grit out. "Shall I tell you what it is, or would you prefer not to know?"

"I can see you want to tell me, and I'm happy to oblige."

"I don't know what sort of hold you have on the Prince Regent, but when I sort it out, you can be sure you won't live to see another day. Are we clear?"

"That's a threat, not a reason."

"The Prince Regent informed me, upon my return from Kress's nightmarish house party, that I was not to touch you."

"And you're willing to abide by our ruler's commands? Good to know."

"Well, unlike some of his subjects, I understand the notion of *loyalty*. You've never understood any part of the concept."

They were beak-to-beak, and neither flinched.

Rory's sense of smell had always been keen, and the scent of his old friend's shaving soap reached his nostrils. His gut clenched.

He took one step back.

James chuckled without an ounce of hilarity.

"How much longer?" Rory asked.

"Will I tolerate your presence?"

"No," Rory replied. "Until you realize you are still pining for someone who did not exist."

Rory could see the muscle of James's jaw tighten.

In one swift motion James grabbed Rory's ill-fashioned neckcloth and twisted it. "If you think I will ever let you have my sister, you are out of your murdering mind. Prinny be damned."

"Catharine never loved you," Rory ground out, despite his limited air supply. He refused to stop James.

James twisted the neckcloth an inch more.

"She didn't love me either," Rory rasped.

James's eyes narrowed.

"But most of all," he whispered, "she didn't love *herself.*"

All at once Verity's brother released him, his face ghostly pale.

"James . . ." He gathered his thoughts. "I told you I accepted full responsibility for her death. I didn't ask for your pardon then and I never will. I don't have the right."

At least James was listening. It was a start.

"The only thing I can do is tell you the truth,"

Rory continued. "She was a wild and beautiful creature whose only passion came from the chase. It was a game. She dabbled in securing a gentleman's love and devotion, and then when she had it, she became disinterested. But the moment a man began to walk away, she'd resume the chase. Yet I understood it, and I understood why."

He waited.

"Don't you remember her parents?"

"What about them?"

Rory shook his head. "The earl was old enough to be her grandfather."

"A respected gentleman in every way," James insisted.

"A respected, rich aristocrat who marries a beautiful destitute lady nearly forty years his junior is a lecherous bastard in my book," Rory continued, "and it creates a mother who teaches her daughters the art of marrying up since security is all."

James crossed his arms over his chest and glanced down at the floor. "When did you begin with her?" His voice was so tense Rory had to lean down to hear him.

"That's not important."

James quickly glared at him. "Of course it is, you ass. She was engaged to me. And you were one of only two men I considered—" James stopped.

Well, the insults were less biting, but sadly

he knew he had to risk the small gain. Only the painful truth would cure his friend. "I fell for her charms when she was fifteen."

A log broke in the massive fireplace, sending sparks in every direction.

James Fitzroy, the premier duke in England, sagged. "Before me," he ground out.

Rory nodded. "A bit."

"Two years is a lifetime when you're that age," Candover said, regaining his posture. "Why in bloody hell didn't you tell me?"

"What did it matter? She was dead."

"No, you idiot. Why didn't you tell me you were in love with her?"

"Because we were juveniles masquerading as men."

"You might be an idiot, Rory, but you were never juvenile. That state was reserved for your parents. You were the only adult in that former crumbling wreck of a manor."

"How soon one forgets your extraordinary talent with compliments." Rory scratched the back of his neck.

The silence in the room was killing him. He knew James so well. Candover was mulling it all over in that mulish nob of his. His pigheadedness was legendary. It was second only to his generosity of spirit.

It was why Rory had always admired him, always wished he was like him when they were young. They were opposites on the first trait, while Rory had always wished to be able to match James's other attribute.

James's face finally relaxed. "This still doesn't mean I'll let you have my sister."

Well, it was a start, thought Rory. He might have dodged death by dagger, but life without Verity was little better. "Understood," said the master of diplomacy and deceit.

James paused, then suddenly squeezed his eyes shut and rubbed his temples with one hand. "No you don't."

Again the silence. Well, Rory thought, it was better than the lists that took forever and a day to read. He shoved that damn thing of hers into his pocket.

"Look," James began, "I won't have her hurt."

"On that we agree."

"She is different from the rest of us—my other sisters and I."

"I figured that out already."

"She might be petite but her compassionate spirit is stronger than the rest of us combined. And her heart is always in the right place. She refuses to see the bad in anyone—even if it is to her detriment. She knows right from wrong to the nth degree and never shies away from admitting mistakes. And she'll do anything to avoid giving pain to another person. And finally, unlike the rest of the scientific and algebraic Fitzroys, she is the most creatively imaginative person I know. I only wish she would harness her talent and put it to use."

"Um, you might want to reconsider that last wish."

James raised his brows.

"And I would describe her creative imagination as more of a desire to bare the truth at any cost—in an original and amusing fashion—except to the unknowing victims under observation." Rory kept his smile in check. "But that part about doing something to her detriment is spot on."

Candover furrowed his brow in anger. "Sounds rather insulting, put that way."

"Absolutely not."

Others, who did not know them, would never guess that the layers of frost between them were melting a fraction of a degree with each passing minute.

Rory took a chance. "Jay?" It was the name he had always used in their youth.

The other man didn't answer.

"I love her," Rory said quietly.

He had never seen the unflappable Duke of Candover startled. This was a first. James was not silent—he was speechless, a vastly different state.

"And I will promise to protect her, cherish her, and guard her with my life." It might just come down to that, the way things were looking.

Her brother still appeared dazed.

So Rory kept talking, but lowered his voice. "I know about the fortune-hunting tooth-drawer's son. And she does not know but I have already taken steps to find the bastard and extract justice."

James cut in. "Don't bother. He's already dead."

Rory started. "I see. Well then. I can only give you my word that I will always love her, protect her, and cherish her until—"

"You know I'm not a minister, right?" James's rare smile appeared for but a moment. "And she has to be present for it to count."

He ignored him. "Jay, I will never bruise her heart."

"*That* is my fear," Candover admitted slowly. "She might be strong, but she has a weakness. When she gives her heart, she does it unreservedly. And if that person dies, a part of her is lost."

"I know someone just like her," Rory murmured, looking directly at his lost friend found, who had eyes just like hers.

"She just—" James exhaled slowly. "—never fully regained her happiness after our mother died a decade ago."

When she had been seventeen. He thought he

might be ill. A sudden certainty engulfed Rory's gut. "During the summer?"

James nodded once. "The June solstice."

God. It was the day after Verity had lost her innocence in the maze. And most likely her mother had guessed but her brother did not know. *And would never know if he had anything to say about it.*

It would kill James if he knew her innocence had been taken by that blackguard.

"Well," Rory continued evenly, "you know I cannot promise not to die. But I can promise to never again drink that bloody frog firewater Kress provided that god-awful night, and I won't swim with swans in the Serpentine again—by the by, wasn't Norwich chased by one of those white buggers?"

When James pursed his lips to hide a smile, Rory knew he had him, and so he muddled on. "Well, Seventeen lived through it so let's not ever let the Duke of Duck forget it. Now, where was I?"

"The list of all the things you will not do to avoid getting yourself killed, and a promise to make her happy."

Lord, Rory thought, he was apparently already making lists like a Fitzroy. "Right. Shall we just cut to the end? I will attempt to keep out of harm's way to the extent possible."

"A true, lying diplomat in every way," James muttered.

The two men stared at each other. Both were of the same height, with the same width shoulders and the same dark, dark hair. The only difference was their eyes. James's were brown and held untold truths, while Rory's were green and world weary.

"So will you honor me with your blessing, Jay—reluctant though it may be?"

"You don't know her at all, if you think my blessing will help you win her."

Rory finally exhaled with a smile. His friend was back. "Shall we have a brandy, then?"

James whacked him on the back in a show of brotherly affection or strength. Rory wasn't sure which, but who was he to care. He had just won the longest stand-off in history.

Candover gestured with his arm in an "after you" movement toward the doorway. Rory led the way toward the ducal study he had once visited on a near daily basis all those years ago.

A growl sounded from his back. "And by the by, *brother*, if I find you again in my sister's bed before the wedding?" James paused. "I will—"

Rory turned and faced his newfound friend. "Jay?"

"Yes?"

"You know I love you, right?"

It was funny how fast one little four-lettered word

could render the greatest of men into mortar statues glued together with horror and mortification.

Yes, Verity had taught Rory well the ridiculous way that one word could paralyze the strongest of men.

For the next day and a half, Rory worked nearly straight through. The serious cramp in his hand began only after the first six hours passed.

And so it went. Sunlight by day, candlelight at dusk, full candelabra at night—all at his desk by the window. His old window, the one in his room from his boyhood. Not that anything had changed since returning here.

He would never reside in the rooms his parents had occupied. They had always been and always would remain people he would never know or understand.

Not by his choice.

His childhood hadn't scarred him. He had thought that all parents lived separate lives from their offspring while residing in the same house— until he met James's mother and father.

His best friend's family had been his salvation then, and now Rory would return the favor and become the Fitzroys' salvation.

He lifted his head from the paper lying on his

desk. He had fallen asleep. He hoped he didn't have ink spots on his forehead. There was only so much sleep a man in his advanced years could miss before he fell like an oak.

He glanced at the words he had written.

The curlicues at the end of each capital letter in the alphabet were going to kill him.

He sighed heavily, arched his back to relieve the stiffness, trimmed the quill, and dipped it back into the India ink. He paused for a moment and studied the crumpled paper next to him.

And then applied words to the page. For another six hours he continued to write, until there were no more words to say.

He rang for his butler.

She still had not finished what she needed to do if she stood a chance of success, and a sense of completion toward her obligations to her family and the people who depended on her. For three days and nights she had worked to finish every last task. She even attended to the future needs of the boys heading to Eton.

Verity sat at the desk she had occupied for so many hours of all the many days since her mother had died and she'd assumed all of the duties of hostess of Boxwood.

At first she hated the role. But it had been her penance.

She had caused her mother's distress that day.

She alone.

And the shock of it had stopped her mother's frail heart. Verity accepted that she was ultimately responsible.

That was why she had sat in this old, empty, beautiful room, away from everyone else, performing the duties her mother had not liked either.

Her mother had constantly said that a moment indoors was a moment wasted. Verity smiled at the memory.

Remembering her didn't pain her nearly so much anymore.

And the oddest thing was, the household duties had taken on a certain charm as the years sped forward. There was a certain rhythm to the calendar of a grand estate such as Boxwood. And rhythm brought harmony and . . . peace.

Verity studied the latest list of things to do that the housekeeper had suggested. It might just be the last time she would do this, and so she took care and joy in the small task.

Her time in Derbyshire was limited. She was balancing the need to carefully plot her course against the worry that Rory would do something he had no right to do.

Her short snatches of sleep had been plagued by visions of Rory running toward the broken form of Catherine Talmadge, whose death had triggered a guilt in him that lasted fourteen years. She would not let that happen again. When she did what she planned, she would not allow him an inch of guilt.

Verity had given herself less than a handful of days to accomplish far too much. She filled short parts of them with Rory for the sheer joy of being with him, and more importantly, to keep an eye on him. She even stooped to wheedling his stable master to send a note if he left the estate.

She also interviewed the three candidates to replace Miss Woods and herself at the school, and during the first night she secretly finished packing her two trunks, even if she still had to figure out a way to drag them out to the stable without anyone seeing.

She also still had to finish the letters to each of her sisters and the longer one to James, and finally had to put on a very convincing act toward Rory that she wasn't going to do what she was, in fact, going to do.

She had already gathered her nerve to write the greatest love letter and good-bye in the history of mankind.

Today was to be a day where she had to endure

the weight of the world with an innocent smile on her face while she entertained a long dinner table filled with neighboring families, now that her brother had become once again the acknowledged crown jewel bachelor in Derbyshire.

Verity feathered her chin with the quill's soft end and reviewed the chef's proposed menu.

She hoped Rory liked roasted asparagus, quail eggs in gelatin, and goose. Of course there was not a single pea to be found. The chef knew better now. Five courses later the menu was done. Another three hours later and everything had been neatly crossed off the long list of duties to see to.

There was really only one last important thing she had to do today before she could escape to the outside world she loved. And it was not on the list.

Verity reached into the drawer with her small key, lifted the board, and removed the stack of red leather volumes.

She ran her fingers over the labor of ridiculous ramblings through the years and could not help but feel pride despite everything.

She carefully replaced the inner workings of the drawer, pushed back her chair, swept her dark blue lawn morning gown's skirting behind her and stood up slowly. Grasping the small stack, she crossed to the crackling fire housed by the beautiful gray marble mantel.

Verity stood before the fire for a long time.

And then she tossed the volumes into the blaze, one by one, and watched her years of work catch fire and turn to cinder.

She should have felt relieved that now she would never have to ensure they stayed hidden again. Instead she felt ill, as if she had lost part of herself. The part no one would ever know existed.

And yet a small part of her sensed freedom. Freedom from the past.

Chapter 17

Dinners were early in the country, even during the summer when the sun warmed the land for far more hours than in the winter.

Verity knew James preferred to entertain early and with military precision.

The Duke of Norwich, Esme, and Rory arrived an hour before the other guests, as prearranged. Verity would try one last time to break through the ill-ease that had replaced the easy manner she and Esme had shared throughout their girlhood. There was nothing like the bond of two wallflowers who had wilted together through the endless Seasons barren of beaux. And yet, ever since Esme had returned far earlier than expected from an ill-fated trip to pursue her artistic passion, and gained a husband mysteriously in the process, their confidences had withered.

Verity was determined to pull the weed of reserve from her garden of friendship with Esme before she left. And so she tugged Esme's hand to pull her next to her as soon as Esme entered the main door at Boxwood, preceding the Duke of Norwich and Rory, who had traveled in the same carriage.

It was amusing to watch three dukes of the royal entourage starched up to the nines, their collars so high and so stiff that Verity remarked quietly to her cousin, "You'd think they'd have scars on their chins from trying to turn their heads."

Esme's return smile was easy.

Oh, she hoped it would continue. She gripped her cousin's arm and stepped slightly away from the three men who had already begun to drift toward a more private nearby salon.

Her brother suddenly turned toward her. "We'll return at the appointed hour."

Verity nodded and turned to her cousin. "Esme, do you mind accompanying me to my bedchamber? I've managed to lose one of my favorite slippers and I want to find it since the ones I've got on now are a trifle too loose."

"Of course, dearest. But, may I say that it would help if you would just start wearing that lovely style of slipper with ribbons that circle the ankle."

Verity pulled a face. "Said the lady whose

mother is on the forefront of fashion." On a whim, she grasped her cousin's hand, and together they mounted the stairs, crossed all the corridors, and finally squeezed past the door frame of Verity's chambers.

She turned to Esme, who had shared every awkward moment of youth with her, as they were the exact same age, and finally spoke. "Esme?"

"Yes, dearest?"

"We've barely seen each other these past weeks. And I know it's my fault. It's just that—"

Esme closed the distance between them and enfolded her in her arms. Verity felt a portion of the weight of her crumbling world fall as she rested her shorter frame against Esme's. There had always been something ethereal, almost magical, about her cousin, whose artwork reflected untold gifts.

"No, Verity. It's my error. I fear that this wretched, disastrous marriage of *inconvenience* to Norwich has made me withdraw from everyone I love." Esme pulled away a bit to examine her.

Verity searched the depths of the ageless wisdom in Esme's gray eyes. "Oh, Esme, please, I am begging you. Will you tell me . . ." she whispered.

"Go on and ask me anything"—Esme stroked her head with such gentleness—"I know I've been distant. Reserved even. I can't explain why. I don't even know myself."

"I've become the same. And I don't know why either."

Esme tucked Verity back into her arms and whispered, "I suspect it's love, then."

"For me or for you?"

"For us both. It's not surprising, actually, when you think about it. We've done just about everything else together."

"Well, not exactly everything," Verity said softly.

"I love you, Verity. Never forget it. While you had four sisters, I had none. I always wished I was your sister in truth, even if we were so much more because we *chose* each other."

Verity could barely speak for the gratitude she felt toward her cousin. The weeks of meaningless pleasantries exchanged between them at the usual round of country social events had worn on her. And Esme always seemed to be able to unravel the mysteries of life, especially when it concerned gentlemen.

"Why is love so complex?" Verity knew her cousin would have answers.

"In my case it's because the man the Prince Regent forced to marry me will never open his heart, or take a chance."

Verity watched Esme swallow awkwardly.

"But I at least can take comfort that I truly believe you and Rory have an immense chance to grab onto happiness. I know no other man like him. Oh, he has always worn dark mystery on top of the suit of armor all men wear."

"I know," Verity agreed.

"Inside, many men are made of marshmallow, others of good solid oak. But in Rory? My dearest, I see nothing but gold: malleable, but strong, and pure through and through."

"I always knew it unconsciously." They moved toward the two damask-covered slipper chairs near the window, which offered an extraordinary view of the earthly delights Boxwood's park offered.

"He loves you, Verity," Esme said quietly. "I saw it as soon as we arrived. It was in the way he watched you every moment when you were not looking."

"Esme . . . Oh, please will you not dismiss what I will tell you?"

"I never do," Esme replied.

"Yes, I know. It's just that I have always been so practical, and I abhor theatricality and what I shall relate reeks of it."

Esme smiled. "Love always seems to be the handmaiden of melodrama. Especially great love."

Verity nodded. "I do love him. I always have, even as a silly girl of three and ten."

Esme bit her lip to stifle a giggle. "I know."

She shook her head. "Was it that obvious?"

"Only to me," Esme said.

"So the thing of it is— You will not tell anyone what I tell you, will you? You promise? It's just that I have to rely on someone to deliver a few letters."

"Where are you going?" Esme glared at her.

"I haven't even told you I'm going anywhere."

"Where?"

"To London. Just for a bit." She knew she was dissembling. "To see Amelia."

"Again?"

"Yes. The thing is, I might not be able to return straightaway." She was careful to keep her tone light, her expression even.

Esme studied her, and Verity felt as if her cousin could see inside her mind. Esme's face turned ashen. "You must trust him, Verity."

"I do!"

"No, you do not. I can see it. Look, each of us has lessons to learn in life. And the only way to become the person we were meant to become, is to take a leap of faith when you least want to veer away from the familiar. Verity, listen to me. You must take a different path if the one in the past led in the wrong direction."

"But I have an excellent sense of direction."

Esme sighed.

"You know I will always take the path which hurts the fewest, and has the best chance of protecting those I love."

"Perhaps you should protect yourself first," Esme ground out. "Specifically now."

"Coming from the lady I have no doubt would lay down her life for me."

"There is a difference, Verity. You and I might be the most independent, strongest females in England. We always give to others. But we have to remember, just sometimes, that it's vital to trust others and allow them to help."

"Esme?"

"Yes, dearest."

"You're right. But this is not one of those times."

"No," Esme said firmly. "Oh, botheration. You are stubborn to a fault, Verity Fitzroy. There. I've said it."

"I know my flaws, Esme." There was not a hint of annoyance in her tone.

"It's not a flaw. It's a strength." Esme leaned forward and gripped her shoulders. "Your flaw, right now, is that you're trying on martyrdom, and I fear you're going to like the fit."

Anger filled her. "I am not! I loathe martyrs. The odds are against selfless actions ever solving anything. I wish you would save your breath for Rory. He's the one primed for self-sacrifice."

"Are you listening to yourself?" Esme said archly. "Look, I know why you're going against your true self. It's love."

Verity trembled. "Esme? Promise me you'll do what I asked."

"No need to say it."

"But I must be sure. You promised you will not—"

"Say anything. My word is my promise."

Esme squeezed her hand and became still, her gaze drifting. "I do believe I should descend. Three dukes in one chamber are two dukes too many. Shall you come with me?"

"No. I have one last thing to do," Verity said, glancing about the chamber for her slippers. "I'll leave the letters at the mill, under the rock where you always sit to paint."

Esme gave her one last hug and whispered in her ear so softly that Verity was not sure if she had really said anything. It was more like a breeze murmuring in the treetops . . . *Take the less familiar path.*

Ten minutes later, still wearing the ill-fitting slippers, Verity descended to join the others in the receiving hall.

The first handful of twenty-eight dinner guests trickled through the door. Verity took her place beside her very tall, elegant brother. It was perverse how the Fitzroy physical traits appeared to far greater advantage in the males of the line. And why had stature seemed to skip over her in particular?

A flurry of "good evening," "lovely to be included," "so good of you to come," mixed with a heavy round of "Your Grace," "His Grace," and even "Their Graces," allowed Verity to lose herself in the familiar ways of her role in her family.

The baron and his baroness were as jovial and kindhearted and loud as always. Verity successfully suppressed a giggle when the baroness actually had the effrontery to kiss James on the cheek in her exuberance.

Verity was never so grateful for all the different characters that flowed through her life.

But gratitude came to a grinding halt when Miss Phoebe Talmadge drifted through the entrance along with her younger brother. The vicar, Mr. Robert Armitage, followed them. Verity peeked at the visages of others nearby. No one took any notice of Mr. Armitage.

Not that she blamed her guests. Phoebe was a stunning vision of beauty, wrapped in elegance.

Never had she appeared lovelier. And while Catharine Talmadge had been a diamond of the first water, Phoebe far surpassed her. She was draped in a very pale ice blue silk gown that delicately clung to her figure, revealing nothing, except everything. A small hint of Belgian lace trailed the longish hem behind her as well as the edges of her very low-cut bodice, which barely skimmed the tips of her breasts.

Back arched, chin tilted, Phoebe's femininity was so achingly beautiful that it was impossible to take one's eyes off of her.

But Verity could. And she did.

Her gaze flitted from face to face of the guests still gathered in the receiving hall. Each person was transfixed—gentlemen and ladies alike. Verity's eyes flew to James when Phoebe floated before him.

Her brother's expression was not one Verity had ever seen before.

Phoebe bowed her head as she slowly curtsied before him. "So very honored by the invitation, Your Grace," she said, her dulcet voice carrying in the silence.

When James did not respond, Verity drifted so close to him they were touching. She shot her hand behind him and pinched him in a place she should not.

He didn't flinch, but finally his gaze refocused and he did the necessary with the grace only a duke possessed.

And then Phoebe was before her, and while no one else would have ever noticed it, Phoebe's smile was a fraction less bright and her expression a fraction less warm than a moment before.

A wallflower gone to seed knew well this treatment. The one thing time had done, however, was bring perspective.

It must be very hard to spend all the hours of every day of one's life trying to achieve and maintain such a level of flawlessness. And yet despite all, time would march on, and other beauties would have their day, pushing the older ones to the edges of the ballrooms, until the night when the former beauties had been forced against the wall to join the wallflowers they had once shunned. Only then, these fading rarities would find it was too late to learn how to take immense joy from the enduring friendships behind the withered faces who knew the freedom only anonymity could bring.

Verity welcomed Phoebe as she would any guest, and Phoebe continued to engage the notice of everyone in her path. Verity watched it all out of the corner of her eye until her gaze snagged on Rory, leaning in half shadow against a column.

His green eyes glittered as he stared right back at *her*—not Phoebe.

Verity had always suspected there would be at least one moment in a plain woman's public life that would shimmer brightly in the small chamber of vanity.

For Verity that moment was now.

And he seemed to know, for he winked at her.

She laughed without a single person taking note.

Rory smiled at her, uncrossed his long, lean legs and walked toward the staircase leading to the grand salon. His wide shoulders strained his unfashionable black coat, which he always had favored. She had always suspected it was to remind himself of his aristocratic family's impoverished circumstances. Only people anxious of staining their garments wore black, unless they were in mourning.

When the last of the guests arrived, Verity accepted her brother's proffered arm and they mounted the stairs to join all the others.

A wistfulness filled her. It might be the last time her brother looked at her with any affection tonight. She refused to dwell on it. She would enjoy every moment of this respite from thoughts of the future.

She left her brother's side when they entered

the elegant chamber filled with the fragrant flowers she had arranged with care. She drifted to
her favored place, beside a large potted palm, in
which she could casually dispose of any mysteriously green hors d'oeuvre chef might have gotten
in his ornery head to slip onto the menu. It was
also the perfect spot to oversee the flow and hum
of the evening.

Esme was engaged in conversation with Sir
John and his tall, thin wife. The vicar was sternly
gazing at Phoebe, who was casting her net at the
only three bachelors in her vicinity. Mr. Armitage
was not one of them.

This is why Verity had loved being an observer
in the corridors of humanity. She spun a hundred
different absurdities in her mind as she gazed at
the tableau before her.

She felt rather than saw someone come to stand
behind her.

"You are quite ravishing tonight."

She could not help but smile. She was immune
to false flattery, but it was indeed, lovely to receive
compliments.

"I would steal a kiss but considering the recent
great strides I've made with your brother, I rather
think I'll not risk it."

She nearly jumped when she felt his warm
hand caress her bottom.

He leaned in closer. "So this is how you did it."

"Did what?"

"Took such excellent notes."

"I don't want to talk about it."

He nipped her shoulder and she jumped. "Perhaps not, but now it's time for you to enter the fray. Come along, then. Take my arm."

And she did. It was lovely, and warm.

He swatted at an arched palm frond. "It's like a damn jungle in here."

"I like jungles." She smiled as she remembered the day she had begun writing the Duke Diaries all those years ago. "I ofttimes give people animal identities."

He grinned. "Really? What am I?"

"Easy. A panther."

"James?"

She rolled her eyes. "Ox. A *drunken* ox, once. "

"I can see I'm making this too easy. Esme?"

"She's the entire zoo."

"Ah, I have you now. Miss Primrose?"

"She's an enchanting combination of only the good animals."

"All animals are good," he whispered in her ear.

"That's not true," she whispered back. "I don't like cheetahs."

He laughed long and loud. "Me neither. Predators through and through and entirely too ugly what with those spots."

She bit back a smile. If she could have loved him more, she would have at that moment.

"All right, time to earn our food. Let's circulate and regroup." He pulled her back as she took a step away from him. "But do not make me jealous of Mr. Armitage again. You know how I feel about vicars."

She was well and true enjoying herself for the first time at an event of her making. Normally, she was too engaged in ensuring the comfort of all her family's endless stream of guests and visitors. The estate was open to visitors nearly year-round. She leaned toward Rory, turned her head and whispered, "Go and talk with the baron. He likes to talk about the war."

He pressed a quick kiss to her temple. "That's certainly more interesting than avoiding ducks with Norwich."

"Ah, the romantic couple," Mrs. Greer announced loudly as she approached them. "It has been far too long since a wedding in our parish."

Verity felt a flush rising from her neckline. "Good evening, Mrs. Greer. And where is Mr. Greer?"

"At home with the gout, poor dear. But you know how he is. He will not allow me to miss a thing. I think he secretly likes to be alone."

Verity glanced at Rory, who had not departed when he had the chance. She knew he was thinking Mr. Greer's secret was not really a secret at all. The man barely said five words to his wife's five hundred.

James drifted toward her, Phoebe casually in his wake.

"So, my dears," Mrs. Greer continued, looking at Rory. "When is the happy day?"

Verity's hands numbed.

"We've been enjoying ourselves a bit too much to finalize—" Rory began before someone interrupted him.

Verity was never so shocked when James cut in.

"July twenty-eighth, madam. I trust you will spread the word."

It was most likely the first time in her life that a duke had asked her to spread the word about anything. Mrs. Greer reacted as if news of the end of the war between France and England had been placed in her hands to be trumpeted to the world. "Oh, indeed, Your Grace," she replied with reverence. "I will not fail you. Oh dear, perhaps I should not stay. It will take some time to circle the neighborhood. Ah, but then tomorrow is Sunday. I shall tell everyone as they arrive to church. Is that not an excellent idea?"

Verity chanced a glance toward Rory, and while

a smile was plastered to his face, there was an odd glint to his eyes, which Verity didn't recognize.

James nodded regally to the flustered, plump lady. "Do what you must, madam. But good news travels fast."

Verity attempted to change the topic. "I like your turban very much, Mrs. Greer. Wherever did you find it?"

"Oh, my dear." The matron touched her hand, "I fashion all my hats myself. Far more original I think, don't you?"

"Oh, yes. Isn't it lovely, Abshire," Verity murmured.

"Absolutely stunning. Perfection. Ravishing," he replied straight-faced. "Is that leopard?"

"No, no." She leaned forward with a conspiratorial wink. "Dyed goat. Far more practical."

"You should make one just like it, Lady Fitzroy," Rory continued.

Verity took a small step back, directly onto the toe of his evening footwear. Hard. "Yes, Mrs. Greer. I shall even promise to wear it on my wedding day." *The one that would never come.*

Phoebe, ever graceful, slipped beside James. "I have been waiting so patiently, Lady V."

All eyes remained glued to their theatre.

"Have you?" Verity replied.

"Oh yes. I have been longing to tell you, on

behalf of everyone in the parish—especially those gathered here tonight . . ." She paused. ". . . how grateful we all are to you for stepping in for our dear Miss Woods to teach our poor tenant children."

"But it is I who is grateful to them, Miss Talmadge. They teach me more than I teach them."

"Yes, but it's such an altruistic endeavor with so little hope for success."

Mr. Armitage joined their circle. "How so, Miss Talmadge?"

Surely no one else, who had not been a keen bystander on the fringe of life's events such as Verity, would notice, but there was the barest hint of something very like fear in Phoebe's posture.

"Why, the cruelties of birth typically hampers their ultimate future. Would you agree, Your Grace?" She eyed James.

James gazed at her, remnants of the past still clinging to his remote expression. "You are both right, I fear."

Rory broke the tide of swelling tension, in his usual well-timed method. "Shall we not take a tour of the air beyond the French doors? I, for one, need it after those magnificent duck confit canapés. What say you, Norwich?"

Norwich stepped up to the challenge without thinking. "I might agree you possess a good sense of direction, as long as one doesn't mind ending up in a bedchamber."

A hush fell anew over the assembled royalty of Derbyshire and stared at her.

And that's when Verity knew.

The rumors from London had arrived at some point in time, and everyone knew why Rory was engaged to marry her.

Chapter 18

A sense of freedom enveloped Verity as she accepted Rory's arm. She didn't need it to steady her as the small crowd parted to then follow them as slowly as decency would allow.

"Don't hover," she murmured. "It's far too obvious."

He leaned down to her as they cleared the doors leading to the gardens. "I like being obvious."

"I know. But I don't." She released his arm and wandered to the railing, where Esme soon joined her.

The rest of the audience staked out their places as unobtrusively as possible.

"There are times I wish I were you," Esme murmured.

"There are times I wish you were me, too," she retorted, a serene smile plastered to her face.

Esme laughed. "Never change, Verity. Please. I don't want to live in a world without someone like you in it."

You might have to, Verity thought, but without poignancy or a single regret.

This was her night. And she knew it. The night air ruffled and refreshed her feathers.

A sense of calm and purpose invaded her spirit as she and her cousin exchanged pleasantries, and the others began to lose hope that more drama was in the offing. The moon moved slowly across the night sky.

"Esme?"

Her cousin linked arms with her. "Yes?"

"I've changed my mind."

"Thank God."

She smiled in the darkness, relieved only by the lanterns hanging in the branches of the trees nearest the ballroom. "The mill is a bit inconvenient, as I have so many duties to attend to tomorrow. And the day after, I have to write letters for the three boys off to Eton."

Esme sighed.

"I'll leave them in my slippers. And I'll even give you leave to toss out these blister-inducing things as well."

"Who cares about your slippers. If you disappear I give fair warning that I will give Rory leave to destroy every last hat you leave behind."

Verity turned her head at the sound of Phoebe's lovely laughter.

The other lady was beside Rory, who was leaning against the balustrade. She leaned in, cupped her hand and whispered something into his ear. An amused smile appeared on Rory's handsome features.

And suddenly Verity was thirteen years old again and back in the old pine tree overlooking the lake. Below her, two painfully beautiful wild creatures were living a life she would never know.

Together.

A sudden visceral change began in the pit of Verity's belly and shot to her limbs.

The familiar within her was suddenly replaced with an exotic need to assert her rightful claim in her domain.

She was not a bloody martyr. She refused it with every fiber of her being.

She marched over to them. And with a single step, she inserted herself between Phoebe and Rory. "He's mine," she said loud enough for everyone to hear.

She caught a fleeting glance of Rory. His eyes danced with humor and . . . and something more, before she heard the sound of laughter retort in the absolute silence of the entranced audience.

Verity turned to see Esme, standing on the railing all alone, laughter still coming from her in waves. She wiped her eyes finally. "Stubborn, through and through." Her cousin caught her breath. "And just in the nick."

"Well, I like that," Phoebe said, meaning just the opposite.

Verity stepped so close to Phoebe that she had to look straight up to meet the beauty's glittering eyes. "And stay away from my brother, too."

Rory chuckled.

Verity swiveled her head and caught him scratching the place on his jaw where the high collar rubbed. "Don't say a word."

He put his hands up. "Never let it be said that I can't listen to my betrothed."

Phoebe sniffed. "My dear Lady V, I fear you—"

"You had better fear me," Verity interrupted. "And I am not your 'dear Lady V.' My mother taught me that one should never assume familiarity unless the person invites you to do so."

"She's got you there, Miss Talmadge," said an anonymous lady from the other side of the balcony.

The Duke of Norwich crossed to Esme and yawned far too wide for it to be genuine. "Lovely evening, Candover," he called out. "But, I do think I prefer the fireworks at my wife's estate. Shall we, Your Grace." He looked down at Verity's cousin, who nodded.

As they took their leave, Esme leaned in to whisper in her ear. "No need for me to revisit your chamber now, as I see it. Keep those slippers. They serve you well."

Verity quickly kissed her cousin.

For the first time in Verity's memory, Esme had not an inkling of the future.

James had the good sense to leave his sister and Rory alone on the balcony as he escorted inside all the guests, who believed they had just witnessed a historic event.

Rory glanced down at Verity, whose face always startled him due to the deep attraction he felt whenever he saw her. "Will you walk with me?"

She nodded.

He offered his arm but then changed his mind. He scooped her up in his arms and carried her down the stairs. She said not a word of protest.

He gently deposited her at the base of the stairs and they walked among the century-old trees by the light of the waxing moon.

The silence was not awkward. He had found peace. Finally.

He halted at the site of the first time he had come to visit her this summer. When he had assumed he could easily convince of the necessity of marriage. He knew better now. She would only do what was in her heart.

Her actions tonight sparked hope within him.

"Verity?"

"Yes."

He paused. She had said that one little word with such finality, not an invitation to continue with his question. "Did I understand you correctly?"

"Yes."

"Yes as in yes, continue?"

She said not a word.

"Or, yes as in yes, you will give me the indescribable joy of truly becoming my duchess?"

"Yes."

He looked down at her face, the face of the person he had come to love with every fiber of his being, and knew. Her yes was really a no. But his life depended on not showing that he knew.

He gathered her into his arms, slowly. Taking such care to hold her, so she would feel his great love for her. "V?"

"Yes?" she whispered.

"I love you."

"I know," she said very clearly. "I love you, too."

They stood there for long minutes. Letting her go was the hardest act he had ever done.

When she slipped from his arms, he knew

not to go after her. As her petite form reentered the ballroom, he could not believe the strongest person in the world could appear so small and fragile.

Verity walked to her chambers, not in a daze, but with a clarity of thinking that had eluded her for some time.

In the quiet of her apartments, she finished her letters to James, Mr. Armitage, Esme, and finally Rory.

It was not really that difficult to say good-bye once a decision had been taken. Especially when the decision was the right one.

She took off her slippers and placed them under her bed, the letters carefully balanced on top of them.

Then she stole into the night, with merely her saddlebags, stuffed with the necessities. Her valises were long forgotten.

She would not need them. Her last hope had died tonight as soon as she realized everyone knew she was ruined. Oh, none of them would ever dare say a word to her if she'd had the opportunity to stay, which she did not because of the diaries. They would be respectful because of her brother's title. Some would whisper about her, others would pity her, but all of them would look at her, and their silent knowledge of her tattered reputation would hover over every conversation.

And because of her brother's name, she would be known wherever she went.

But that was the least of her problems.

Esme was wrong. She was not being a martyr. She was being incredibly selfish.

No matter what happened in the end, she would know he existed. He was genuine and true and he loved her for herself, just as she would forever love him.

She stole into the stables, using the secret gap in a board that emptied into the old harness room. Sneaking past a slumbering stable boy, she silently entered Captio's stall with everything overloaded in her arms.

Her mare nickered softly and nuzzled her side, searching for a cube of sugar, which Verity provided as she saddled and bridled her. She was the only thing of value Verity was taking with her, along with an inordinate amount of gold coin, which she now knew better how to hide than the last time she was in London.

She rode Captio in a southerly direction. She was bathed in the warmth of the night.

It was the exact right way to remember her mother the night of the tenth anniversary of her death. "Mother," she whispered into the darkness, "I've missed you so."

Little did she know, but in her haste to depart far sooner than she had planned, she had forgotten her least favorite cliché of all time: The future did not wait.

Chapter 19

Verity arrived at the White Horse Inn on the outskirts of London in record time. It was not due to her riding skills. It was due to the outrageous amount of gold coin she pressed into the hands of an ostler ten miles from Boxwood, who mysteriously appeared twenty minutes later with a very smart phaeton and insisted on driving her to London himself.

She rather feared he had nicked the fast vehicle and even faster horses from some poor gentleman at the inn.

Did she really worry? No. What was one more broken law when the penalties she had already accumulated would have put over a hundred hardened criminals in Newgate for the rest of their lives?

And she was tired of worrying and was ready

for the story to be over—until the outlaw ostler and she drew into the well-maintained yard of the White Horse. The innkeeper winked at her and insisted a penny was well worth the price for the *Evening Herald* from last night.

"And the *Morning Post*?"

He shook his head. "The *Herald* be what everyone reads now."

Not that it mattered anymore. How much worse could it get?

A lot worse, it turned out.

Her shriek from the neat little ladies' withdrawing room was most likely heard all the way to London.

She stormed out of the inn, grabbed the reins from her lawless accomplice. By the look on his face, and his silence during the rest of the journey to Town, it seemed he regretted not insisting on twice the rate he had gleefully taken from her two days ago.

Verity drove them straight to Carleton House, politely returned the reins to the white-faced ostler, and dismounted without any aid. Both driver and passenger hoped never to encounter the other again in their lives.

She slowed as she marched toward the royal guards fronting the prince's new-famed residence. The size and elegance, but more than anything the cost to redesign and refurbish, and re-gild the vast majority of it before Prinny had deemed it acceptable for royal occupancy, was what drove the masses armed with rotting fruit (but no peas, it should be noted) in their hysteria to these very gates each day after the first of her entries in the *Morning Post*.

And then she halted mid-stride. Stumbling forward and then righting herself, she slowly turned. There was not one single protester behind her. Where were all of the produce-wielding marauders, decrying the excesses of the aristocracy?

Was she hallucinating due to lack of sleep? It was entirely possible.

She walked to one of the guards. "I want to see the Prince Regent."

He raised one brow.

Did they teach all males that trick? She hoped the three nice boys from her family's school in Derbyshire would not adopt it. It was very unattractive. And rude.

A very thin man crossed the stone pavers from one of Carleton House's eight arches. He elegantly showed a leg in deference to her. "Is that you, Lady Verity Fitzroy?"

She nodded without thought.

"Oh, we've been waiting and waiting for you. His Majesty was on the point of sending out a small regiment to comb the route from here to Derbyshire for you." He again bowed low.

Yes, she was obviously ready to be placed in Bedlam. *Voluntarily.* Had the world gone mad when she had blinked at some point?

She was certain she had never met this strange little man before her. And why was he treating her like the queen reignant, or at the very least a foreign head of state.

And she had thought the tricky part would be "knocking over" a large man. She hoped that was the popular jargon of criminals in the know these days, because if she had to break the law, she wanted to do it with style. Fashion, she might not care about, but lexicons were another matter altogether.

"So glad I did not put the prince to any trouble." He might have very different feelings when it concerned a whole lot of trouble instead. And so she curtsied to gain this squirrelly man's favor. "Um, is he—" She should have prepared for this better, she feared. She just wasn't sure how to phrase it. "—or rather, is His Majesty at home?" She paused.

He stared at her, a smile overspreading his face.

"Or receiving?"

Nothing.

"Taking appointments today?"

He finally put her out of her misery. "He's waiting for you, madam."

"He is?" She feared she'd just squeaked for the first time.

He nodded and invited her to follow him.

Fourteen rooms, seventeen corridors, four sets of stairs, and untold number of doorways later she found herself ushered into the royal bedchamber. She was so in awe that she only realized she was alone with the future king of England when she heard a heavy door close behind her and wheeled about.

Perhaps beheadings were held in private in this day and age.

"Come here, my child," a deep voice called from an immense bed in deep shadow.

Was he ill? Why, it was half four in the afternoon.

"Let me see your face," he said gently.

She raised her chin and boldly strode forth. She would not be described as a coward in the history books. A fool or an idiot, perhaps, but not a coward.

She stopped midway. In her fluster, she had forgotten that she was looking for *him*. That lying, living, soon not to be breathing, masquerading conniver who was soon to be known as her ex-fiancé if she had any say in the matter. And, yes, she rather thought she had quite a lot to *say* or *write* about it.

Unless of course the prince regained his senses and cut out her tongue to shut her up and her hands to shut her down.

Then again she had nothing to lose. "Where is he? I know he's here."

The prince smiled in a great show of munificence. "All in good time, my dear, all in good time."

Was there anybody in the story of her life who could be original and go through their chapter without a cliché? These were the sorts of observations that her siblings never understood. Then again, most people did not either.

Except Rory. The bloody imposter.

No. He was really just a taker, instead of the giver she had originally taken him for. He took ladies' hearts. He took people's secrets, and worst of all, he took people's blame that they had earned through years of toil and sweat. Well, maybe not sweat, but toil certainly.

"Take your time, my child." A teensy-weensy hint of an edge bordered the prince's voice. "But not all day. I have things to do, places to go, and celebratory events to attend. And if you are to go with us, time . . . vast amounts of time must be spent on your appearance." It was very hard to make out, but Verity thought the royal head suddenly leaned forward and rolled his eyes. "I had not believed him when he said three hours would not be enough time for your headgear alone, but I fear he was right." He paused. "Then again I should know better. He is always right."

"Not always," she said without thinking.

A quick grin splashed across the only part of the royal face that she could see—the lower half. "Do you have proof he has ever been wrong? I should pay you handsomely for it if you do."

She thought long and hard. And then a little longer. "May I get back to you about that, sire?"

" 'Get back to me'? Is that some sort of colloquialism from Derbyshire? Strange land, the Peak District. I often wonder if the thin air affects the mind. But I should not have told you that. Your brother becomes all puckered and starched up whenever I've hinted at it in the past. How is Candy, anyway?"

Candy? The royal nickname for James was *Candy*? She nearly cried for the want to start scribbling again. "Uh, 'Candy' was doing very well last time we were together."

"Sent a note to him, by the by. Can't have his nerves in a bundle at this moment. Why, the bachelorhood of the majority of the royal entourage hangs in the balance. And your brother is the key chessman on the board game of my life at present. Why, the fashion in which the last month or so has unraveled has made it patently clear that we must be on full alert for a return to chaos at any moment." He yawned. "My life is in imminent danger."

She squinted her eyes and leaned in closer to try and see him better. "So you will still make them all marry?"

He sat up straighter. "Do you have a better idea? He said you might. Something about dangerously creative with imagination run amok." He belched.

The devil. Well, Mr. I-love-you-even-if-you-are-stubborn-and-your-hats-are-hideous had just veered 180 degrees south in the complicated algorithm—or was it geometry?—that ruled her particular not-so-feminine mind. She put on her best demure smile, clutched her hands in a begging position. "Oh, no, sire. I think you are absolutely correct. There is no other way out of this sad, sad affair. They all *must* marry. Except my brother, of course. Two failed engagements is enough punishment. But as for the Duke of Abshire, my *former* betrothed, the self-proclaimed author of the Duke Diaries, the usurper of my—" She stopped. Prinny was famous for being fickle. *Think before speaking.* "—my . . . my . . ."

"Innocence?" the prince offered with another yawn.

Righteousness filled her. "No. Rory would never do anything like that."

The royal arm circled in the universal motion to indicate she was to speed up her harangue.

"Well, I think, for this particular duke . . ." All the fury that had ignited within her upon reading Rory's proclamation that he was, indeed, the infamous and—and—and *tittle-tattling, gossip-mongering, prattling, blabby chatterer of the century* . . . dissipated in the thick air of London's upper stories.

She bowed her head and whispered, "Did he learn how to listen from you or did Your Majesty learn it from him?"

He chuckled. "I think you already know the answer to that. I would tell you that an old dog can indeed learn new tricks but I understand that you have a queer aversion to clichés. But why haven't you asked me why I am willing to show patience, and, ahem, quite an extensive amount of time, to the real person behind the words that nearly caused a revolution not one week ago? Is that not the real question?"

She exhaled roughly. "I fully accept any and all punishment Your Majesty decides in his royal wisdom to mete out." She paused.

"Go on."

"I would only ask if I could accept full punishment in a fashion that would not harm the reputation of my family."

"Yes. Yes. Yes. And so on and so forth. And all around the mulberry bush. The answer is no."

"No?"

"No."

"No, there is no way not to harm my family, or no, you refuse to punish me even if I deserve and even demand it?"

"Sacrifice is tedious, don't you think? I know you do for it's your brother's favorite discussion. And I agree. Martyrs are not very successful at succession."

She didn't dare say a word.

"But perhaps I should go against C's request. Perhaps I should exact some sort of punishment for your immensely foolish . . . what did he call it?"

" 'Tittle-tattling, gossip-mongering, prattling, blabby chatterer of the century,' Your Majesty," she ground out.

"Indeed, Lady V. He's an absolute genius, don't you think? You must ask him how he memorized every nuance of your handwriting, then spent hours writing new diaries he made look ancient. But the most brilliant part of his plan was taking the blame, and earning a fortune to boot, by selling the entire set to the *Evening Herald*."

"I would have thought that the brilliant part was how he made everyone, ahem, especially Your Majesty, into a veritable hero using my style of lexicon, and painted the columnist as a liar and a thief."

Prinny blinked. "I see why he likes you. Courage bordering on stupidity. Shall I confide the biggest secret of all, my dear? I only tell you this in the strictest of confidences, of course."

She blinked and then nodded, still surprised the future king wasn't truly going to sentence her to a lifetime at Newgate for the embarrassing royal things that had been made public.

"Do you know why that anarchist for a columnist retracted all he had quoted and printed?"

She leaned in to hear him better.

"Your intended terrified the little traitor. He told him that he would hang for trespassing and stealing from the Crown if he did not print an immediate apology, admitting to changing and embellishing Rory's nonexistent diaries to incite chaos. Rory even made him suggest he was French."

"And he did it remarkably fast," she said peevishly.

"Oh, he is famous for planning, don't you know? Arranged it all in advance. He only had to corner that weasel columnist when he returned."

She shook her head, both annoyed at her inability to plan as well as he—despite all her years of training—and also proud of Rory's extraordinary abilities.

"By the by, Lady V, was Sussex really Middlesex's washerwoman for an entire month when he lost a wager?"

"Every Tuesday and Friday." She nodded gravely. "The Duke of Middlesex spent most of those days on the third story of his townhouse, facing the mews, while Sussex labored before him. The garden was fairly blue with interesting oaths I never could quite understand. Especially Fridays."

"Why Fridays?"

"As far as I understood it, Sussex would have preferred to go to Tattersalls with my brother for the Friday auctions."

The Prince Regent clapped his hands together in glee. "You should have added that in your description."

"I daresay, it was bad enough," she replied.

The prince half lowered his lids over his eyes. "I should enjoy reading the rest of your writings, my dear. When may I expect to have them?"

It was no idle request, and they both knew it.

"I am so sorry, Your Majesty, but in the interest

of succession I burned them before I came here."

He leveled a glare that would have withered a bigger man. "Too bad." Prinny readjusted his cap. "Let's see, where was I?"

"Punishment. Mine. "

"Right. Yes, I have it. You are to relearn the hazards of martyrdom from your brother, who will reeducate you on the importance of remaining who you are by means of regular beating, with a rod not more than one-inch thick, and solitary confinement in a dungeon."

She swallowed. "I see."

"I'm not finished, my dear. You demanded punishment and I shall gladly bestow it even if it saddens C. So the last part is simple. After your confinement, you shall enter a new state of confinement. You'll marry the boy and bear his heirs. We need more C's in the world. You're on your own regarding his martyrdom. He's in complete denial."

"Uh . . . Right. Um, and who is C?"

He snorted. "With a naturalist mother such as yours, surely you know all about that creature with a prehensile tail, independent eyeballs, and the ability to blend into surroundings."

She stood stock-still.

"You may tell him that he has earned his retirement." The Prince Regent rubbed his nightcap, exposing an inch of graying stubble on one side of his head and long strands on the other.

"Are you telling me—"

"Absolutely not."

"But—"

"My dear Lady V, if you say one more word, I may just change my mind and have you thrown in *my* dungeon with nothing to eat except . . ." He looked at her with a question in his wise but weary eyes.

"Fig tarts?" she said with hope.

"Excellent . . . another liar to add to my list."

At that precise moment someone—someone identified by his prehensile tail, independent eyeballs, and the ability to blend into surroundings—crashed through the royal door.

He slapped one hand against the other. "Finally . . . I was getting a bit worried about my abilities in my declining years."

Prinny chuckled. "'Act old later' has always been my motto."

Their eyes met, and she could not feel her hands.

The prince chuckled again. "All right, all right, enough of that . . . one could hope you have the Special License with you, C. I'm not sure I can stand one more round of gossip concerning C's and V's and so on and so forth, and round and round. My God, have neither of you any respect for my nerves at all? Scandalous. Find a chamber. But be ready in six hours. And find her a real hat to replace that bird's nest falling to pieces, C. That is a royal command."

Chapter 20

The return ride to Derbyshire was the exact opposite of his ride to Town. He would not let her gallop. And he would not leave her side.

They stopped at every inn, as early in the day as he could wheedle from her. And she had let him. If only to prove that she could keep that Fitzroy obdurate nature in check now that she was a Lennox.

Up to a point.

Forty miles from Rutledge, to be exact. All evidence of an obedient wife in the making disappeared that late morning.

Thank God.

"Rory?"

"Yes, my love."

"I'm not stopping anymore."

"Sorry?" He smiled to himself.

"Look, I'm tired."

The smile fell from him and he rushed on, "Let's go back to the inn. I'm tired, too," he lied.

"No," she said. "You misunderstand. I'm tired of all these villages and stops in inns. I want to go home."

"I sent word on ahead to James that we'd arrive at Boxwood the day after tomorrow."

She halted her mare. "No. I want to go to your home."

"Our home," he corrected. "But it's five miles farther."

She smiled. "Then we'll just have to race the last five miles. Last one there forfeits whatever the other wants."

He just couldn't deny her when she looked at him with a huge smile on her face and the corners of her eyes crinkling with laughter in her heart.

Of course he let her win. There wasn't another option.

As they rode past the end post, she wore the same expression. But said not a word.

They rode side by side into the stable. Dawn was streaking pink tentacles in the sky.

As they rounded the corner from the stables, a short distance to the main entrance, she stopped.

Her mouth fell open.

The door was gone.

"Oh my God. We've been robbed."

He grasped her waist and pulled her close. "No we haven't. I asked Cheever to do it when I left."

"Are you out of your mind? We'll be robbed blind."

"Who in hell cares? It's just things, Verity. Replaceable."

She shook her head. "Where are the servants?"

"I sent word ahead from the last inn. I gave them leave for the next two days. I think they were glad to go, to be honest. They think I've taken leave of my senses."

"You have."

"Your cousin doesn't think so."

"Pardon me? When was she here?"

"Jealous?"

"Be serious, Rory."

"She told me to open the door to my cage. And I find—unlike you, apparently—that she gives excellent advice. You would do well to listen to her."

"You're right."

"Sweetest words in the English language." He picked her up and nuzzled her head, relishing the feel of her in his arms and the scent of her in his mind. "By the by, I haven't told you the latest gossip in the county."

She stiffened in his arms.

"It's not what you think."

"Really," she retorted, doubt dripping from the word.

"You'll like it very much."

"Well, are you going to tell me?"

"I'm trying to learn how to maintain suspense, in the same fashion you managed in your diaries."

"I see." She did not go on.

He waited. And waited. And finally sighed as he climbed the stairs to his bedchamber that was now hers. "I see I haven't quite mastered the art of it."

"I wouldn't say that," she whispered.

He stayed silent.

She finally could not hold back her laughter another moment. "Enough. I can't stand it. Tell me!"

"All right, then."

When he did not go on, she beat his chest with her fists. She was stronger than she appeared.

"Far too curious, in addition to being far too stubborn. A quite lethal combination."

"Very nearly, in your case," she said dryly. She said not another word.

He carried her down three more corridors, made a left past the Blue Room, filled with war trophies that boggled the mind. It was the only door he had not personally removed from the hinges. That one would stay locked. Forever.

"Rory?"

"Yes, my love."

"The thing of it is . . ."

"Yes, my love?"

"You see . . ."

He sighed. "You're so much better at this than I."

"It's all in the timing."

He gently tipped her to regain her footing in front of the opening to his chamber. Then he kissed her. He gazed into her eyes and kissed her again.

And once again with more feeling.

"Stop." She finally pushed against his chest. "I give up. You are much better than I could have possibly known."

"Well, you are a good teacher."

She smiled at him.

"So shall I tell you finally?"

"Yes."

"Are you sure?"

"Rory?"

"Yes, my love?"

"If you have any intention to make love to me before I fall dead asleep—and I think you know that when I say dead asleep you understand the full nature of the probability—then you had better just spit it out."

He smiled.

"Is it that important?"

"Well, I think so. If we are going to live on this gossip-infested peak, which puts London to shame, I had better learn how to whisper over scandalbroth with the best of them."

She arched a brow and leaned forward in the overt nature of a gossip of the finest water. "So?"

"Miss Phoebe Talmadge is soon to exchange her name for another."

"Really?" She obviously did not believe him. "And who told you this?"

"The ostler's daughter at the last posting house."

"Then it's true," she said, quite serious now. "And who is the lucky, very rich man?" She paused. "If you tell me it's James, I might have to go back to the posting inn and do bodily harm." She stared at him with those big brown eyes of hers. "And then find a snake-charmer for James."

He finally let her out of her misery. "Mr. Armitage. Your vicar." He shook his head like a seasoned magpie.

Her eyes widened. And then she laughed. "Do be serious. Gossip has to resemble something that could actually happen. Plagues in jungles, revolution in London, me with you." She whispered the last.

He kissed her tenderly again. He didn't know how much longer he could wait. He had been too long without her in his arms.

"Seriously?" She began to laugh again.

"That is not how I expect my wife to react to my kisses."

"No, Rory." She wiped her eyes. "Tell me the truth of it."

He crossed his hand over his heart, just like Mrs. Greer had the night that was the best and worst of his life.

"But how could it be?" Wonder filling her voice.

He arched a brow and whispered in her ear. "I saw them talking by the water goblets in Boxwood's alcove."

"You'll do very well here," she said in a matter-of-fact tone.

He watched her tug on one end of his neckcloth, which fell open. He felt her fingers on his skin and then her lips in the hollow of his neck.

It was his undoing. He picked her up and carried her to his bed.

"You know, Rory, you are going to have to stop this picking me up business. I'm beginning to feel like an infant. I do know how to walk."

"Not until the day after tomorrow you don't." He plopped her down onto his bed. God, he wanted her. He needed her.

Hell. *Want* and *need* were words that didn't suffice for the sensations he felt when he saw her in his bed.

He placed his knee on the edge of the bed to climb in after her.

"Wait!" She sat up suddenly.

"No more," he ground out.

"No really," she said, her eyes sparkling.

"Verity, my love, I can't wait any longer."

Her eyes softened. "All right, Rory, but promise me that the first thing you'll do the day after to-morrow is to return what is rightfully mine."

"You already have my heart. You had it at 'cheetah.'"

She burst out laughing. God how he loved her laugh.

"So you're not referring to my heart, I take it."

"No. I want my hat back."

He still hadn't quite figured out this particular species known as woman.

She rolled her eyes. "The one you held as black-mail all those years ago under my pine tree."

His eyes widened in disbelief. "It was you?"

"Of course it was me. Who did you think it was?"

"I didn't see anyone. It was so hideous, I thought someone had put it out of its misery by leaving it to molder. You know, ashes to ashes and all that."

"You *love* my hats."

"Indeed," he replied. "I would even die for them."

It was the last coherent word that was heard by either of the sole occupants of Rutledge Hall for a good long time.

Unless one considers broken phrases, punctuated by pleading and much laughter, as coherent.

Only one thing was certain.

Goodness of spirit proved it triumphed in the end as long as one part charm is mixed with a large pinch of wit, with side helpings of courage and perseverance. It was, indeed, a perfect recipe for happiness.

Next month, don't miss these exciting new love stories only from Avon Books

Kiss of Temptation by Sandra Hill

Condemned to prison for the sin of lust, Viking vampire angel—or vangel—Ivak Sigurdsson is finding centuries of celibacy depressing. When temptation comes in the form of beautiful Gabrielle Sonnier—who needs help breaking her brother out of prison—Ivak can't help but give in. But as the two join forces, they both begin to wonder if their passionate bond is really only lust, or something more.

Stolen Charms by Adele Ashworth

Determined to wed the infamous thief, the Black Knight, Miss Natalie Haislett has no trouble approaching Jonathan Drake—reputed to be a friend of the Knight—for an introduction. This may be difficult as Drake is the Knight himself! While traveling together in France as a married couple in search of the Knight, passions bloom and the daring bandit sets his sights on the most priceless treasure of all . . . Natalie's heart.

Sins of a Ruthless Rogue by Anna Randol

When Clayton Campbell shows up on Olivia Swift's doorstep, she's stunned. No longer the boy who stole her heart, this hardened man has a lust for vengeance in his eyes. Clayton cannot deny that the sight of Olivia rouses in him a passion like never before. But as tensions between them rise, the hard-hearted agent will face his greatest battle yet . . . for his heart.

*At Avon Books, we know your passion
for romance—once you finish one of our
novels, you find yourself wanting more.*

May we tempt you with . . .

- **Excerpts** from our upcoming releases.

- Entertaining **extras**, including authors'
  personal photo albums and book lists.

- Behind-the-scenes **scoop** on your favorite
  characters and series.

- **Sweepstakes** for the chance to win free books,
  romantic getaways, and other fun prizes.

- Writing **tips** from our authors and editors.

- **Blog** with our authors and find out why they
  love to write romance.

- **Exclusive content** that's not contained
  within the pages of our novels.

Join us at
www.avonbooks.com

AVON

An Imprint of HarperCollins*Publishers*
www.avonromance.com

Available wherever books are sold or please call 1-800-331-3761 to order.

FTH 1111

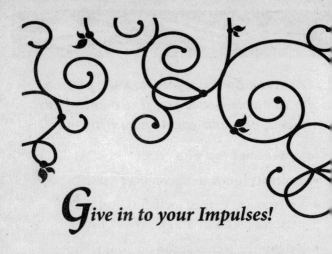